Kif: An U...

Elizabeth Mackintosh
(Josephine Tey)

Josephine Tey and Gordon Daviot, were de pseudonyms used by Elizabeth Mackintosh (1896–1952) a Scottish author best known for her mystery novels. She also wrote as Gordon Daviot, under which name she wrote plays with an historical theme. In 1990, The Daughter of Time was selected by the British-based Crime Writers' Association as the greatest mystery novel of all time; The Franchise Affair was eleventh on the same list of 100 books.

Kif: An Unvarnished History

1

The boy stepped into the chill dark of the winter morning and closed the door quietly behind him. Quietly because the wife of Farmer Vass was apt to be unreasonable if she were wakened betimes. It lacked an hour till dawn and there was neither earth nor sky, hedge nor horizon. Only the all-enveloping dark, immediate, almost tangible—the blackness that hems us in with ourselves and annihilates philosophy. And it was bitterly cold. The boy clutched at his coat collar as the thin sterile air struck at his bare throat. His hobnailed boots echoed irrelevantly—a dreary sound—as he made his stumbling way over the cobbles of the yard and fumbled for the lantern that hung at the stable door. His sleep-sodden brain which had brought him thus far mechanically was wakening to its daily passion of revolt.

God! what a life! What a bloody dam-fool life! A day that began with fumbling in the dark and ended fumbling in another dark, and in between a long procession of monotonous jobs, impersonal and void of interest. A life of fastening buckles, he thought venomously, as his rapidly stiffening fingers refused their office. Buckle-fastening! When life was so short and there was so much of the world. Even those high new-born pearly dawns of summer that lifted his heart with their wonder were but urgent invitations to set out and see. He wanted—passionately wanted—a life where things happened; where the unexpected swung at you with a terrifying beauty and events were not, since every hour brought its event. The phlegm, the appalling for-everness of the fields and hills roused in him a desperate consciousness of his own evanescence, and a rebellion that any part of his short and so precious time should be given to their thankless service. And what was there beyond his work to make it worth while? To sit in winter at the farmhouse kitchen fire while Johnny, the other hired man, scraped on his fiddle and Mary the 'girl' flirted ineptly with a surfaceman from the railway or a shepherd from the hill? Or to go once in three weeks or a month to a dance at the nearest schoolhouse—an affair of polkas and boots? Or on summer evenings and Sundays to join the gathering at the bridge-head and exchange gossip and smutty stories, to make one of the self-elected tribunal which sat in sly judgment on the manners and morals of the countryside, utterly content with themselves and their lot? Even when he capped their stories and earned their appreciative laughter and their admiring 'Ay, boy, you're the one!' he had waves of angry disgust, not at the subject of his triumph, but at the spiritual poverty of his audience.

The only events at Tarn were the New Year and an occasional calving. And last autumn the little Jersey had got bogged in the low grazing; an affair which had caused one day at least to be vivid with the meeting of emergency which is life, and which, like lightning at night, had left the succeeding moments darker.

Beyond the occasional kissing of a girl at a dance the only thrill of positive pleasure that he knew was provided by the threepenny 'shockers' which he bought with his scanty pocket-money when in Ferry on carting-business and absorbed in bed at night to the accompaniment of Johnny's snores. It was usually a battle between the swift sleep that falls on the open-air worker and his thirst for colour and movement. That his need for at least vicarious adventure was great was witnessed to by the repeated trouble with Mrs Vass over the unwarrantable burning of candles. Johnny, not being cast in martyr's mould, had no hesitation in absolving himself at the price of his companion's secret, with the result that candles were rationed thenceforth. If it had not been for the kindheartedness of the flirtatious Mary—to whom a male thing in trouble, even if it were only a long-legged sulky-mouthed boy, was quite unthinkable—his one escape from a too drab reality might have been seriously hindered. But Mary's generous supply of candle-ends—and Mary had royal ideas as to what constituted ends—saved the situation.

At this moment she came to the kitchen door and called into the darkness 'Kif! Are you there, Kif?' her voice subdued in deference to the unawakened household. The boy, who had seen the light appear fifteen minutes before in the blank house and had been hoping for the summons, came clumping to the open door that emitted a friendly stuffiness to the frozen yard and followed her into the kitchen, where the fire had graduated from the first stage of merely spectacular flame to a glowing heat, and a steaming bowl of tea stood on the table.

'There's a cup of tea that will keep you going till breakfast,' she whispered, and added the time-honoured formula, 'You'll not let on to herself?'

Kif grinned and gulped the scalding tea, his shadow between the oil lamp and the firelight swinging ghostly across the wall and ceiling. He would make a handsome enough man, thought Mary. No one to look at him now would think he was only fifteen. Pity he was so plain, though. And his quiet ways were nice if only he had a little more back-chat.

They made desultory conversation in that happy comradeship savouring of conspiracy of two people who alone are awake while others sleep, until the shuffle of feet on the stone-floored passage proclaimed the arrival of Johnny. While his senior was being fortified with tea against the rigours of the morning Kif withdrew to his work. But at breakfast he said:

'Are the two carts going to town for the meal?'

Johnny paused with a spoonful of porridge and milk half way to his already open mouth.

'And what if they're not?' he said, eyeing Kif's carefully expressionless face with cheerful malice. He swallowed the porridge, and since the boy was silent he added: 'Well, since you're so curious, only one's going.'

Not a sign rewarded his expectant scrutiny of the face opposite. In another country Kif would have made a reputation at poker. His inside might be turning over in sick disappointment in a way that defied the ordinary laws of anatomy, but that was no reason that daws should peck. He pushed aside his emptied plate and cut himself a hunk of bread with apparent indifference. The hope of a visit to town had been to him what the prospect of a meal is to a hungry tramp. Its sudden obliteration was a thing that did not bear immediate contemplation.

But Mary, coming from the hearth with the teapot, said to Johnny:

'You're the fine teaser, aren't you? Can you not tell the boy and be done with it? It's only one cart that's going, sure enough, Kif,'—in her soft western voice his name became Keef—'but it's yourself that's going with it. That *amadan* is going west to Little Crags for the new pony. Didn't I hear Himself telling him in the byre last night.'

She passed him his cup and affected not to see the dull flush that came to his dark face and that he tried unsuccessfully to hide in the bowl-like proportions of his cup. What a shame to tease him when he wanted to go like that! She had a moment of mushy warmth towards him. If his hair had been live and curly instead of the lank thick stuff it was she would have run her fingers through it as she passed behind him to the dresser. As it was, she contented herself by putting a plate of scones down in front of him to the pointed exclusion of Johnny.

And Kif, on his part, had for her a permanent if mild regard—the only approach to affection he knew in his singularly unattached existence. He had in the highest degree that unemotional attitude to his fellow beings that is common in members of a large family in poor circumstances. When his parents had died two years previously and his family had been scattered to the ends of the kingdom, the younger to homes—the capital H kind—the older to situations, he, in common with the rest, had accepted their separation with equanimity. Personal relationships had very little meaning for him. Since the day of his birth no one had singled him out for special attention or consideration—except with a view to punishment occasionally. He had been a unit in a family at home and at school he was a unit in a class. That it might be otherwise had never occurred to him. He was conscious of no lack of human contact in his existence, no desire for a confidant. He was, on the contrary, more than ordinarily self-contained. No one had ever shown any interest in his possible thoughts or desires; there was no reason that he should expect that anyone should. When he was twelve he had rebelled unconsciously against this anonymity by being as wild at school as circumstances in the person of a fairly competent master allowed. His master, who rather liked him, deplored to a colleague the fact that he was difficult to appeal to. It did not occur to him that personal appeal was a thing so strange to the boy as to be almost meaningless and certainly open to suspicion. On going to Tarn as farmer's boy he had lapsed again to his habitual reserve and was a model of behaviour. That he was passably efficient in his work, however, was due to the fact that his whole life had been spent among farms and farm work and not to any good will in the doing of it.

Sitting on the edge of the cart on the way to Ferry he reviewed the situation—a little more philosophically now since there was the prospect of town in front of him, and the sun had thawed the ice that was horror to a carter on the sloping roads and was warming his back agreeably. For a mind unpossessed by other visions an ideal day lay ahead. He was to collect the meal from the grain store, do three errands for Mrs Vass, wait for the three o'clock train from the south and bring back the packages it would presumably deliver. Easy, pleasant, leisurely. But it was Kif's tragedy that the easy and the leisurely had no appeal for him. That he should do this thing for years to come without the hope of deliverance was a thought that stopped his heart with its poignancy. The appalling waste of time!

What he would do instead was not clear. He had not sufficient knowledge of the world to apportion himself a definite rôle. What he could do was equally vague. If he had had any ideas on that subject Tarn would not have known him for the two years it already had.

On the outskirts of the town he had to descend hastily and go to the agitated mare's head as the third battalion of a Highland regiment swung down on him led by their pipes and drums: wild, defiant, deliriously triumphant. Even while he was remonstrating with the animal he was hypnotised by the splendour and the rhythm of them. Long after they had passed he stood gazing after them as one involuntarily stares after a lighted train which has thundered past one in the dark, caressing the mare's nose with an absent hand.

'Lucky chaps!' he thought. 'Lucky chaps! France in a fortnight probably.'

That something more than France waited for them he did not consider. At least their lives would not have been uneventful.

He left the horse and cart at the goods station and repaired to an eating-place patronised by his kind—a place of benches, oilcloth table-covers and cracked but mighty china. While he was waiting the appearance of the tuppenny pie and strong tea which was the regular farmhand's lunch (Shades of famous trenchermen, behold your sons!), a red-headed youth opposite, whom he knew as a herd and odd-job man on market days, brushed the last crumbs of pie from his garments, sucked his teeth appreciatively and said to Kif, to whom he had nodded on entrance:

'Thinking of joining up?'

Kif was so taken by surprise that he blurted out:

'Me? I'm only fifteen.'

The red youth grinned as at a pleasantry.

'I don't think!' he said expressively, and continued to regard Kif with a look in his bleached blue eye which obviously placed Kif among the knowing ones.

'Well, well,' he said at length, 'every man to his taste. Far be it from me to press you. I come of a military family myself. My great-grandfather was the only man who ran away at Waterloo. So I sort of feel that this show wouldn't be complete without me. Sorry you haven't leanings that way. We might have done the deed together. However! Wish me luck. So-long!'

And the door swung to behind him.

Kif gazed unseeingly at the food the slatternly attendant had set before him, his mind opening on new and amazing vistas. Did he really look like that? He must get out and see. He devoured the pie, drank half a cup of the scalding liquid and paid his bill. Halfway down the street he paused at a confectioner's, where a looking-glass formed the back of the window, and dispassionately considered himself. He saw a tallish youth whose ill-fitting old coat could not conceal the breadth and muscularity of his shoulders. Heavy lids and thick brows gave sophistication to the bright dark eyes—the only animated part of a face that had missed good looks through its lack of modelling. It was certainly not a boy who looked back at him from behind the little mounds of chocolates and 'mixtures'. And that being so all his problems were miraculously solved.

For the first time since he was hired at Tarn, Kif went home without a threepenny 'thriller' in his pocket.

2

Kif joined the army on the twelfth of December, 1914. He enlisted at a recruiting office in Ferry, where his statement that he was eighteen was received without comment. His request that he should be sent to a Highland regiment had not so happy a fate. The sergeant in charge affected surprise and demanded to know the reason for so curious a predilection. Since Kif's only reasons were the unforgettable vision of the other day and a vague memory of fine stories in his history book at school he had not an answer ready, and the sergeant seized the opportunity to lay before him a brief *résumé* of the attractions of his own regiment. So Kif, who was largely indifferent to the means as long as the end was achieved, became one of the Carnshires—known throughout the service as the Half-and-Halfers, not from any lack of thoroughness either in their spit-and-polish or their exploits in action, but because being recruited from both sides of the border they were neither wholly Scots nor wholly English. He started out to the horizon of his dreams with one spare shirt, two pairs of socks, a Testament of Mrs Vass's, an untidy packet of scones and cheese which the tearful Mary had thrust into his hand at parting, his pay up to date, and his master's blessing.

This last had been obtained at the end of an interview which had left Kif rather surprised at himself, and his master wholly surprised at his employee. Kif had broken the news of his intended enlistment in the stable as he was unharnessing the mare. Patriotic fever being then at its height, Mr Vass saw in the proposition only the age-old glamour of a uniform and war hysteria, and promptly vetoed the suggestion.

'Not a bit of it,' he said. 'You're engaged to me and engaged to me you stay, see? Time enough in three years from now to fight for your country. By that time you'll have time to think about it and you very likely won't want to.'

Kif hung the bridle carefully on a protruding nail and steadied it with a deliberate hand before he turned.

'That may be true enough,' he said, 'but I'm going now.'

'Don't be a fool. Don't you realise that you can't? Supposing you go and enlist to-morrow. All I've got to do is to tell them your age and they'll throw you out without thanks, and I'll have you back in a day.'

And he turned to go. But before he had taken the first step, Kif stood between him and the door.

'Look here,' he said, 'the sooner you understand the better. I'm going. And there's nothing in Heaven or earth that's going to keep me. I'll stay till the end of the week so's you can get someone in my place. But not a day after. You can go and tell them my age if you like, but it won't bring me back here. So you might as well keep your mouth shut. I'd just go somewhere else and enlist where you couldn't interfere. *I'm going.* Is that clear now?'

The staggered farmer sought for words. He experienced a queer uneasiness which had something to do with Kif's presence between him and the door. There was no threat in the boy's attitude. He was standing easily before the half-door, his hands hanging limply at his sides. But his face in the lamplight was very white, and there was that in his eyes that gave a man of peace, even if he were still muscular and little over forty, most furiously to think.

'And do you expect me to pay you wages when you go?' he asked feebly.

'That's as may be. I haven't any right to them, I suppose, since I'm going without notice. But the wages don't matter.'

'So-ho! You're the first person I ever met who thought that. Well, well! Who will to Cupar maun to Cupar, I suppose. You're being a big fool, but it's you that'll be the sufferer. We'll see what we can do before the week's out.'

Kif had taken that, correctly, as capitulation, and as the days passed Mr Vass by some queer logic of his own had come to look upon the pending enlistment as his own doing. He was letting Kif go, was he not? Putting himself to endless inconvenience so that he might serve his King and country. And the fact that a boy of fourteen had been found to take Kif's place added the last ounce of satisfaction. So that when, on the last morning, Kif received not only his full pay but his master's benediction as well, he was more amused than gratified. What did gratify him and remained with him as a strange warm feeling under his ribs was the recollection of Mary's wet eyes. It was a new sensation to be the centre of interest even temporarily, and the more he licked the more he liked the taste.

That prominence, however, was not to be his for long. At the Carnshire's depôt he found that he counted rather less than did one of the hens at Tarn. In those days huts were not yet thought of, and the incipient battalions of the new army were billeted with more regard to space than suitability in the choice of location. Bewildered tyros in the art of self-preservation were harried by openly contemptuous and inwardly resentful N.C.O.'s through the unspeakable discomfort of life in drill halls, concert rooms, riding schools, garages, breweries, anything that had floor space and a more or less weather-tight roof. To the old N.C.O.'s of the Half-and-Halfers this incredible collection of odds and ends—mostly odds, as one confided to his crony the sergeant tailor—was a desecration of the fair fame of the regiment. A nightmare. War they understood. It was their business. But it was their own affair. Losses were deplorable but to be understood. This influx of an untutored mob was a tragedy. It was the end of the Regiment. Only the heart-breaking need of that same regiment made the situation bearable at all. That being so they had to make the best of that unnameable rabble.

When the fifth Carnshires marched out of barracks three months later, the sergeant tailor, standing by the gate to watch them go, jerked his head sideways in a gesture of admiration and remarked to a month-old corporal striding past him, 'Man, the swing o' yez!' That that miracle was possible was due in equal proportion to the faith, hope and philosophy of the volunteers and—let us not forget it—to the much cursed and much cursing N.C.O.'s of the old army who, lacking faith and almost devoid of hope, had yet sufficient charity to agonise over us to the end that that multitude of individual worth might not be made null for lack of a welding power.

During those months Kif was perhaps the only entirely happy man in the battalion. He had never lain soft, and what was hardship to the majority was but mild discomfort to him. Even the peeling of 'spuds' and the scrubbing of floors and tables, the cutting up of meat for the endless stew, the fetching and carrying—all the everlasting fatigues which were such a bitter trial to the ardent spirits of the others, who had entered the army with but one object in view, to get to France as soon as possible—were done by him with a relish that endeared him to the hearts of the weary corporals so beset by martyrs and protestants. Nothing came amiss to him. What did it matter that to-day he was scrubbing out a dixie when he could rejoice in the certainty that to-morrow he would be doing something totally different, that every varied day brought something new? Even inoculation did not damp his cheerfulness, though he was decidedly ill for the first time in his life. For two days he lay on the doubtful comfort of nobbly 'biscuits' and let the world pass round and over him, while he dawdled in a universe that was partly real and partly dream.

His nurse-in-chief during the two days that he 'went sick' was the red-headed herd from Ferry. When Kif with five other newly enlisted was ushered into the barrack-room at the depot the first person his eyes lighted on was, to his dismay, the author of his happiness. That the dismay was not mutual was evident by the surprised glee on the face of the offspring of soldiers.

'Hullo, hullo, hullo!' he said, making a little song of it. 'If it isn't little Fifteen! What bit you, childie?'

Kif's heart stood still. In a moment they would all know. Someone in authority would hear. Inquiries would be made.

9

He put down the brown-paper parcel which contained his possessions and walked down the length of the room.

'If you get me heaved out I'll kill you,' he said simply, but with such intensity in his quick undertone that the youth's laughing face became grave. He looked at Kif intently for a moment and then said wonderingly:

'Coo! D'you mean to say it was true what you said? God bless me! Well,' he added after a further scrutiny, 'you're safe enough, kid. Take it from me. No one'd ever believe it.' And as he saw Kif's mouth opening with the inevitable question: 'As for me, I'm your man. I wouldn't split on you not if they gave me a commission. You're a sport. Come across to the canteen and celebrate. Think you must have had military ancestors as well, somehow.'

'What's your John-Willies?' he asked when beer was set before them.

'Archibald Vicar,' said Kif.

'Do they call you all that? That's not what the chaps at Ferry market call you, is it?'

'No, everyone called me Kif.' Quite unconsciously he used the past tense.

'What's that short for?'

'Don't know. I've been called that ever since I was little. I think it's the way I used to say my name. Your name is Struthers, isn't it?' He had just remembered it.

'Private James Struthers.' The red-headed one rolled the name delightedly. 'But the "private" is only temporary, so to speak. And I'm going to introduce you to one of the best, so that when I depart from the ranks in my upward career I won't be leaving you lonesome. He hasn't much chance in the army, but him and me's pals.'

The prospectless one proved to be a young stockbroker, London born and bred, with an understanding eye, a humorous mouth, and literary tastes. He was the complete antithesis of Jimmy Struthers, who seemed to provide him with an immense amount of private enjoyment. Both were typical of their class and professions, and that they should have foregathered even in that polyglot assembly was due partly to the possessive habits of Jimmy and partly to Barclay's attitude of *laisser faire* and readiness to be amused with whatever came his way. And Jimmy was certainly an entertainment. There was a strange appeal about him, too. One had the same warm feeling for him that one has for a particularly valiant mongrel pup. He had broad cheek-bones and a narrow jaw, and his mouth in repose had a half-pathetic, half-disgruntled droop which was not borne out by anything either in his character or his history. When he was not talking his eyes had a half-asleep expression that was almost dazed, but in one moment he would rouse from apparent indifference to an argumentative and gesticulating animation.

It was with these two that Kif spent the leisure moments of his first months in the army, and it was Jimmy who shooed the solicitous Barclay away from Kif's mattress and constituted himself physician, consultant and nurse where the sufferer was concerned. He had himself been inoculated at the same time as Kif and regarded the proceeding as a direct insult to his status as a human being. Apart from the hurt to his dignity—'like dipping a lot of ruddy sheep'—it seemed to have had no effect on him.

Kif became a first-class shot and developed a real talent for scout and intelligence work. He cursed night manoeuvres with point and proficiency because it was the custom to abhor them. But secretly he delighted in them. There was something in the darkness and expectancy that vibrated an answering chord in him. Anything might happen. Any one of the dragging palpitating minutes might break suddenly into flaming moment. Night was pregnant with event.

That ninety-nine per cent. of nights on manoeuvres were merely a protracted boredom of cold and discomfort never damped entirely the expectation with which he set out on them. He would sit in the lee of a dry-stone wall—and if you have ever sat behind a wall built of unmortared stone you will realise how very little lee there is—with the rain soaking through the shoulders of his greatcoat and a half-gale coming through the chinks at his back, swearing mechanically and enjoying himself to the top of his bent. He made his tall and by no means slight figure a part of the murky world about him, and for a little glorious hour would live as he had prayed to live, his mind alert to meet the unexpected and throng with plans to counter plans.

Barclay liked him and was interested in him to an unexpected degree. It was on night manoeuvres, lying in reserve on the edge of a sheltering firwood, that he stumbled on the knowledge of Kif's unattached condition. Kif had expressed his intention of not taking the usual leave before going to France.

'But what will your people think?' asked Barclay, to whom one's people were an integral part of one's existence.

'People?' said Kif vaguely, not because he did not understand the term, but because his mind was on other things.

'He means your folks,' said Jimmy, with the air of one condoning a slip of the tongue.

Kif explained his situation.

'And don't you want to see the people at the farm again?'

That was what Kif had been considering. *Did* he want to see the Tarn people again? It would be rather nice to swank before them in his uniform, which certainly became him marvellously. And there was Mary. He would quite like Mary to see him.

That was Kif. He would consider going back, not to gratify any need to see someone who had been amiable to him, but to taste again the magic of someone's approval. Sentiment at that time did not exist in him. He approved of Barclay and understood Struthers, and was happy with them, but he had no definite affection for either.

He had once, seeing Barclay reading, asked him tentatively for the loan of a book. Barclay, who had been reading *Pater*, had sent an urgent message to his sister, with the result that for the next week Kif was absorbed in Owen

11

Wister's *Virginian*, and in the succeeding weeks discovered Kipling. Kipling he approved of unreservedly, and it became difficult to drag him out of an evening to the almost nightly entertainments organised for the troops by the enthusiastic civilians of the neighbourhood.

'Come on, my son,' Barclay would say, cuffing the black head, the only visible part of which was the nape of the neck appearing between two bony big-jointed hands, 'come and hear charming ladies sing.' At the second cuff Kif would come to the surface and exhibit resentment. Occasionally he was really angry; but he always went in the end. Not because of *force majeure* but because, being thoroughly wakened out of the dream land of adventure, the attractiveness of the real world of his inhabiting was once more patent to him. Concerts had so far bored him mildly—but you never knew. The glory of not knowing—of living a life that was a succession of corners!

In the end Kif elected to take his leave—the battalion were then at Bulford—but it was not spent at Tarn, nor did Mary ever have an opportunity of admiring the uniform. Stronger than Kif's desire to taste again the unaccustomed sweets of playing lead was his longing to go out by himself for to admire and for to see'. The helpless restlessness which had characterised his existence at the farm had left him when his life leaped from stagnation to movement. That he had by his own doing become a pawn of unseen forces did not worry him. He had taken the stone away, and life moved, and that was all he ever asked of it. Being master of his fate was no ambition of Kif's.

But he had no intention of refusing heaven-sent opportunities of embroidering it.

He had meant to leave the others under the impression that he was going back to the farm, but Barclay's solicitude frustrated the intention.

'Will you stay at the farm?' he asked. 'I mean, will they put you up?'

Kif, after a microscopic pause, said airily, 'Oh yes, I expect so.' But his airiness was so ethereal as to be suspect. Barclay looked up from where he was employed with button-stick and polish and favoured Kif with a long and doubtful scrutiny. Kif bore it well for a moment or two, and then a very faint dull flush came up from his collar. Barclay looked a moment longer and returned to his buttons smiling.

'Where are you going, Kif?' he asked.

Kif laughed. 'If you hadn't said you had only a sister I'd have said you were a seventh son.'

'Second sight isn't necessary when you give yourself away by looking as guilty as that. You'll never make a successful criminal, my lad. Is your destination a secret?'

'It isn't a secret. It's just that I don't know anything about it. I'm just going to look-see, you see.'

Barclay forbore to probe further beyond hoping that if he came to London he would come and make the family's acquaintance. Kif, who had no intention of doing any such thing—the very thought of it made him sweat—thanked him politely and the subject was dropped.

Kif began his *ave valeque* to Britain by going to see a boxing tournament in Salisbury. At Tarn he had read with avidity the boxing news in the newspapers. After that he had read the racing news. Football interested him very little—there was little of adventure in anything so redolent of the village green—and, for similar reasons, cricket not at all. Horse-racing and boxing fascinated him, and boxing came an easy first. When he found himself actually and incredibly a part of what he had so often seen pictured, his joy vent itself in a prodigious sigh which led the man next him—a private of Marines—to say:

'Fed up, mate? It do seem long when you're waiting. They oughter 'ave a band or something.'

Kif assented absent-mindedly. He was not going to tell anyone that the mere fact of being in the building, of being one of that waiting crowd, was almost sufficient joy without the prospect of the spectacle to come. He listened in a daze of happiness to the fragments of talk which dropped out of the hum of conversation. Behind him three men were giving each other riddles. He heard one say, 'I'll give you one now. When is a . . .' Everywhere round him men were arguing, discussing, explaining:

'. . . knocked silly in the second round.'

'. . . three in the cook-house . . .'

'. . . and I said, ses I . . .'

'. . . far better in the Strand . . .'

'I'll lay you six to four . . .'

From his seat near the ring-side the huge house soared into a thick blue haze in which the medley of voices seemed to be caught and to hang suspended. Where roof met walls there were heavy violet shadows. Nothing had form or definition. Vague voices, vague shapes, vague shadows. Nothing real except the focal point of the ring, a square of drowned brilliance in the merciless light of the down-shaded arc lamps.

The ring-side seats filled up. A man in evening clothes came and made a little speech, to which Kif did not listen. Another came and made an announcement about a substitution in the programme. Seconds appeared, tremendously important, with basins, towels, and sponges. A slim youth in a blue dressing gown climbed into the ring and sat down in a corner very much as if he had lost his way and was too tired to go any further. He took no notice of the hand-clapping which greeted his arrival and merely nodded vaguely to the animated remarks his second addressed to him. A chunky youth in a paisley-patterned robe, with a flat-topped head of stiff upstanding hair alarmingly reminiscent of a curry-comb, climbed through the ropes, bowed jerkily to every part of the house, and subsided thankfully on the opposite chair. Someone came and introduced them, holding them tightly the while as if afraid of their slipping through his fingers. They shook hands with every appearance of doing their duty in the face of tremendous odds. A gong clanged, and they came to life.

13

To Kif it was primarily a fight, and a good one. He saw nothing consciously of the beauty of those poised dancing figures in the flooding light; nothing of the ripple of biceps and deltoid, of swung torso and quick feet, of light sweat that made silver high-lights on the golden bodies, of the gracious appeal of a perfectly trained thing in complete relaxation. But long after the night's entertainment was over the recollection of it caused him a satisfaction that was not due wholly to the excitement of contest.

In the third round the 'curry-comb' floored the slim youth with an upper-cut which his habitually crouching position had masked until it was too late for the slim one to parry. He went down heavily and the umpire had counted eight before he had struggled to his knees; but he was on his feet in time, blindly fighting off the elated 'curry-comb', who was out to make an end of an easy thing.

Much good sentiment has been wasted on the man who will fight on when in pain. Pain, instead of evoking the desire to give up, incites to action by a direct appeal to temper, as any animal trainer will bear witness. But the man who has the will to make himself fight when dazed, sick, and half blind is a hero. Something of that Kif felt in the suspense of the moment. He had no pity, as most boys of his age would have had, for the staggering figure fending off attacks he could hardly see, but he had the most intense admiration—an admiration that speared him like a knife, an admiration that began in unaccustomed hero-worship and ended in envy.

'Game chap, that!' said the marine to Kif when the gong had saved the object of his admiration from extinction and he was being revived by anxious seconds in the corner. 'The black chap looks to be about half a stone heavier, though he can't be.'

The fourth round found the slim one so far recovered that the 'curry-comb' reverted to the cautious tactics which had lost him the first two rounds. His supporters became vocal in their disapproval. Victory had been his for the taking, and he had failed to grasp it. With the ingenuity of their kind they aimed their blow-arrows where they stung most maddeningly. Their victim became angry, and twice his opponent's right landed smartly in his ribs through a too impetuous movement on his own part. More and more he lost his coolness. In the sixth round he lost his temper entirely. The slim youth saw his chance and took it, and the bout was over.

Always afterwards when Kif heard the word 'boxing' he had a lightning picture of these two in the ring.

Kif left the building when the last bout was over, drunk with satisfaction. Of all heady drinks the achieving of a much-wanted ambition is the headiest. Love, the most vaunted of the intoxicating beverages, is a poor thing, sharp with fear, flat with doubt, bitter with longing. But this realisation of an ambition—even if it is only tobogganing down a grass slope behind Authority's back to the detriment of microscopic shorts—this achieving! To have been, to have seen, to have done! Nothing makes a man so fey, so god-like.

And Kif, his head buried in Y.M.C.A. blankets, was fey because he had attended a boxing match.

3

Kif set out for London next morning snuffing the wet spring air on his way to the station as a terrier snuffs at a rat-hole. Any morning is a morning for setting out, but two are ideal: a damp spring morning when the little wind is full of the scent of growing things and the sky has lifted from forgotten horizons; and an autumn morning, still and faintly frosty and full of mellow sunlight when the hedges are cut and the trees tidied from the walks. One sings: 'Come and see! Come and see!' And the other says: 'It is over; let us go.' Kif on that spring morning trod the moist pavements as a king enjoying his own.

In the warmth of the railway carriage he grew sleepy again, and for the first half hour watched a strange country wheeling by in a mildly interested somnolence. A fat elderly countrywoman seated in the middle of the opposite seat regarded him with obtrusive benevolence. She had cheeks like the apples in her own orchard and round china-blue eyes. Her grey-brown hair was parted in the middle and sleeked down in a thin shining enamel under a degrading and meaningless erection of net, lace, wire, feathers, sequins and flowers which was probably the pride of her heart. She sat clutching to her bosom a well-filled basket, though the next stop was a good hour away. It rested uneasily on the steep escarpment of her lap and every now and then slid slowly and was rescued by its owner in a convulsive hitch. With the air of one invaded suddenly by a new idea she now started a search in this receptacle and after some exploration produced a crumpled little paper bag. She unrolled the top, gave a reassuring glance at the contents, and with an embarrassing disregard of her nearer neighbours she strained billowing over her basket and proffered the bag to Kif. Kif, amused and gratified at the marked preference, smiled at her, awkwardly inserted his big hand into the trifling scrap of crushed paper and with infinite difficulty withdrew a sweet.

'You're young to be serving,' she said, offering the sweets to the soldier on her right, but keeping her eyes on Kif.

'I'm eighteen.'

'Oh, dear, dear. Just a baby. What about your mother? What does she think?'

'Haven't got one.' Her eyes reminded him of Mary.

'And are you going to the front now?'

'Not me,' said Kif comfortably. 'I'm going on the spree.'

This left her rather in the air. She looked doubtful, and was obviously moved to warn his motherless innocence of the dangers that awaited him, but did not feel equal to it in face of such an audience.

But she had broken the ice of railway-compartment good manners and presently the conversation became general. Under cover of it the soldier opposite Kif—the recipient of the old lady's belated charity—said to him:

'Going to spend your leave in London?'

And they talked together, the desultory unaccented talk of strangers who have yet a common bond. Kif found that his new acquaintance was almost more unattached than he himself. He was an Australian who, beyond the larger ports of Britain, knew nothing at all of the country. In spite of the martial bravery of a Cameron kilt, he was, and always would be, a sailor. He had been the mate of a wind-jammer which put into the Clyde in October. Overcome by the prevailing fever and fired by several drinks to a sublime pitch of military fervour he in one mad moment turned his back on the sea which had been his world literally since his birth, thrusting his freedom royally if insanely into the maw of an insensate machine and becoming a thing of no account to

be chivvied about in strange duties by infantine lance-corporals with the down still on their cheeks. That the bitterness of the inevitable awakening had not drowned his worth was obvious in the three stripes which adorned his upper arm.

All these facts Kif learned severally and in the course of time. At the moment he saw only a 'Jock' who regarded him with childish eyes, whose colour reminded him of heather honey—or was it wet sawdust?—and whose mild expression was astonishingly contradicted by the long line of the ruthless mouth marked with the faint perpendicular lines of old cuts. He looked with his fresh colouring and dreamy eyes ridiculously like a baby in a perambulator until one noticed his mouth; when he smiled, too, his teeth showed broad and short with a queer sawn-off look that was somehow cruel.

Kif liked him; liked his quiet soft voice, his half-shy air and the suggestion that hung about him of things seen and done. And he in his turn liked the boy with the bold dark face and eyes that could laugh so readily at the sentimental vagaries of fat countrywomen. When he discovered that Kif had no plans beyond staying 'at a Y or somewhere' he fell silent, and when they tumbled on to the platform at Waterloo, two stray mortals in a purposeful world, he said:

'Look here, I'll show you London if you'll keep me away from the docks. Is it a bargain?'

'It's a bet!' said Kif after a moment's surprised pause, and together they went out into the streets.

Travenna—for that improbably but actually was the Australian's name—decided against a Y.M.C.A. 'I've had enough of the barrack-room for the moment. I know a woman who'll take us in. I used to stay with her when we were in the river and I had time to burn.'

He took Kif to one of these little streets of two-storey houses below London wall. A woman answered his knock—a middle-aged woman with a frizzy Alexandra fringe and a forbidding expression which was due more to absence of mind than to presence of intention.

'Hullo, Mrs Clamp!' he said, 'can you give us a room?'

She looked at him coldly for a second or two. Then her beady black eyes broke into twinkles and she beamed welcome and amusement.

'Well, my! well, my!' she said, 'if it ain't Mr Travenna! Well, you are a one!' she added, still holding the hand she had shaken and using it as a lever to push him away from her for the better examination of him. 'And you do look a treat in them Scotch clothes. Bit of a change from nyvy, hy? And why isn't your friend a Scotchman too?'

This was her polite way of including Kif in the conversation.

'Me? I got knocked over in the rush,' said Kif.

'Weren't in time in the queue, hy? Well, well, come in and 'ave something to eat while I see about your room. Of course you can 'ave a room. Changed days an' no mistake,' she went on as she ushered them into a front room. 'There's Arthur somewhere in the country'—the country to Mrs Clamp was a nebulous region the only positive quality of which was that it wasn't London—'getting the most 'orrible indigestion trying to eat horse. It ain't in human nature, I 'olds, to assimilate stuff like that. In sausage, maybe, I wouldn't wonder. But not in slabs. Now I'll cook you something you can eat. I bet you ain't had a steak an' onions like mine for a bit, hy?'

She disappeared in laughter at the heartfelt sally her remark had provoked, delighted to be cooking for hungry men again. Before she married a Quartermaster and gave four sons to the sea's service she had cooked for more fastidious palates with entire success and equal enthusiasm.

Travenna sprawled on the minute sofa while Kif fingered the curiosities that crowded every horizontal surface and overflowed on to the walls.

'What do you want to do first?' asked Travenna. 'It's your call.'

'I just want to mooch round first and then I want to go to a theatre.'

'That's a good programme.'

'And I would like to see some racing if there is any near.'

Travenna whistled. 'That's not in my department. Never happened on any. But I'll certainly go racing now it's been pointed out to me. We're going to have a bonza time.'

That the time was a bonza one is proved by the fact that Kif spent the whole of the rest of his leave in London. It was perhaps the happiest week of his life. Every day was a succession of new things, of ambitions achieved. Things which he had wanted and which had appeared to be vain dreams six months ago suddenly crystallised to reality. And the reality was in most cases better than his dreams. London which in the first hours seemed drab and ordinary had become before he left it the all-satisfying thing it is to its lovers. Travenna with his colonial desire to see things and his native readiness to do anything once made a companion after Kif's own heart. He was a mass of contradictions, but fundamentally he was a sentimental child. And in some of their expeditions they were ridiculously like a couple of good children. They spent an instructive morning being solemnly conducted over the Tower, and a very hilarious afternoon at the Zoo. They gave tea to a couple of girls who ogled them as they were wiping their eyes in front of the monkey-house, and bade them farewell outside Selfridge's after having paid their bus fare home, since they had booked seats for a musical comedy and had no intention of 'wasting the evening on a pair of skirts', as Travenna remarked. That Kif's nights were spent in blameless slumber in one of the beds at Mrs Clamp's was not due to any desire for chastity on his part, but to the direct intervention of the wind-jammer's mate, who knew the most fashionable dives from 'Frisco to Hong Kong and who was not going to have it said that any boy found knowledge in his company.

So much has been written—and charitably condoned—concerning the conduct of final leaves that I feel it behoves me to present this picture of a typical evening at the Clamp establishment. Kif and Travenna had come in hilarious and slightly elevated from witnessing a revue so soaked in military sentiment and studded with patriotic tableaux as to be unbearable to more sophisticated palates—Kif had borne the sentimental parts for the sake of the spectacular and Travenna the spectacular for the sake of the sentimental—and after a large supper, retrieved from the stove where it had been left to keep hot, and eaten among the curios, they had retired for the night. Travenna was in bed and Kif was trying on his kilt. The secret conviction that one would adorn a garment considerably better than one's neighbour extends from crowns to cast-off trilbys, and though more blatant among women is by no means peculiar to them.

'It droops at the back,' said the critic from his pillows. 'You'll have to stick out behind more.'

But Kif was not listening. He was wrestling with the difficulty of beholding an adequate portion of himself in the minute swinging mirror on the toilet table. He would adjust its angle and retreat hopefully a few steps only to advance again and patiently persuade its stiff and too-sudden joints through a microscopic arc. After several futile attempts he mounted a chair and tried to solve the difficulty on Mahomet's principle with recalcitrant mountains. This gave him for the first time an excellent view of his be-spatted feet but of nothing else. He sat down on the chair and laughed helplessly.

'If you sit on my pleats wrong ways on I'll put you to sleep for a month,' warned Travenna.

'Can you box?' asked Kif, suddenly interested.

'No,' said the ex-mate, 'I can hit.'

'Oh, well, I can shoot, myself. But I'd like to be able to box.'

'Look here,' said Travenna, not interested in mock warfare, 'I'll work the mirror for you if you go down and get that other bottle of beer.'

Kif assenting, he got himself out of bed and solemnly worked the mirror up and down while Kif delighted in a fragmentary but continuous reflection of himself.

'You're a sport,' said Kif. 'It's a fine rig-out. I wish now I'd been firmer and joined a Highland regiment. But I couldn't leave the Carnshires now. There aren't any flies on the Half-and-Halfers.'

'It still droops at the back,' said Travenna. 'Buzz off and get the beer.'

Kif, in spite of his country upbringing and ancestry—or perhaps because of it—was a town lover, and London laid her spell on a willing victim. After the first hours of vague disappointment he had capitulated with the suddenness of one who has for a moment failed to recognise a friend in some new garb. From a bus-top he surveyed his kingdom and found it good. From the street level he surveyed it and found it almost familiar. In all his perambulations, in all his crowding new experiences one quality singled him out from the army of countrymen who come to view London for the first time. Kif never gaped, mentally or physically. Even he himself realised that everything was surprisingly as he had expected it to be. And he drew as much satisfaction from that fact as the gaper does from his wonder. His calm acceptance of things which had never before entered his actual experience was due partly to his reading, which if indiscriminate had been sufficiently copious, and partly to a constitutional lack of awe. Kif's bump of reverence was, to say the least, ill-developed. He strode the alien pavements full of a little warm chortling joy that London after all was only this. He had the feeling of having come home.

On the third day Travenna announced that, having exhausted the more obvious pleasures of the town, they would now go racing.

'If there is any near London to-day,' amended Kif doubtfully.

'If there isn't we'll go where there is some,' said the Australian.

Mrs Clamp, coming in with the breakfast tray, brought a morning paper, and was drawn into the discussion. Where was Kempton Park? How did one get there?

She replaced the cover which she had been in the act of removing from a large dish of bacon and eggs and surveyed them mock-sorrowfully.

'So that's the latest?' she said to Travenna. 'As if you 'adn't lost enough fortunes what with poker and what not. An' 'orses are a deal wuss than cards, that they are.'

'*Are* they?' said Travenna, interested. 'Well, as I haven't touched a chip since I left Boston, I think I'm due a little gamble. They don't play cards in the British army. Only kid's games.'

'Well, if you take my advice you'll either stay at 'ome or else leave your pocket-book with me. If you don't lose it betting you'll lose it the other way. There's a nasty lot goes racing.'

'You seem to know a lot about it, mother.'

'Oh yes, I been to the Derby many a time. But that's different.'

'How, different?'

'Well, the Derby ain't racing in the ordinary manner of speaking. The Derby's all right. But Kempton! 'Ere, 'ave your eggs before they're cold.'

'Well, it seems my education's been neglected in some ways, and that's going to be rectified this very day.'

'Don't forget to leave your vallybles behind and don't say I didn't warn you,' she said as she went out. A second later she thrust her head in again to say: 'And don't back the favourite.'

Halfway through breakfast Travenna's mind took one of its childish and unexpected turns.

'I'm damned if I'm going to a social occasion in this damned uniform,' he said suddenly, laying down his knife and fork for the better considering of the situation.

Kif looked up in surprise. 'Why, I thought you liked it?'

'I like it all right in its proper place, but I'm damned if I'm going to a race-meeting in it.'

'What can you do?'

'Haven't thought yet. Tell you after breakfast.' He resumed his eating with an indignant expression on his face which would have been funny to a less concerned observer than Kif who was afraid, not knowing Travenna, that the plans for the day might be brought to nothing because of this unforeseen whim of the Australian's.

But half an hour later the sitting-room was strewn with the garments of the male members of the Clamp family which their delighted hostess had drawn from moth-ball cupboards. They lay across the sofa and hung, limp and grotesque, from chairs, like marionettes drained of their stuffing, each still keeping strangely the impression of its wearer's characteristic. Mrs Clamp introduced them after the manner of Mrs Jarley, and eyed them with the complacence of a terrier who has produced a bone, a conjurer who has proved the miraculous capacity of a hat. Travenna with his chin tucked in stood in the middle of the floor like a bull about to charge, while his mild golden eyes went back and fore over the array. At last he picked up some navy blue garments from the sofa. 'This may do,' he said, and was making for the door when his gaze in passing fell again on a grey broken-checked cloth known as Glen Urquhart. He hesitated in his stride and without remark gathered the grey suit to him.

'Come along, Kif,' he called from the stairs. 'Come and see the fun.'

'Shout when you've got the first lot on, and I'll conduct a general inspection,' said Kif, and retired into the scullery with Mrs Clamp, where he dried the breakfast things in spite of that good lady's protests and much to her admiration.

He hung the last cup on its nail, spread the towel carefully to dry and disappeared up the stairs two at a time like a small boy released from school. He entered the bedroom just as Travenna was in the act of hurling a grey-checked waistcoat into the far corner by the washstand. The grey trousers which he was wearing outlined too lovingly his heated person.

'It's a mystery to me,' he said to Kif, 'how such a fine upstanding pair as old Clamp and his missis produced such a set of under-sized sissies as their sons seem to be.'

His indignant eye together with the clinging trousers were too much for Kif. He subsided on the edge of the bed and laughed tearfully. And Travenna after a moment's hesitation joined him.

'What do you want trousers for when you have a kilt?' Kif asked presently, sitting up and drawing a khaki coat-sleeve across his wet eyes.

'I am going,' said Travenna, with a pause between each word and an edge to his speech that his platoon knew well, and that slovenly deck-hands had known of old, 'to Kempton Park as a private individual—as a gentleman. As myself, in fact. Not as Number 123456789 of any army in the universe. I am now going out to buy a suit, and you are coming with me.'

In the Strand Travenna bought himself a complete outfit and was inclined to be offended that Kif would not accept his offer and let himself be garbed afresh at his friend's expense.

'What's the use of me getting myself up like a liner captain ashore,' he observed pertinently, 'if you're going to hang on to these togs?'

Kif felt the truth of the argument, but was immovable. He hardly knew why he refused. It was partly pride, partly shyness, partly a half-born and unacknowledged loyalty to the uniform which had released him from slavery. He longed to see himself clothed as Travenna was clothed in delicate brown cloth and fine shirting, to see the effect on himself of these trousers which hung with so ravishing a line straight to the thick smooth brown shoes. And yet he refused, and could not have told why.

He even suggested to Travenna that, since by his sartorial glory he had raised himself out of what he called 'plating class', they should go separately to the races. This restored Travenna's good humour. He cuffed Kif lightly on the side of the head. 'Come on,' he said, and left a bowing shop-keeper raining refined blessings. They walked all the way to Waterloo and Travenna admired himself blatantly in every window.

But Kif from the minute he entered the railway carriage forgot all about clothes. Even Travenna's passage-at-arms with the stout elderly gentleman who thought that he (Travenna) ought to be serving his king and country instead of going to a race meeting faded into greyness beside the dazzling fact of another

21

ambition about to be realised. And nothing in the realisation damped his happiness.

There was sunlight on the thick green of the trees, on the flat pale green of the course. Sunlight on the white rails and the white stand. The warm air in the paddock was full of the frou-frou of voices that came and went above the murmur which was all that remained at this distance of the clamour of the ring. Warm air full of pleasant smells: bitter cigarette smoke, the faint fine scents of well-dressed women, the sweet smell of crushed grass, the good clean smell of horses. Now and then a high far voice called the numbers of the runners, a voice that floated out over the crowd as mournful and plaintive as any muezzin calling the faithful to prayer. And within the magic white circle of the parade ring, stepping daintily, fastidiously, tolerant for the most part of the crowd that leaned in critical appreciation along the rails, went the objects of Kif's adoration. Chestnut, bay, and brown, they filed sedately round the tan-bark track, the sunlight shivering along the high-lights on their coats, their tails floating gently behind them, their eyes acquiescent, their ears inquisitive. Here a bay snatched at his bit, pulling, and the lad who was leading him remonstrated mildly with him. Here a filly shied away like a blown feather from a suddenly opened sunshade, stood quivering, gazing, and then, reassured, dropped her head and followed her minute custodian into file again.

Kif leaned against the rail and sucked it all in as a thirsty man takes water. Nothing was strange to him. He had done this in imagination many times. He could tell the eager Travenna everything he wanted to know of the where, the what, and the when, and quite an impressive amount of the why. More than ever, he had come home.

Travenna had recognised a spiritual resting-place if not a home in Tattersall's and spent his time in joyful excursions between the paddock and the Ring. In the Ring, tips were confided to him by chance acquaintances or a name was bandied about, and he would reappear at Kif's elbow demanding 'Where is Crimson Baby? I want to see Crimson Baby'. Having seen, he would look interestedly at the medium of his investment and go back to put his money on. Kif refused to have a bet in each race. He was saving up for a gamble, he explained. When he saw something he really fancied he was going to put all he had to spare on it. He stayed habitually in the paddock till the last jockey had been thrown into the saddle and led through the gate. He was back in the paddock to see the winner unsaddled, while Travenna, who was astoundingly lucky, was collecting his due from disgusted bookmakers. And five minutes later he was propped against the parade-ring rails in his old place watching the placid procession, watching the personalities gather in the sacred circle for the next race; first a trainer or two, spare, hard-lipped men, with clear, wrinkled eyes, quiet, indifferent; or a lad doing proxy, neat, stiff-legged, conscious of his hands; then the owners, well fleshed for the most part, genial or haughty as their temperaments were, full of jests or dropping a curt remark. A pause in the influx, and lastly the jockeys, smiling, careless-seeming, more or less self-conscious, crossing the space with their jerky, straight-footed walk as quickly as possible, and spilling as they went a riot of colour that danced and flamed among the drab. Another pause, and mounting time. Kif regretted that one pair of eyes was not adequate to absorb so prodigal an outlay of beauty and incident. Sidling, pirouetting horses, horses standing still and proud, jockeys tossed, a flash of colour, on to shining, uneasy backs, patient lads, anxious, efficient men, the almost imperceptible movement to the gate that merged the dizzy kaleidoscope into a single glowing silken string.

Before the big race of the afternoon Travenna flung himself breathless against the rail by Kif's side with an enthusiasm which shook the stout wood.

'Well, I'll say this is a great game. I've won seven pound ten so far. Found your fancy yet?'

'Yes,' said Kif, 'there he is. Number eleven.' He pointed to a smallish bay, almost a pony, with black points. 'Wilton trains him. Not So Fast, he's called.'

'That's a fool name for a horse.'

'Well, you see, he's by Investigator out of Cautious Dame.'

Travenna regarded his friend's choice a little longer and then remarked:

'You can't be said to have a flashy taste in horseflesh, anyway. Where's this Strathnairn they're all talking about? They won't give more than evens.'

'He hasn't come in yet.'

'What's extra special about him that they're so frightened?'

Kif enumerated as well as he could remember the achievements of Strathnairn. 'He was fourth in the Derby last year,' he finished, and even as he spoke there was a sudden crescendo of the crowd's murmuring followed by a hush. Strathnairn had come into the ring.

Quiet lay like a spell on the four-deep sophisticated crowd as he made his slow way round the track. Black except for a white diamond, sixteen hands, magnificently muscled, almost impossible to fault, he moved proudly, a king enjoying the homage of his subjects. Hardened race-goers gaped in silence, or uttered a monosyllabic and blasphemous appreciation. Kif, attune to wonders, had not anticipated anything like this. Travenna, after having watched him round the ring in silence, said:

'I didn't know they made them like that. And you said he can do things as well as looking like that?' He looked a little longer. 'Well,' he said, heaving himself off the rails and rubbing his ribs tenderly, 'I expect you've changed your mind about what-d'you-call-it—Not So Fast?'

'No, I haven't.'

'What! Are you going to back him to beat *that*?'

'*That* is going to carry nine stone and mine has only seven stone two. And— — Oh well, I said I'd wait till I found one I liked, and I've found him, that's all.'

He took out his wallet and gave Travenna two notes. 'Put that on for me and take up two men's room in the stand till I come.'

Kif was back in the stand in time to see the parade. Strathnairn, as befitted the top-weight, led the glittering line that trailed its slow length down the middle of the course, Flannigan, the leading jockey of the day, sitting upright and pleased on the superb back.

'You're a fool, Kif,' said Travenna amiably as the cherry and gold jacket was borne past them. 'I don't know the first thing about horses, and you probably know quite a little, but you don't need to know anything to see that that thing's the icing on the cake.'

Kif did not answer. His eye was searching down the lovely line for the green jacket and orange cap. There they were, Not So Fast demure but alert; neat, beautifully turned, well-proportioned—but a mere pony. His jockey, an about-to-be fashionable apprentice, made in his unexpected beauty a fitting pilot for so gracious a thing. His small face under the orange cap was carved like a cameo, delicate, aquiline, pale like ivory. He went past easy and grave, his small bright eyes on his mount's dark poll.

Kif drew a long breath. Something was hurting in his chest. 'If that kid'—the kid was four years his senior—'only did the little horse justice he would show that sultan up at the top a thing or two.'

They were cantering now, the colours fading rapidly into mere specks far down the course.

'I got a hundred to seven for you,' said Travenna. 'Strathnairn is odds on. They offered me evens and I went to scout for a better price, and when I came back he said it was eleven to eight on. He'd give a 'Frisco dealer points and a beating.'

He unslung the glasses with which Mrs Clamp had furnished them, and which the vicissitudes of many Derby days had wrought to the battered polish considered *de rigueur* in racing.

'A man gave me a tip for Firth. Do you know what that was like?'

'Yes, he was that queer whitey-grey, fourth in the parade.'

'They're frightened of him too. Two to one was all they'd give, so I left it. Change your mind and have something hopeful before it's too late?'

Kif grinned and shook his head. He watched the heated jostling throng in front of him, and was blissfully sorry for them scrambling to and fro there for a point above the odds, and caring not at all, so that their money was well placed, what carried it. *They* had no little bay with black points. Calculation was in their eye, and *Racing-up-to-Date* bulged from their pockets. He was about to tell Travenna how superior to him and to everyone else there he was feeling when the roar of 'They're off!' swamped every other consideration. In the ensuing quiet, late bettors fled from the ring to what vantage point they might find in the packed stand. Travenna, whose turn it was, had focussed the glasses on the far bend when he turned suddenly and shoved them at Kif. 'Here you are, kid,' he said. And Kif took them. This was his hour.

Far down there at the bend the course lay sunny and tranquil, quite deserted. While he could have counted six he watched the distant trees and listened to his heart thudding. A blur of swiftly moving colour swam into the green and fled along the back stretch to the bend.

'Badly off,' the murmur went round, 'something badly off.'

24

At the bend the blur resolved itself into its elements and the smooth effortless of its progress gave place to the visible striving of horse and man. Out from the ruck came a grey horse riderless. Kif remembered that Firth's jockey wore colours of French grey and his heart resumed its place. Second by second the distance between the field and the grey horse widened. Firth . . . the word was bandied about . . . Firth.

'What's that fool doing?' said an irate voice behind. 'Does he think he can keep up that pace with eight stone three?'

'He's crazy, or else the colt's bolted.'

But still the grey came on and there was a distinct green hiatus between him and the rest. Then two horses came out in pursuit, a red jacket and a magpie one, and presently a third. They had come to the grey's quarters without making any impression or causing a falter in the machine-like stride of the leader when a black whirlwind broke from the shifting mass and swept irresistible up the course. A roar from the stands. Flannigan and the favourite! They passed the third of the challengers as though he had been standing still. The jockey in the scarlet lifted his whip twice and faded out.

'Flannigan's bringing him early.'

'Afraid of Firth, I expect.'

Now the grey, the bay carrying the magpie jacket, and Strathnairn were racing side by side. The bay's jockey was sitting down to it and the bay was struggling gamely. But it was a struggle. With still more than a furlong to go he dropped back beaten. Strathnairn and Firth were left to fight it out. It was incredible that the grey could keep in front much longer. The pace had been a good one. But still his rider had not moved. And then without apparent cause he brought out his whip and the crowd read the signal and roared again. Strathnairn!

But Kif's heart was heavy. He turned the glasses again on the ruck, despairingly, and saw what none of the absorbed crowd looked for. On the outside, coming up from what seemed an immense distance in the rear was the green jacket and orange cap—flying! Kif had not realised that anything on four legs could cover the ground like that. The excited murmur of the crowd wavered, broke. They had seen. In a heavy-breathing silence they watched the new-comer while the sound of the hoofs grew in the silence. Would he do it? Firth was still holding Strathnairn, but they knew that Flannigan had his measure. He could beat Firth, but what about this with the green and yellow?

'What's that thing?'

'It's that Investigator colt of Rayner's.'

Kif's heart was suffocating him. The apprentice was sitting motionless on Not So Fast, crouched down with his face alongside the flying dark mane. Someone called an offer in Tattersall's. It fell unheeded into the silence. Speech struck from their lips, they watched him come. He was only four lengths from the leaders now, and Flannigan woke to the danger. He urged Strathnairn. There was no response. Thrice his whip fell and Strathnairn leaped forward. But Not

So Fast was level with him. In front of him. Half a length. A length. Half a length.

The post flashed by.

Kif's knees were trembling. Travenna looked at him delightedly.

'Well, I'm damned, but he deserved it, and so do you for backing him,' he said. But Kif was already shoving through the dazed crowd to the exit where the policemen had but newly drawn aside the barrier. He tore along the path to the paddock. There would be a crowd from the Club side, and he must see the little horse once more.

Pressed against the rail of the unsaddling enclosure he saw Not So Fast come back, still demure, still alert, sweating but not distressed. The apprentice, his ivory beauty flushed and a little tight smile playing round his mouth, patted the wet neck lovingly before he carried his saddle into the weighing-room. The trainer was trying to look as if he had not cared much one way or the other. The owner had given up any attempt to hide his feelings and was beaming on all and sundry. Round about, the varied crowd talked in Kif's ear.

'Deserves it. Left lengths, he was.'

'Good advertisement for Investigator.'

'. . . someday for that boy if he keeps steady.'

'Bred him himself.'

'What was the price?'

'Weighed in!' shouted a voice, and the little bay was led out of Kif's sight. He went slowly back to Travenna, who presented him with a wad of notes.

'Here you are, Rockfeller. You'll be able to take a tram now when your feet ache.'

Kif, bewildered by the sight of his wealth, handled the wad doubtfully.

'Count it if you want to, I don't mind,' laughed Travenna.

'I was just thinking that I'll have to bet on the other races after all to get rid of some of this.'

'Come on!' said his friend. 'I've just discovered that the man who trains *that*,' he pointed with his stubby forefinger to a name on the card for the next race, 'is an Australian, and I'm going to put my shirt on it.'

If the rest of the afternoon was rather an anti-climax Kif was not aware of it. He was wrapped in a happy dream.

In bed that night he decided that some day he would own a thoroughbred, bay with black points, and he would call it—what would he call it?

He was asleep before he had chosen a name.

_____

The 6.10 at Waterloo, a wet evening, and the end of his leave. Travenna, who had been ordered to Chelsea barracks for a course of instruction, was on the platform to see him go.

For the first time Kif had a real pang at parting from a fellow-being.

'Good-bye,' said Travenna, giving him his hand, but not looking at him. 'Good luck!'

'So long,' said Kif.

They never met again.

Kif was half way back to his battalion when he remembered that he had meant to send Mary a picture postcard from London.

4

Kif left England in June on a grey still evening when the sea was a level floor of lavender and Folkestone lay dreaming and lightless, a mere gathering of the greyness where the white cliffs still glimmered. The subdued bustle of readjustment which was the backwash of embarkment faded into a little silence as the dim coast vanished, broke out again, and eventually settled into the low hum of conversation which was one with the faint thud and wash of the *Arundel* nosing her way indifferently towards France. Kif leaned against the rail and thought of nothing in particular. The calm of the night was in him and some of its dreaminess and unreality. On one side of him Fatty Roberts, the company buffoon, was calling heaven to witness that if he died it would be from tobacco starvation and not from bullets. On the other was Barclay, very quiet and whistling snatches of something under his breath. Further away was the voice of Lance-corporal Struthers insisting—Kif could almost see the gesticulation—that it was 'the principle of the thing, sergeant.'

Jimmy had put up his first stripe shortly before he went on leave. The promotion elated him not at all. It was in his estimation the natural order of events and he treated it as such. He had spent his leave lording it over his admiring women-folk—five sisters, a mother, and a grandmother—and showing off blatantly before his elder brother, who had not yet torn himself from his browsing life among the sheep. 'One of these days he'll take root, mark me,' he had said. He had come back to the battalion with three recruits in his train whom he had proceeded to adopt, bully and mother, very much as he had Kif. There was no limit to Jimmy's fostering propensities. He was the complete company-sergeant-major in embryo. He had not wet his promotion beyond a mild exchange of drinks, but on the night that the battalion heard definitely that they were 'for off' he had come back to camp so riotously drunk that Barclay and Kif had hard work to save the infant stripe. At the cost of twenty minutes' hard work, some desperate expedients and some shin bruises, they did it, however. Jimmy had asked next morning, 'Who put me to bed last night?' but had offered not a word of spoken thanks. He had made a little eloquent gesture with his head, and left the matter there. In the months that followed he paid his debt in divers ways and many times.

Barclay had refused in spite of urgings from home, cogent arguments from his superiors, and the oratory of Jimmy Struthers, to consider taking a commission.

'It isn't my job,' he would say. 'I'll form fours, and march, and with luck register an outer, but I'm not going to mug up drills.'

What he really hated, though he would never say so, was the thought of responsibility. It was a thing his mind shied away from. If he took a commission he would be saddled with it night and day—an old man of the sea on his shoulders, perpetually clutching and weighing him down. It would be disastrous, he felt, to attempt to make himself into something he was not by nature. Disastrous not only to his own peace of mind, but perhaps to those unfortunates whose safety would depend on a man who had no confidence in himself. Therefore he stayed a private. And Kif was wholeheartedly glad, though he said nothing. Kif was popular enough in his platoon not to have necessarily missed Barclay if he had gone, but the fact remains that Kif was happier with Barclay, whom he did not always understand, than with Jimmy, whose language and habit of thought resembled his own. Barclay had twitted him gently about his failure to reach Golder's Green during his visit to London, and Kif had been perfectly frank about his doings with the exception of the visit to the zoo, which he suppressed, partly from an inward conviction that it was a childish proceeding, partly from fear of Barclay's amusement.

'Well, well,' said Jimmy—it was in the canteen and he was propped against the counter behind them—'you couldn't fairly expect him to posh himself up for the "afternoon tea" business on his precious leaf. He was out to see all he could in the time. And I bet he didn't leave anything out,' he added feelingly.

Barclay, who had been half saddened and a little foreboding somehow at Kif's rapture with the world, expressed more in his obvious happiness than in his account, smiled and said:

'Oh, as long as he didn't see more than there was. . . .'

Jimmy's eyebrows went up. 'I suppose that's awful clever,' he said. 'I never read anything but the football results myself.'

Only brigadier-generals impressed Jimmy, and they not seriously. But Kif had wondered, going to sleep, what exactly Barclay had meant.

He looked down at him now in the dark and wondered what he was thinking. He had a family to be sorry about; a mother and things. It must be rotten to have other folks to consider. Thus Kif, all unaware that he should be feeling the want of someone to be sorry for him. His roving eye caught a familiar profile outlined against the sky and the direction of his thoughts changed. He considered the profile admiringly: the stubborn set of the head, thrust slightly forward so that the jaw was lifted, the grim upper lip which made a very slightly convex curve, and the short straight line of the lower one to the suddenly jutting chin. That Murray Heaton, ex-horse-breeder and occasional cross-country jockey had earned the unqualified approval of as mixed a company as ever was brought together, was due not to any fortunate sally at a critical moment, but to their shrewd recognition of his worth as a leader. His men not only obeyed him unquestioningly, admired him, quoted him, and imitated him, but they looked on him as their own property; than which is no better testimonial. Barclay admired the man's efficiency and envied him his complete self-confidence. Kif approved his lack of fuss, and the way his eyes smiled when his mouth did not. And Jimmy adored him in secret, and spoke possessively of him in public.

It is popularly supposed that proximity to horseflesh leaves some peculiar and indelible stamp on a man; a metaphorical straw in the mouth. I have never been able to see it. Apart from the draught-board-breeches-and-yellow-waistcoat brigade—which is limited, and in any case insignificant—your horseman, professional or otherwise, in mufti looks just like an admiral, a detective, an actor, a boy-in-buttons, or a stockbroker, as the case may be. Heaten looked rather like a lawyer until you noticed his hands. He had an uncanny capacity for seeing things which appeared to have happened behind his back, a fact which was partly responsible for the veneration in which he was held.

Kif, considering him, wondered for the first time what the possession of power would be like; what it would be like to order people about and to have them say 'sir' and look respectful. He considered it gravely. To decide instead of being decided for. And you'd have to see that the thing you decided on was done, of course. The whole thing would be a hell of a nuisance, now he came to think of it. Having other people dependent on you. You'd have money, of course. Money would be good. But you couldn't have a really good time, somehow. In which case the money would be of no use. No; being the boss was as far as he could see a dam' poor business.

So by devious routes did Barclay and Kif arrive at the same conclusion.

And with such unheroic thoughts did Kif journey to France.

5

This is not a war diary; it is merely the history of Kif. And Kif's experiences on the western front differed not one whit from those of any other private who went to France in 1915; they need not, therefore, be given in detail, since the details are known either by experience or hearsay to every soul who may read this book. Principally he learned in all their moods the verbs to scrounge, to wangle, and to take cover, and became proficient in all of them. He also learned to talk the lingua franca which obtained behind the lines, and which stood to the troops for French, and to the French people for English. He was at Loos in the autumn, and came scatheless through that welter of incredible bravery and monumental mismanagement, and was duly ribald in billets afterwards over the thanks of the Higher Command.

Ribaldry was a weapon which he needed rather less than the others, to whom it was often their only hold on that sense of proportion which is sanity. He used it rather as he had cursed night manoeuvres; because it was the fashion. It was not that he was insensible to the loss of his chums—though Jimmy and Barclay were still safe—nor to the horror of things, but some of the horror was mitigated by the fact that he still kept, in spite of the possibility of death and mutilation, that thirst for the unexpected that characterised him. He hated his tour in the line as everyone hated it; but he invariably volunteered for a raiding party, and would drag himself over the mud of no man's land, terrified but ecstatic. Before an attack or during a bombardment he waited in as palpitating suspense as the rest, until the danger was over; but after a short period of safety and boredom he had a vague desire to experience the moment again. Which is the quality which distinguished him from his fellows. Even the continuous mining in the Hulluch area which sapped in every sense one's morale left him less exhausted than it did the others. The possibility that the piece of trench which he occupied might at any moment be blown skyward—a possibility that most men found infinitely more unbearable than being shelled—was to him but a mitigant of the monotony of the eight-hour shifts of mine-carrying. It added a spice of chance to the prosaic labour of carrying bags of spoil—knobbly lumps of chalk that hurt his back—through inadequate passages and up indifferent stairs.

His two friends had to battle with the unspeakable conditions unhelped by any natural aptitude. To them ribaldry was a necessity, not an indulgence. Barclay's natural philosophy stood him in good stead where discomfort and danger were concerned, but broke down over dirt. There were times, stumbling down Hulluch alley through the wearing uncertainty of knee-deep mud and worn by a battering time in the line, that he could have wept aloud because he was filthy. But there was invariably a saving distraction at the crucial moment: Fatty Robert's panting observations on the inadequacy of communication trenches where a man of his generous proportions was concerned, or the total disappearance of the man in front of him into the mud and water. And the mining villages behind the lines were usually well equipped with baths, where a shower restored his good humour.

Jimmy, a bundle of nerves and devotion, was a model of efficiency, the model being as near the original Heaton one as Jimmy could make it. When things grew too thick he became short-tempered, and his tongue had a more caustic quality than usual; but no one had ever seen him 'rattled'.

At Béthune, where the rest billets were, and where life was fairly normal still, Kif had a mild flirtation with a buxom waitress at a café. That it was merely a mild flirtation was again not due to any excess of virtue on Kif's part, nor to backwardness on hers, but to the fact that his rival was a sergeant of his own battalion. Simone rightly felt that to achieve a double *affaire* in a place the size of Béthune with two men who were invariably out of the line together was possible but not politic. And if it was a question of a choice between a rather inarticulate private and any sergeant whatsoever she had no hesitation. The French have never been a sentimental nation, and their logic is beyond reproach. So Kif helped her to wash up, learning the names of dishes and pans in the process, and receiving a kiss now and then for his pains, and the sergeant took her walking.

In the spring of 1916 both Kif and Barclay got leave for Britain, and Barclay insisted that Kif, who obviously intended spending the whole of his in London, should stay at Golder's Green. Kif for the first time in his life was torn in two, and for the first time since he came to France he lost sleep. He had slumbered happily with the cold of a stone floor striking through a single blanket, with rain trickling down on him from between crazy tiles, with the enemy putting down a barrage half a mile away, with men moving backward and forward over his prostrate body and stumbling into it occasionally, with rats exploring his clothing and lice enlivening it. But now he stayed awake and thought about going to Barclay's people.

Barclay was sincere in his wish to have Kif spending his leave with him. Kif knew that. He even had a spasm of pride at the thought. If Barclay had been an independent individual and had asked him to spend his leave at his rooms Kif would have consented immediately. But there was this business of meeting and living with Barclay's people: his mother, his sister, his father. And though Barclay for some incredible reason wanted him it was extremely likely that to these people he would be merely a nuisance, something to be put up with for Barclay's sake. They probably wouldn't show it, of course. They might be very obviously nice to him. That would be worse, much worse. And if it was like that and he had accepted their invitation he would have no excuse for leaving them before his leave ended. And yet—they might not mind so much. Some of those ladies at the depot canteens had been quite easy to talk to. He would not always be round and in the way. And if they were all as nice as Barclay. . . .

So Kif turned it over and over, staring into the dark, wanting to plunge but fearing the depth of the water. For the first time his nerve failed him. He was still hesitating on the brink when Mrs Barclay's letter came. Kif had no correspondence except an occasional note from Mary or Mrs Vass with socks or sweets, in return for which he sent postcards, chosen with the help of Simone, on which the Union Jack and the Tricolor flourished amid roses of an indescribable pink. Barclay was with a working party when the mail arrived. Kif regarded incredulously the vivacious writing, so different from Mrs Vass's careful angularities and Mary's painful scrawl. He fingered the envelope doubtfully. There couldn't be a mistake. There was his name in full and his designation in every particular. He tore open the flap.

'DEAR KIF' (wrote Barclay's mother), 'I feel I must call you that because Tim never refers to you by any other name. Tim says that you are expecting to have leave very soon, and that you have no friends in London. Whether your leave coincides with Tim's or not we should be so glad to have you with us. That is, if you have made no other plans. You and my son have been such friends that I feel that we half know you already, and we are all keen to know you better. If you come we will do our best to give you a nice time in spite of little war-busy London. If you know in time tell us when to expect you—a procession goes through our spare room just now—but if not, don't let that keep you away. Walk in and we'll find a bed for you and be delighted to see you.

Yours most
sincerely,

M
A
R
G
A
RE
T
B
A
R
CL
A
Y.'

'Kif's had a love-letter,' said Fatty, regarding Kif's crimson face with malicious enjoyment.

'More like a bill, I'd say,' said another, puzzled to analyse the boy's expression.

"Is missus' 'ad triplits,' suggested a dapper little cockney known as Wigs, not from any artificiality about his sleek fair hair, but because his name was Clarkson.

This was received with *éclat*.

'Triplets yer granny!' insisted Fatty. "Oo ever blushed so coy-like over kids? It's a skirt.'

Kif consigned them all cheerfully to perdition and walked out of the barn in a hail of ribald suggestions. At a safe distance he sat down on a heap of bricks and read the letter slowly, twice. Then he replaced it in its envelope, smoothed it thoughtfully, and put it carefully away in his pocket-book.

The working party had returned by the time Kif came back to the barn. Barclay was reading a letter and two more were lying on his knee. The top one of the two had an envelope like the one Kif had received. Kif crossed to him and subsided crosslegged on the floor a few feet away. He picked up a straw and absently broke it inch by inch its entire length. As Barclay shoved his first letter into its envelope Kif, twisting the straw painfully, said:

'I had a letter from your mother.'

He threw away the tortured straw, and as Barclay turned to him he bent to pick up another one so that his face was not visible.

'Oh?' Barclay regarded the top of Kif's service cap with a smiling glance. 'Nice woman my mother.'

'If you really mean it about wanting me at your home, I'll come.'

'Good man!' said Barclay. 'That's settled.' And he tore open his second letter. Then, remembering, he picked up an unopened weekly paper and handed it to Kif.

'Here you are,' he said. 'I've two to read yet. Don't pass it on till I've had a squint at it. Wigs cut out the pretties ones in the last before I'd as much as had a glance at it.'

Kif split the wrapper and rolled the curling paper backwards with absent-minded care. He turned the pages conscientiously, but he saw nothing of the contents. There was something he must ask, and he did not know how to do it. He considered waiting until it was dark ; when they were going to sleep, perhaps. But he must see Barclay's face. If he were going to know for certain—and he must know—he would have to ask now. He shut the paper and rolled it tightly between his hands. Barclay was finishing the reading of his mother's letter and the amusement on his face nerved Kif to the point.

'I say,' he said slowly, 'did you ask your mother to write that letter?'

'What letter?' asked Barclay, looking up with the delight of far-away things still about him and only half comprehending Kif's presence.

Kif swallowed audibly. 'The letter to me,' he said.

'Not I!' said Barclay, thoroughly roused now and thankful to be able to be truthful. 'That was entirely off her own bat.'

He was suddenly conscious of the need to be facetious. 'If she's dragging you into the family circle against your will, don't blame me. She's a leech when she gets an idea into her head.'

Kif smiled and rose, but said nothing. He put the paper down gently by Barclay's side—some of the deliberation of the countryman still hung about his movements—and went out. In another minute he would make a fool of himself. He regarded two bare and scoliotic poplars opposite in hot disgust. What the hell was the matter with him ? Getting soft like this for no ruddy reason. What the . . . . A stream of oaths chased themselves through his brain as he whipped himself to composure.

He was merely an old campaigner who needed his leave very badly. He was just sixteen, and he had never had a letter like that from anyone before.

6

It was thick fog and one in the morning as they walked out of Victoria Station. They stood on the kerb and considered. Kif drew what was meant to be an ecstatic breath and choked. Barclay stamped his feet automatically. It was certainly a chill reception.

'After all,' said the Londoner suddenly, 'it can't be much more than four miles. Queer how far away you think the suburbs when there are buses and tubes, and you've never done a route march. And after all it's only a mile or two. I'm blowed if I'm going to spend the night here when there's a perfectly good bed only four miles away. Let's hoof it.'

'But we'll be rousing them in the middle of the night?'

'They'll be thrilled to the marrow,' predicted the son of the house, and stepped off into the fog.

They tramped steadily without remark for some time, both fully conscious of the wonder that the shadowy world about them was the London of their dreams. To Barclay this world of vague tall shapes had a silent watchful awareness. Aloof but aware. He had a sudden recollection of Torridon mountains as he had seen them during a Highland holiday, a slight scarf of mist rising slowly but with uncanny deliberation from their still, awful faces. Withdrawn but aware, he thought. To Kif the town was a sleeping place, and he the only aware thing in a world that dreamed. The thought intoxicated him. The town was his and the freedom of it. A royal thought. All round him a dim oblivious world, uncaring, negligible, and he alive, potent, eager.

Not that Kif analysed it that way. He analysed very little and himself not at all. If he had been asked what he thought of London on that foggy early morning all he would have said would have been that it 'gave him squirms'.

At the top of Baker Street it lightened suddenly and a minute later a stray taxi appeared. Their simultaneous whoop attracted the attention of the somnolent driver even more than their dash to him. If he had not been crawling circumspectly in the darkness there might have been two casualties that had not furthered the national cause in the least, a fact which he pointed out to them with a sleepy querulousness. It required all their powers of persuasion, monetary and otherwise, to make him abandon the thought of the bed that had seemed so near and turn back to the chilly northern heights. When he harped a third time on the little time he had had in bed for the last week Kif lost his temper.

'Blast you,' he said, 'when d'you think we were in a bed last? You turn your bus round and take us where my pal says, and be thankful you're doing it for dollars and not for fear, see?'

'Oh, well,' said the man, as Barclay, in answer to Kif's indicative elbow, climbed heavily with his kit into the taxi, 'if it wasn't that you were serving I wouldn't do it. As it is, I've no doubt I'll live to see you hanged, my lad.'

'You won't,' said Kif, 'you'll be the cause.' And he slammed the door behind him.

As they chugged slowly through the dark Barclay said: 'If the sound of this Methuselah doesn't waken them I'll knock up old Alison. She sleeps above the door, and she can get us some food without routing them all out. You'll like her. We've had her for ten years. If she left I think mother would go straight into a nursing home. She runs everything.'

He lapsed into silence. The taxi snuffed and snorted its distressed way northward and the two sat withdrawn, each busy with his thoughts. Presently Barclay stepped out on to the running-board and directed the driver through the gloom. After much fumbling they drew up definitely and Kif climbed out on to the pavement. He could see nothing but the black mass of a house that was evidently one of a row. The taxi-man mentioned without emotion the price of his services, a sum which had been the subject of his sleepy cogitations for the last fifteen minutes, and which was placed artistically within a shilling of what the weary warriors might be supposed to be willing to pay. Kif was quite ready to argue, but Barclay, to whom parley at that moment would have been like haggling at the gate of Heaven, shoved two notes at the man and led Kif away. They stumbled through a small garden and Kif stood breathing in the smell of wet earth and green things, and not realising why he felt welcomed, while Barclay felt about for appropriate missiles. As the gravel sprayed on the window for the second time the sash was gently raised and a melodious Glasgow voice inquired softly: 'Who is i'?'

'It's me—Tim, and I've got a friend. Come down and let us in without wakening the house, there's a dear.'

'Goad bless us, is i' you?' The voice mounted on the last word in a swoop of amazement. 'Ay, well, stop you a minute just and I'll be down to you.'

It was less than a minute after that the light was switched on in the hall and the door carefully unbarred. It was opened by a little woman with her dark hair bundled hastily into a tight knot at the back of her neck. Barclay's 'old' must have been an epithet of affection, for she was not over forty. She seized both Barclay's hands and shook them endlessly while she gazed at him, but uttered nothing but one long low liquid 'Well!'

Barclay laughed at her under his breath and said: 'Well, Ailie, there'll be toffee-making to-morrow!'

Her big brown eyes twinkled at him. She smiled over his shoulder at Kif and led the way into a small dining-room at the back, a place of cream walls, gleaming mahogany and shaded gold lights. As she lit the gas fire she said:

'I doubt the bath wa'er won' be ho', bu' by the time you've had something to ea' i'll be all right.'

'Glory! Anyone staying? I suppose Mr Vicar can have the spare room?'

Kif wondered for a moment who Mr Vicar was. Someone else to meet! Then he realised with a shock that Barclay was referring to him. Mister! How funny! He, Kif Vicar, had suddenly grown up. Mister!

'Ooh ay,' she said, 'it's all ready. I'll away now an' see about yer food.' And she left them.

The fire, a large one of simulated coals, was already glowing. Barclay pulled up a chair and indicated one to Kif. Kif, following his host's example, added his belt to the heap of accoutrements in the corner and sat down. He regarded with a faint horror the indifferent way Barclay used the cream tiles as props for his army boots and refrained from following him so far. These were the things Barclay was used to, he thought; the kind of thing he had grown up with. All the years he, Kif, had been eating his meals off a rough table in a flagged untidy farmhouse kitchen Barclay had eaten his here. His eyes wandered over all he could see without moving his head. He gravely considered a framed piece of *petit point* that hung beside the mantelpiece, wherein two shepherdesses eternally toyed with a plump and ruddy swain over a stile. Was that beautiful? Why had they framed it? On the mantelpiece itself were two yellowish jars covered all over with a queer pattern, and another shepherdess whose bodice was not as modest as her demeanour, and a roughish blue and yellow bowl exactly like the one Simone kept her soap in in Bethune. What did they have that there for? And over the row of china there was a picture in a thin gold frame. The picture was so dark that it might as well not have been a picture, but it made a nice dark restful patch on the wall. The whole room was restful. The whole house. Beatitude filled him. Presently he would sleep in a bed.

There was a faint sound as of a breeze outside, and the door swung open. A girl in a dressing-gown stood in the dark oblong for an uncertain moment, and then came in to them with a glad cry of 'Tim!'

Barclay met her halfway and kissed her resoundingly.

'Hullo, Ann, old lady,' he said, 'have we spoiled your beauty sleep? We meant to sneak to bed and appear "the morrn's morrn", as MacIntyre says.' He turned to Kif, who was standing awkwardly by the fire, but before he could begin an introduction she had crossed the room with her hand outstretched.

'It's Kif, isn't it?' she said. Her handshake was firm, like a man's. 'It is nice to know you are not just an invention of Tim's.'

Her eyes went back to her brother and lingered on him, and Kif's lingered on her. The black silk garment that wrapped her writhed with sprawling dragons and contrasted oddly with the demureness of the smooth brown hair parted in the middle and coiled in plaits round her ears. Her hairdressing, in turn, contrasted with the aliveness and strength of her face; a piquant, short-nosed, wide-mouthed face with a low forehead, level brows and a stubborn chin. In this garb she looked about twenty, but was in reality twenty-two. Kif's eyes slid shyly away from her bare feet thrust into slim things of scarlet leather.

'Who is MacIntyre?' she was saying as she pushed her brother back into the chair from which he had risen, and seated herself on the arm of it.

'MacIntyre is a private of the line and a natural philosopher whose acquaintance I regret you may never make. When he says "morn's morn" you could grind a knife on the noise he makes. But his real *métier* is scrounging.'

'No, swinging the lead,' amended Kif. "'Member his broken toe?"

Ann was about to inquire further into the prevarications of MacIntyre when Alison returned with the beginnings of a meal and she said instead:

'Before you start eating I am going to tell Mother you are here. She'd never forgive me if I didn't waken her. Quite apart from missing a precious minute of you, she never approves of an act she's not on in, as you know. Father's in Birmingham for the night, by the way. I'll be back in a minute.'

'Little did I think I'd live to see the day that I should trail muddy boots over a carpet and not have Alison as much as glower at me,' said Barclay, stretching his legs to the glow again and giving the maid a sideways glance.

'Ay,' said Alison reflectively, laying forks and not looking at him. But there was a world of meaning in her monosyllable.

'Mother says would you go up to her, and would Kif forgive her if she doesn't appear till morning,' said Ann, returning. She shut the door behind her brother and settled herself down opposite Kif. 'I won't offer you a cigarette because Ailie thinks that anyone who will smoke immediately before a meal of her cooking is damned everlastingly. You're only having what she calls "cauld kail het again", but I'd rather have Alison's "cauld kail" than a Savoy luncheon.'

'And this'll be by way of asking me t' starch they belts you forgoat t'send t'the laundry,' remarked the maid as she departed to fetch another trayful.

Ann twinkled at Kif. 'One up to Alison. You haven't told me how you got here. It's pretty foggy, isn't it?'

Kif gave her the history of their arrival. It was wonderful to him to have this girl talk to him with the natural ease of a sister. She took him for granted so utterly. Not once did he catch a scrutinising look, an appraising glance. He had hoped for kindness, but he had not anticipated this. And when Barclay returned and they drew in to the table she helped Alison to bring the dishes and waited on their needs with such complete matter-of-factness that it helped Kif to resign himself to the strangeness of having a being like this, in a garment the like of which he had never seen, play waitress to him. When they had been supplied she sat down at the bottom of the table and drank weak tea while they disposed of Alison's 'kail'—fried sole that was to have been for breakfast, and stew tasting and smelling of all the flavours under heaven in just proportion, to which Alison had added leftover potatoes from last night's dinner.

The talk was all on the surface, laughing, bantering talk. To a stranger looking on it would have seemed that these three had come back from a theatre or a dance, and in the course of a belated meal were recounting the amusing incidents for the entertainment of each other. Only the uniforms spoke of war. Between them and the spearing reality of things as they were hung the armour of their British self-containedness. Where their Gallic allies would have laughed and wept and embraced till emotion was spent they covered up their vulnerable places with a protective shell of flippancy. It is not the prerogative of breeding or education, that play of not caring. It is due to the Briton's constitutional aversion to a scene, which is his fabled stolidness, his weakness and his strength.

'I have to be at the hospital at half past seven,' said Ann, 'so I'm going back to bed. If you hump your kits upstairs, though, I'll see you settled in before I go. I have sent Alison back to bed.'

They followed her up the stairs, and on the landing Barclay tossed Kif for the first bath and won. There was no host and guest relationship between these two veterans. Barclay disappeared to turn on the water and Ann led Kif to his room.

'This is yours, Kif,' she said as she switched on the light. 'I hope you'll find it comfortable. We are not going to call either of you in the morning, so you can sleep till the day after if you like.' She shoved her hand between the turned-back sheets to make sure that a hot-water bottle had been put in. 'If there's anything in the world you want that we might be able to supply, ask Tim for it when he has finished soaking himself. Sleep well!' and she was gone.

The quiet of the room flooded round him. He lowered himself gingerly on to the edge of the bed and considered it: primrose lights, daffodil curtains closely drawn, thick pale carpet—he moved his boots uneasily—and unpatterned pale walls warm in the glow that somehow filled the room. He slid contemplative fingers over the amber taffeta of the eiderdown and the cool uncreased bed-linen. Then his gaze went again to the carpet. He unbuttoned his tunic hastily and applied himself to the unwinding of his puttees.

7

Alison put down the tray and drew aside the curtains so that the noon sunlight invaded the room. She looked gravely at the still sleeping Kif.

'Save us!' she said. 'It's a bairn! Her eyes noted the uncrumpled state of the bed; he had most evidently slept as he had lain down, immediately and continuously—and came back to the young face from which sleep had washed the last hint of sophistication. In spite of his size and the muscular arm protruding from the sleeve of a pair of Barclay's less hectically coloured pyjamas his youth was patent. Alison sighed as she wakened him.

'Here's a bit breakfast to you. I've just wakened Mister Tim. Mrs Barclay said you'd probably be verray angry with her if she allowed you to sleep any longer.'

Kif smiled sleepily at the thought of his daring to be angry with his hostess for any reason whatsoever, and hoisted himself into a favourable position for attacking his first breakfast in bed. Alison seized his boots and was departing with them when he said:

'Oh, please, I'll clean them. I——'

'You'll do no such thing,' she said. 'This is yer holiday!' and the door shut behind her.

Kif looked at the poem in silver and gold which was breakfast as conceived by these people. The toast, the fillets, the marmalade, the butter, the pale yellow china all glowed golden among the shining purity of silver utensils and white linen. Delicately his long fingers slid among the crowded perfection, lifting and pouring and setting down. He had reached the toast and marmalade stage when Tim, radiant as to person and raiment, came in on his way to the bathroom.

'If you go vamping old Alison like this you'll be having her join the regiment as a vivandière or something. I hear she is dropping salt tears in the scullery over your boots and demanding "how a lad could be expected t' walk in they boots?" Now all she said to me was, "You'll no' be needin' so many pairs o' shoes nowadays, I'm thinking!"'

Kif grinned at the apt rendering of Alison's accent and manner. 'It's a bonza day,' he said, his eyes on the window.

'It is, my son, and we parade for luncheon at one-thirty. Ann has victimised someone into taking her place at the hospital for the duration of our leave, and the family is talking of taking us down to the coast in the afternoon, or anywhere else you'd like to go. So stir yourself. I shan't be five minutes in the bathroom.'

Kif made the best toilet that can be achieved with the British private's service uniform of the 1916 pattern. He had to rely for effect, in the absence of the wiggle of breeches or the swing of a kilt, on the brightness of his buttons and the degree of smoothness and polish that could be imposed on his thick hair in the process of brushing it back. (Hair was worn straight back in those days, you may remember.) But the ultimate result was fairly satisfactory. He took up a silver hand-mirror that lay on the dressing-table and proceeded by dint of several experimental positions to enjoy entirely new views of himself. He wished his chin had not such a straight up-and-down line; it would look so much better if it stuck out a little more, like Heaton's, or Travenna's. He wondered where Travenna was now and if he were alive. One stray letter was all that had ever reached him from that world's vagabond.

DEAR FRIEND (it had said),

How are you I hope you have managed to dodge boche bullets so far. At the moment we are in reserve near censored. That is all I can tell you. It is just about as bloody a place as all the other places in France. And Belgium is a whole lot worse. To think I used to like Antwerp and never guessed what was behind it. Well, how are you? I certainly hope you are well and not too fed up with this war. That was a good time we had in London. It would be a good plan to have another. What do you think?

Yours,

The thought of Travenna made him deplore afresh the lack of zip in his attire. Solemnly considering his image he sought for any means of brightening his person that he might have overlooked. He had not nearly exhausted the possibilities of double reflection when Barclay came to fetch him, and he went downstairs reminding himself how nice Ann had been and hoping for the best.

Barclay ushered him into a living-room full of comfortable chairs, space, and the smell of a wood fire. On a sofa at the hearth sat a plump smallish woman whose wiry grey hair was parted in the middle and drawn to a loose knot at the back of her neck and whose broad shrewd face seemed to be composed of curves.

'Mother,' said Barclay, 'this is Kif,' and she rose and came to meet them.

Margaret Barclay's long suit was motherliness. She preferred mothering male things, but was always delighted to act as mother confessor, adviser, and on occasion Providence to any young girl. The only stipulation was that the recipient of her favour should be perennially conscious of her superior wisdom, surer instinct, and more complete knowledge of the world. Any failure to realise this, any evidence of a tendency to think for oneself, or advice sought and disregarded, was succeeded not by any lack of kindliness—Margaret Barclay was invariably kind—but by a subtle waning of interest. This acceptance of her infallibility was more common among men, a fact which probably accounted for her preference for them as members of her suite. She was exceedingly popular with her tradespeople and with all shop assistants. Her gracious and unaffected manner left them feeling somehow that they were in her debt since they had been allowed to serve her. Where she was a regular customer she took an unfailing interest in the various histories of the staff, and when illness or matrimony overtook one invariably marked the event in a practical manner.

As might have been expected, her son adored her unreservedly. Her daughter, who had inherited much of the hard practicality which was the basis of Margaret Barclay's being, recognised the quality in her mother. She had inherited also her mother's capacity for taking her own line, which did not tend to complete understanding between mother and daughter. Where they differed most radically was in the fact that Ann Barclay never desired to take anything or anybody

40

under her wing, and the, to her, obvious pleasure of her parent in the admiring obedience of her followers roused in her a faint contempt. On occasions it almost nauseated her to see what she mentally characterised as 'grown men and women' sitting at the feet of a woman with no more brains or knowledge than they had themselves, but who had the courage of her personality. And yet that personality was directly responsible for the continuance of smooth relations between mother and daughter. It was not possible to quarrel with Margaret Barclay; to any assault she offered her impenetrable front of sweet reasonableness, her patience, and her tacit assumption of superiority.

'My dear boy,' she said quietly, 'we are so glad to have you. I hope everything has been as you would like it, and that Alison has been looking after you well? And that you forgive me for not coming down to welcome you last night?'

She had a very beautiful speaking voice, which she used With deliberation and very perfectly. Her pronunciation of the English tongue was what every purist and musician Would have it be. She used slang now and then when the 'pally' attitude of the moment needed emphasis, and always with good effect. Kif fell at once. If the charm of her voice had not done it the obvious welcome she extended would have been sufficient to a boy who had hesitated so painfully over his possible reception.

'It is very good of you,' was all he could think of at the moment, but she seemed pleased with him.

Alison announced luncheon, and with a light hand on his arm she drew him into the dining-room of the night before, still talking deliberately and gently. As they seated themselves Ann joined them in her V.A.D. uniform. She acknowledged Kif's presence with a smile and a little gesture of her hand.

'If nobody minds but myself,' she said, 'I'll not change into mufti. Joy-riding even with troops on board is looked on askance, so the more uniforms we have to blaze at the great B.P. the better.'

They discussed the destination and route of the proposed joy-ride. The women naturally elected that the men should choose. Kif was eager to go to the coast, but, that granted, was indifferent where. Tim agreed to the coast, but stipulated that there should be cliffs. The conversation went via motoring through the commonplaces of roads, gradients, scenery, accidents, first-aid, artificial respiration, swimming, and the Channel. Some of it was witty, most of it was amusing, and all of it was light-hearted, and in all of it Kif managed to keep his end up without difficulty. He was habitually quiet but he was not slow-witted.

As soon as the meal was over Ann brought round the car—the Barclay clan's one extravagance, as Mrs Barclay said—and they set out for Birling Gap, Ann driving with Kif beside her, and Barclay and his mother behind.

Surrey and Sussex! What terms of week-end sophistication they are become! And even now, with the red rash of villadom creeping over them, there is no country in Britain so satisfying in its settled loveliness. Cold hills and windy skies of the north, sodden fields and smoky horizons of the midlands, even the little orchards and flowery meadows of the west, what can they put against this?—this little kingdom of forest, weald, marsh and down, with its everpresent sea. Nowhere are horizons so seductive and so generous in fulfilment. Would you have brisk heather and peaty turf, bracken and twisted fir-trees? They are here. Would you have thick hedges, and roadside farms that drowse in forgotten valleys? They are here. Would you have tall skies with a level land from edge to edge, etched with grey willows that attend slow streams? They are here. Or would you have high green hills of thymy turf that have blue distances for ever at their feet and have still on their brows some of the glory of the world's morning? They are here.

Barclay, defending his demand for cliffs, said: 'I have a constitutional aversion to a seaside place where the land and sea seem to have met by accident, as it were. You're walking along a perfectly ordinary bit of turf when a wave comes wollop at you and you say rather surprisedly, "Oh, yes, the sea of course. I knew it was round here somewhere." I like a place where the sea comes up against more than it bargained for and makes a song about it.'

When Kif, the car being parked on the cliff top, descended the chalk-hewn steps of the gap to the white shore and beheld the Sisters smiling their siren loveliest in the afternoon sun he agreed with Tim. Shining, aloof, and incredibly fair they stood along the lonely coast. The sea, no assailing force to-day but a prostrate lover, kissed their white feet in an ecstasy of abasement.

Tim put down the tea-basket and said: 'I once took a cousin, a girl, here for an afternoon, and all she said was, "Gosh, isn't it just like a postcard?"'

Said Ann, busy unpacking: 'Sylvia never said "Gosh" in her life.'

'Am I to conclude by that remark that you admit the major indictment?' asked her brother.

'Oh, well, I wouldn't put it past her, as Alison says; she never did show symptoms of soul, but she most emphatically has chronic ladylikeness.'

'Hospital work has had the most disastrous effect on Ann's metaphor,' said her mother. 'When first she started motoring it was the same, you may remember. Everything was described in terms of cranks and spanners. Tim dear, would you get me the other cushion from the car if no one is just pining for it?'

They spread tea on a patch of tawny sand below the white boulders that the cliffs had cast as sops to an importunate sea, and ate in the unequalled content of people who are living wholly for the present and who find that present good. There was no wind to make a murmuring in their ears when the talk died; only the sleep-inducing repetition of the sea filled the silence. Now and then a gull swooped, or a pebble slid from the cliff in a little rattle of scudding fragments. A ship, hull down, made the only human finger-mark on a shining elemental world.

When they had lit cigarettes Mrs Barclay and Tim strolled away along the beach while Ann and Kif stayed where they were, given up to the lassitude that invades the most active on a spring afternoon. Ann lay on her side watching the gulls that swooped and eddied apparently meaninglessly about the cliff face. Kif sat propped against a boulder, his service cap tilted forward, his eyes, shut to black slits, on the dreaming sea. Presently Ann said:

'Tim says you know all about farms. I am thinking of taking up that kind of work when the war is over.'

She was not. It is true that she had decided to have a career of her own when her country no longer had any need of her. But she had not considered the medium. At the moment she merely thought that it would be nice to show an interest in something this quiet boy might be supposed to be familiar with.

To her surprise the quiet boy twinkled down at her and said unimpressedly: 'I think you'd better think again.'

'Why?'

'I don't know,' he said, not because he did not know, but because he was searching for words that would explain. 'How would you like a day like this?' he said at last, and began an account of the farm-worker's average day. As he talked, some of the bitterness of his life on the farm came back to him, and through his matter-of-fact phrases there emerged some of the futility, the barrenness, the endless expending of oneself on the thankless earth that will be there unchanged and unchangeable when the labourer is as if he had not been.

'And you don't get anywhere,' he finished. 'You just go round in circles. If you don't want to get anywhere it might be all right. But I should think you'd want to get somewhere. And anyhow it's awful work.'

'But don't you love animals?' she asked, rather taken aback.

'I like horses, yes. And dogs. But you wouldn't go to work in an engineering shop just because you liked the smell of oil. Animals are only a little bit of a farm—at least the kind of farm I worked on. If you're fond of animals a stable would be the place to go to. Have you ever been to a race-meeting?' And on hearing that she had not,'You'd like it,' he assured her, and proceeded to give her an account of the day he and Travenna had spent at Kempton, while she lay and watched him, her rather small merry blue eyes unwontedly grave. She had met many men of many varieties and all classes in the last two years and had learned to judge them fairly accurately. Her opinions were habitually clear-cut and she usually knew the reasons for them. And now she was wondering why she liked this boy. His physical attractions cancelled each other out, she decided. He had a pleasant voice but a bad accent; his body was good to look at, but his face was plain; good teeth but an ugly mouth; and nice eyes if only the lids didn't give them that reckless look. Was it only his quiet manner that attracted one? But Tim had liked him; and Tim, though easy-going, had his standards. Perhaps she had liked him by proxy.

'Yes, I'd rather like to work in a stable,' she said. 'I learned to ride when I was at school, but it was only the trot-out-one-canter-and-trot-back type of thing. I must do something in the open air. If I had a job indoors I'd regret every fine morning to such an agonising extent.'

'But if you had an outside job you'd probably be sorrier still on every bad one. And there are about five bad ones to every good one.'

43

She had a moment's spasm of annoyance that the conversation was not running quite as she had unconsciously planned it; but her by no means scanty humour came to her aid. She laughed and said: 'You're not being very encouraging, are you? What would you suggest that I should do with my abounding energies?'

This direct appeal rather turned his flank. He smiled at her, but in a moment he said quite simply: 'I expect you'll get married.'

She had not expected that, so she merely shook her head and asked: 'What about you, Kif? What do you want to do after?'

It was Kif's turn to shake his head. He did it quite gravely, but in a moment the imp in his eye was laughing at her when he said: 'What would you suggest for me?'

'I don't know. I don't even know your requirements.'

'I want something that makes no two days the same. Something so that you never know what's going to happen next.'

'Great heavens!' said Ann unaffectedly.

'Do you want to make money at this queer business?' she asked after a short pause. 'I mean must we consider that an indispensable part in choosing?'

'I don't want a lot of money, if that's what you mean. I'd want enough to go to a show or a boxing match or a race-meeting once a week perhaps.'

'Better go racing every day and be a bookmaker. They say that it's the unexpected that happens there, though judging from my friends' experiences the failure of the favourite seems to be common enough to be monotonous. But you wouldn't mind that if you were a bookie. The only alternative seems to be picking pockets in the Strand. You'd have the double excitement of not knowing what you were going to take out of a pocket and never knowing the minute you were going to be pinched.' She took a cigarette from the case he offered her and considered. 'I don't know, Kif,' she said seriously at last, 'you stump me. I don't think there is such a job. Not unless you made a few millions first and then proceeded to juggle with them. That would meet the case.'

They smoked in silence. The almost brimming tide gave little exhausted pants of achievement, the gulls swooped and cried. Into the girl's mind came the good things her brother had told of this boy at one time or another: his courage, his good humour, his unselfishness. 'It is strange,'she remembered his writing, 'he has any amount of initiative, but no capacity for leadership.' What kind of work could his good qualities be harnessed to in peace time? With the greater part of the earth's surface as well explored as the downs the day after the Derby there was little scope for physical courage and endurance in these days, it seemed. But then—this hypothetical future?

As if he read her thought he said: 'Well, we needn't be bothering our heads!'

His remark being delicately vague enough for her to ignore its probable meaning she said: 'It's a good enough game for a sunny afternoon. I don't expect you'll discover the ideal profession——'

'I don't expect so.'

----'any more than I shall get a job out of doors with every day a fine one.'

They smiled at each other.

'But it is something to know what you want, Kif.'

When Mrs Barclay returned with Tim she found her charming but difficult daughter playing five-stones with two pebbles and three shells under the expert tuition of the ex-farmer's boy. They were both completely unselfconscious and entirely happy.

Kif helped to pack the tea-basket with the neat-handed efficiency that was always so astonishing coming from his loose, big-jointed hands, and carried it up the cliff while Tim assisted his mother. As she came to the car Mrs Barclay said:

'I think Kif will come behind with me this time if it would not bore him dreadfully, and you, my dear boy, can change places with Ann if she gets tired of driving.'

So Kif, nothing loth, climbed in beside his hostess, and as they rolled through East Dean—a dreaming hollow filled with warm sunlight—Ann could hear the boy's low voice answering the musical one more and more readily. The mothering process in full swing, she thought; but it was more in amusement than contempt to-day, for she was happy. There was sun and spring air and Sussex, and beside her sat the being she cared most for on earth, reprieved for a little from the horror over there. And a little mothering probably wouldn't do the present subject any harm. He didn't appear to have had much of it so far. Perhaps her mother would find his ideal job for him. But no! It would be much more likely that she would gently dissuade him from so primrose a path with careful and unanswerable arguments about the advisability of a safe profession, a stable income. The Orthodox and the Expedient were the gods of her mother's idolatry—though she would have been sorrowfully forgiving if the suggestion had been made to her.

'What are you smiling at, Ann?'

'I'm smiling because I can't help it. It's such a refreshing sensation to have one's muscles do it of their own accord instead of having to do it for them that I'm just letting them carry on.'

Her brother patted her knee, but said nothing. He, too, appeared to be listening, though probably with different emotions, to the voices behind.

'How did you two get on?' he asked presently.

'I like him. He's not so shy as you said he was.'

'He isn't so much shy as quiet. He evidently found you not too terrifying.'

'Oh, no; he wasn't in the least blate. (Alison asked if you would like almonds in the toffee, by the way, and I forgot to ask you!) He vetoed farming as a career for me after the war in no uncertain manner.'

'I expect he would! . . . I'm almost frightened for him sometimes, and I don't in the least know why. I think perhaps because he is so tremendously in love with life. People who are that are simply asking to get hurt. Life's a rotten spec. at best.'

'But, Tim! you found it good enough once!'

'Yes, good enough. And I was perfectly happy. But with a difference. Kif—I can't explain; I just have the feeling.'

It was dark by the time they reached Croydon. Kif, who had been calmly happy in the sunlight and the companionship at the Gap, was roused to something more than content by the glamour of the evening streets: topaz and ruby spilled on the purple of the earth and strung across the blue-dark of the night; narrow streets full of light and sound where tram, bus, dray and barrow nudged each other in expostulating impatience; wide dark boulevards where the surface gleamed and reflected as if wet. The diamond light of a searchlight, unearthly and chill, swept a cool finger over the bustle of the town. Kif watched it for a moment and then tried not to see it. They were running into London, London in the evening; surely that was joy sufficient to blot out the cold reason of a thousand searchlights. For the rest of the way his independent spirit soared from the toils of his companion's sympathy and was away again on the horizon. And Mrs Barclay, who was growing a little sleepy, shrank further into her fur coat and thought of dinner.

Mr Barclay, whom Kif met at dinner, was the leader and Grand Master of his wife's admiring train. He was a little pink man with upturned grey moustache which in Lombard Street gave an uncompromising briskness to his appearance, but in his wife's presence made him look still more like a faithful small terrier. He welcomed Kif with a heartiness which was a queer blend of shyness and pomposity. Ann and Tim seemed to have inherited little from their father except their smallish bright eyes. Both children had their mother's wide humorous mouth and curving chin, though even in Tim's case the lips had a fuller curve than hers.

If Mrs Barclay was subtle there was nothing suave about her spouse. He fired questions point blank at Kif until Tim, noticing what he called his father's prosecuting counsel manner in full blast, obtained Kif's release from the witness box by beginning a story about MacIntyre. Mrs Barclay had made war talk taboo, but even her edict was not sufficient to achieve such a miracle where the central thought and major experience of everyone present was war. Mr Barclay laughed appreciatively over the MacIntyre tale, and turned immediately to Kif with another question. This was merely what he would call 'showing an interest in the boy'.

'And what has been your most thrilling experience at the front?' He belonged to the brigade who liked the sound of 'at the front', and stuck to the phrase long after it had passed into dis-use outside the illustrated press.

Kif, rather at a loss, grinned. 'I think it was the time Fatty Roberts put the brazier on top of the box of Verey lights and the dug-out went up,' he said.

This was so unexpected from Mr Barclay's point of view that he was momentarily speechless. Kif caught a doubtful look in Ann's eye and said to Tim: 'Back me up. Miss Barclay doesn't believe me.'

46

'Oh, rather!' said Barclay, who had been smiling at the memory. 'Old Kif's quite truthful. You wouldn't have thought that anything as wet as that dug-out was would have even smouldered, but it blazed like a match factory. There was more than one entrance to it, of course, so there was a fine draught. We started making a barrier with sandbags, but with the Verey lights popping all over the place you never knew the minute they were going to set fire to the boxes of bombs or something like that. And when Murray Heaton came along to superintend Jimmy nearly had a fit and told him to get out of it because it was no place for him. I don't suppose Murray ever had that said to him in his life before.'

'What did he do?' asked Ann.

'Well, the moment was too hectic for anyone to observe much. He didn't take any notice with his face. His face, in any case, is about as noticing as a Red Indian's. But I think he was amused.'

'Amused!' said Ann. 'I thought he was an awful stickler for discipline!'

'He is. But he stickles in the right places, if you know what I mean. There are no flies on Heaton.'

'That is the Heaton who rode a lot before the war, isn't it?' Mr Barclay asked, though Tim had told them in letters and in person all about his captain, and all the family knew that he knew. It gave him a childish delight to trot out a piece of information, however tattered. 'He seems to have done well?'

That word loosened the bonds of their self-containedness. If Murray Heaton, playing poker at a kitchen table in a blue haze of cigarette smoke that dimmed the candlelight, felt an ear burn at the moment it was the right one.

'I am going to send you straight off to bed, my children,' said Mrs Barclay as they finished their coffee. 'You have all arrears to make up.'

She herded Kif and Ann upstairs and allowed Tim half an hour for a talk with his father. Kif was in bed, his nose in a Kipling that Ann had provided, when Mrs Barclay came in with a tin in her hand and laughter in her eye. She laid the tin on the bedside table.

'Alison's offering,' she said. 'Her most luscious "Taiblet". Don't eat it all to-night, or the rest of your leave will be of no account. Have you everything you want? I really think Tim has the most deplorable taste in pyjamas,' she added as her eye came to rest on Kif's sleeve.

Kif laughed at her. 'They look all right to me,' he said. 'I certainly never wore anything silk before.'

She patted his arm lightly. 'Good night, my dear,' she said, and left him.

He lay for a full minute with his eyes on the door. Then he humped the bedclothes over his shoulders and returned to Kipling. A moment later he remembered the tin. He sat up and peered into it, selected a piece of the sugary brown sweetmeat and popped it whole into his mouth. He lay down and pulled the clothes up again. As he crunched the mouthful his gaze wandered absently round the piece of room visible between the pillow and the sheet. Then he

47

propped the book once more into a convenient position and, still chewing, fell to its perusal, utterly content with the world.

8

It would not be true to say that Kif did not enjoy his leave with the Barclays as much as his first one with Travenna. It is not possible to compare them; it would be as possible to say that one preferred chalk to cheese, their properties being in no wise the same. From the orthodox point of view his week with Tim's people was packed fuller of entertainment and well-being than anything his life had so far contained. For the first time he ate daintily, slept soft, moved in an atmosphere of leisure, and was wrapped round with consideration and kindness. And he liked it. He was sybarite enough to appreciate the softness, and the consideration appealed to his unaccustomed and naturally egotistical soul. He enjoyed to the top of his bent the theatre parties; the supper dances in the carpetless drawing-room at Golder's Green when he fox-trotted expertly with charming beings who seemed to take him entirely for granted since he was a soldier, a friend of Tim Barclay's, and could dance; the motor drives through an England sweet with spring; the games of badminton on a lawn too small for tennis. But if he had analysed his sentiments—and he did not, for he was happy—he would have discovered that the day on which Tim, Ann, and Mrs Barclay went to the country to visit a grandmother and which he spent mooning round his beloved London by himself held, as well as happiness, a quality that the others had lacked. It was the quality which had made his leave with Travenna the unforgettable thing it was. It had something to do with the freedom to go and do and see at the bidding of no one and without consultation with any but his own spirit. When he was alone—and Travenna had been so perfectly his complement that they had moved as one—he was lord of the earth.

If Kif was vaguely conscious that being one of a jolly party packing the present with its maximum content of joy could still leave him looking for he did not know what, gratitude to his hosts and his habitual lack of introspection smothered the thought. Had his leave been longer the soft wrappings that held him might have chafed and gratitude might not have been strong enough to melt entirely the intolerance of sentimental bonds that characterised him. As it was, Kif reached the end of his leave in a passion of gratitude to these people for their goodness to him. In his perambulations round town his mind had been exercised over the desire to give them something in return. He would have liked to give both Ann and her mother a souvenir, but the difficulty of finding the appropriate something confounded him. What did women like that like? Any ornament that he might buy, he decided, would almost certainly not find favour in their sight. He retired to the Park and analysed for the first time that outer shell that woman presents to the world. In the hour that he spent gaping at the passing show the only article that met with his approval was a pair of silver shoe-buckles. But he had never seen Ann wear anything like that. Perhaps they weren't in fashion. He took his problem to an A.B.C. shop and over sausage-and-mash considered it afresh. The crowd at the marble-topped tables were not productive of ideas in one devoid of them. It began to be borne in on him, however, that he lacked the courage to present even a box of chocolates in person—especially to Ann. He was shy about presenting anything at all to Ann, somehow. He wanted very badly to give her something, but she might not like it—the giving, not the gift. A remembrance of her cool matter-of-fact charm came to him and he saw in imagination the involuntary lift of her brows. He grew hot and decided that a sin of omission was better than one of commission. He would make the gift to Mrs Barclay only. There couldn't be anything against that. He repaired forthwith to a Piccadilly fruit-shop and squandered what remained of his pay on a basket of fruit—Mrs Barclay did not eat sweets—with instructions that it was to be sent two days later, when he would be gone. He laid such stress on the condition that it was not to be delivered before the stipulated time that the amused assistant watched him out of the shop and speculated idly as to the nature of the intrigue.

Tim and Kif were due to leave in the early morning. Ann was to drive them to the station, but Mr and Mrs Barclay were to take leave of them at home. There had been dancing on the last evening, but the guests were gone. At the best of times a used and deserted room is a sorry spectacle: a desolation of crumpled cushions, cigarette-ends, and disarranged furniture; but when the end of the party is the imminent end of everything the situation is unbearable. Kif helped Ann to straighten things, patting cushions back to enticing plumpness with dreary assiduity, and then said good night. When he attempted to take leave of Mrs Barclay she said: 'I shall come in later and see that you have everything.' So Kif shook hands with his host, who was once more pompously shy, and left them.

As he sorted his kit on his knees on the amber carpet Ann came in and said: 'Anything I can do, Kif?' She was looking very lovely in some kind of green stuff that didn't shine. Nothing shone about her but her eyes and her hair. He understood why she had come—partly because she was sorry for him, but mostly to give her parents their last while alone with Tim—and wished she would stay, but could think of nothing to keep her. She picked up a pair of his socks, and finding an incipient hole sat down on the edge of the bed to darn it. Kif folded and arranged and placed and replaced while they dropped little friendly remarks into the quiet. Ann folded the socks carefully and saw them stowed in their appointed place. Then with the little gesture of her hand that was characteristic of her she said a smiling good night and was gone.

Alison succeeded her five minutes later. 'I' 's noa' such a big tin as I wid ha' liked,' she said. 'Sugar's gey hard t' come by. But I'll have some more to send you in a week or two.' She extended the tin of toffee to him in one hand while she put the hot-water bottle in its place with the other, and before he could thank her had taken her departure. 'I'll call you in good time in the morning,' she said at the door, 'so sleep sound.'

Lastly Mrs Barclay, her serene self, perhaps a little more deliberate than usual. Kif sat up in bed and attempted to give utterance to some of what he felt.

'I don't know how to thank you——' he began, but she laid a restraining hand on his arm.

'You are not to try,' she said. 'If you have been happy with us we are more than paid for the little we have done for you. To do something for some of you boys is surely nothing that we need thanks for. It would be our bounden duty if it were not our pleasure. So let us call it quits—with the debt decidedly on our side. And now, is there anything I can do for you?'

There wasn't.

'Well, I want you to promise me that if there is anything you want in France you will write to me and ask for it as if I were your—aunt, let us say. Is that a bargain?'

Kif promised, with his first faint definite feeling of rebellion against the gossamer toils of human obligation. She rose from the bed's edge. 'Au revoir, my dear boy,' she said. 'I hope you will come to us any time you feel inclined to. There will always be a bed for you, you know.' She bent over and kissed him lightly on the forehead. She made a remark about the electric lamp and went away.

Kif shoved a desperate palm against one eye which threatened to disgrace him, swore in a fierce whisper, and put out the light. But as he fell asleep, deep down beneath the level ache of parting and ending, were little sharp shoots of anticipation that he was going back.

It seemed to him that he had only just fallen asleep when Alison wakened him. Even washing did not dispel his lethargy. He stumbled into his uniform dazedly, devoid of thought, of emotion, almost of identity. He picked up his kit, switched off the light without a backward glance, and made his cautious way downstairs. Though everyone in the house was awake it was full of the subdued movement of those who are up betimes. He found Ann pouring out coffee and Tim helping out bacon and eggs. The glow of the shaded table light struck down on them, but through the uncurtained window the outline of roofs showed against a lightening sky. They ate in a business-like silence; light conversation in the dawn is usually a failure and on occasion may degenerate to hysteria. Neither the Barclays nor Kif had a hysterical side, and so no one attempted the ghastly farce of being amusing. Ann, who was once more in the V.A.D. uniform, since she was going on duty that morning, went out for the car and Tim went up to take leave of his parents. At the door Alison came to help Kif with his kit. As he shook hands with her she said: 'See and take care of yourself. And keep an eye on Mr Tim.'

As Ann let in the clutch both boys turned to wave to the dim white blur in the doorway that was Alison, and that typified to both of them all that they were leaving.

It was a damp morning and a wild red sky showed above the black housetops. The cañon of the road was still in semi-darkness with the slender silver threads of the tram-lines stretching out into infinity. Nothing inhabited the world but a groaning dust-cart. Here and there a lighted window showed, a golden square in the flat neutrality of the house-fronts. It should have been a cheerful sight, a lighted window, but it was not. To Kif it was merely a suggestion of more early rising, a part of the complete joylessness of the hour. To Tim it spoke of the security and comfort he was leaving, the sweet safety of things dear and known. And Ann did not see them. She saw nothing but the long straight road stretching ahead of her—remorselessly. The mournful music of their horn floated out into the morning and was one with the red sky and the golden windows and the long dark road.

At the station the swarming khaki made it somehow easier. Bustle and the elbowing of a crowd covered up a little of the stark nakedness of fact; muddled a little their perceptions with thronging irrelevancies. Only at the last moment, as its way was, did the thing leap and tear them.

Kif's throat suddenly hurt him, so that speech would not come. He faced Ann—Ann who looked as though she were going smiling to her death—fighting for words.

'You've been so decent to me! I can't thank—I——'

He shook her hand crushingly and left her with her brother.

9

Kif went back to summer conditions and a bereaved and indignant company. It was a new sensation to feel a soft carpet of dust underfoot after the ubiquitous mud. As for the company, it was indignant to the point of mutiny. The powers that be had given Murray Heaton a majority. This was looked on as a violation of their rights that nothing could condone. That Heaton had several times lately refused the honour did nothing to mitigate their bewilderment and wrath. And Heaton, who if his lot had been cast as a dustman would have been a prince of scavenging and who had been torn in two between love of his company and his ingrained ambition, understood the situation and went about his work at battalion headquarters looking, it was reported, like the sphinx with a toothache.

That was some slight balm to the deserted company who rolled the information on their tongues and approved of it.

Jimmy also had gone up a step on the way to that proverbial baton; though Jimmy's highest ambition in life was the glory attached to a regimental sergeant-major. Than which, when one comes to consider it, there is no greater glory. A colonel certainly is nominally his superior. But a colonel is so far away as to be almost mythical in his power; no more terrifying than God. Whereas the R.S.M. is a very present and actual deity: omnipotent, awe-inspiring, omniscient. Oh, an R.S.M. every time! Jimmy had achieved his second stripe through a direct hit on the part of the enemy artillery. He was sorry about Fatty Roberts, and the other five who had gone west, of course. Fatty especially, as the company comedian, was a loss to be deplored. 'An' he occupied more than two men's place in a front line trench,' he said. 'What a goal-keeper he'd have made!' But it was all in the day's work, and things were 'cushier' now, he informed them, than the battalion had ever known them.

Apart from the change in weather conditions a change in scenery had also been vouchsafed to them. Instead of the utter desolation of the Flanders plains— a level sea of mud from sky to sky—they revelled in the gently rolling hills and little woods of Picardy; a kindly, pleasant land with the gold of the charlock over its fields and its white chalky roads rolling away into blue distances; a land in which war was an alien incongruity. At Loos, in the Salient, the earth was not the earth they knew; war had made it so much its own that the horror of it was one with the horror of war. But here death was an outrage. Billets had roses in the gardens, and up in the line grass waved and there were cornflowers, stitchwort, charlock and the red splashes of poppies. Always poppies! Who that knew Picardy in '16 will see poppies and not remember it? Larks sang in the hot skies. Aeroplanes droned in place of the absent bees. So when a man coughed and fell forward, and a little dark trickle ran along the earth like a dusty worm, minds waked to surprised protest against such an invasion.

Those were the days before the Somme country was a churned-up rubbish heap crowned with the broken skeletons of woods—those little fatal woods.

Kif sat on the bank with a writing-pad on his knee and a stub of indelible pencil stuck behind his ear and idly chucked little pebbles into the still water. The sun came through the high branches behind him and made little hot places on his back, and a movement of the warm air that was hardly a breeze trailed light fingers over his bare throat. The calm water curved away to his right, blue and green and silver, with its tall row of attendant poplars. On the opposite bank, further down, a few garments lately washed and stone-held now to dry made a little patch of motley. Somewhere an aeroplane droned and far away there was an intermittent murmur, but the world was very quiet. He looked again at the 'Dear Friend' that adorned in careful backhand letters the virgin page, and sighed lazily. He took the bit of pencil from behind his ear, cogitated a while, twisted the pencil propeller-wise once or twice between his fingers and put it back again. It was very warm.

He was seventeen to-day, but no one knew or remembered the fact but himself, and he was not at all inclined to sentimentalise over it. Retrospection he might indulge in at the prompting of such an event as an anniversary, but introspection never.

Footsteps came along the path, footsteps too light for army boots. Kif turned his head mechanically, and almost as mechanically smiled at the girl as she came. Her steps slowed to a stop. She hitched the basket she was carrying to a firmer position on her hip and regarded him with a grave little smile.

'You are lonlee,' she said. Her L's reminded him of Alison. His grin widened.

'I'm stuck,' he said. 'Come and help me write a letter.'

She moved slowly over the grass to him, her skirts falling away like water from each forward-swung limb. She was tall and broad-shouldered and firm-bodied, and her neck rose proudly to carry the round, dark head with its salient cheek and chin bones. She was clad in the age-old and ageless dress of the peasant—a fitting bodice and a full skirt, the latter part of the garment being several inches shorter than her grandmother's would have been, but still showing not more than a length of ankle.

'Stuck,' she repeated. "ow stuck?'

'I don't know what to say.'

'Then it is not for me to say to you what to write.' She spoke English with a strong French accent, but very fluently.

'You might help a chap,' said Kif. The golden afternoon was made for dalliance.

'It is to your fiancée, perhaps, the letter?'

'Me? Gosh, no. I haven't got a girl.'

'Is it not to a lady that you write?' she asked, genuine surprise in her tone.

'Yes, it's to a lady, but she's old enough to be my mother.'

'Then write to her what you write to your own mother.'

'Haven't got one.'

'Ah!' She made a little sound of commiseration which embraced in its monosyllable the whole gamut of sympathy.

'It's too hot an afternoon to go carrying baskets that size about. Stay and help me.'

'I go to return the laundry of *Monsieur le Colonel*.'

'Well, but Monsieur le Colonel'—he mimicked her pronunciation—'won't need a clean shirt for another two hours at least. And this letter will have to be written by then.' He patted the grass beside him.

She laid down the basket and seated herself a foot or two away from him with the deliberate grace of a great lady and with complete unselfconsciousness.

'You speak awfully good English,' said Kif.

'Before the war English people come every year to the Chateau at my home, and the little girls I walk with them and they teach me English.'

'Where is your home?'

She nodded her head in the direction of the low murmur. '*Là-bas*,' she said. 'It is not any more.'

'Rough luck!' said the boy to whom sticks and stones were nothing and the horizon everything.

'*Eh bien*,' she said, 'it is of no use to weep. I say like you, "Fat lot I care". The little Marjorie she say that *continuellement*.'

Kif gave a shout of laughter at the unexpected phrase in her charming accent, and she smiled in sympathy.

'You say that, no?'

'Very often,' Kif admitted. 'What is your name?'

'Marcelle Fleureau.'

'That's pretty. Mine is Archibald Vicar, but they call me Kif.'

'Keef,' she said, and Kif, who was looking at her cheerful brown eyes, saw nothing for a moment but the bare flagged interior of the kitchen at Tarn.

'You have been long in France?' she asked, and they talked the simple serious personalities of two simple beings while the pad lay neglected on the grass by his side and the sunlight grew more golden.

It was the redness of the light on the water that recalled her to the passing of time.

'*Hélas!*' she said. '*Le colonel!*' and got hastily to her feet. Kif rose with her and took the basket.

'Ah, *non, alors!*' she protested, and held her hands out for it. But Kif carried it to the edge of the town.

'And you have not written your letter. That is too bad,' she said as she took it from him. 'I have hindered instead of helping.'

'Help me to-morrow,' said Kif.

The battalion were out at rest, and for another fortnight Kif met Marcelle every evening, and every evening they walked by the water solemnly exchanging experiences and views of life through the long June sunsets. Kif was seized with an attack of diffidence that annoyed him. He had known her a week before he had summoned up courage enough to hold her hand. When he did she took the gesture so calmly that he was at a loss to know whether she had been expecting it, or whether she found it so unremarkable as not to be worthy of notice. She puzzled him and fascinated him. She was neither coy nor forthcoming, and she had none of the little airs that the girls of his acquaintance—with the exception of Ann—invariably used in the presence of men. And yet she was not in the least reminiscent of Ann. She was strangely self-sufficient, in the best sense of that mis-used term. She was deeply interested in Kif and all he had to tell her about himself, but she never wanted anything from him. Her unselfconsciousness hung like a veil between her and his eagerness. And Kif, who had made one of the bridge-head gatherings at Tarn and whose country upbringing had not inculcated in him any reverence for the female of the species, would go back to Barclay's twinkling eyes and Jimmy's pungent remarks wondering at himself, wondering about the girl, and swearing to himself to be bolder on the morrow. But on the morrow when face to face with her serenity the old diffidence drowned his resolution.

Barclay was inclined to look with kindly toleration on what he mentally called 'Kif's little affair,' but Jimmy, it seemed, was worried. Barclay ran into him one day in the little bar in the side street that leads down to the water. His blue eyes scanned his friend without any sign of recognition and his mouth had a more than habitually mournful droop. No one looking at him would have believed that inside Jimmy's bright head lay anything more than an addled sleepiness.

'Good evening, corporal,' said Barclay in mock humility.

Jimmy's eye travelled mechanically over his friend's buttons and came back to his face. 'What's this girl that Kif's got hold of?' he asked.

Barclay understood that he was being taken to task.

'Haven't the remotest idea.'

'Then you ought to,' snapped Jimmy.

'Am I my brother's keeper? And I always thought that Kif had an excellent taste in females.'

'You know quite well that the boy wants looking after. Because he's gone quiet all this time is not to say that he's not going to bolt at all. A country kid like him. Never seen anything more than lumps of girls at home.' Thus Jimmy the cosmopolitan! 'And now he's parlayvooing every night with God knows what, and you haven't as much as cast an eye over her.'

'Well, supposing my eye, having been cast, found nothing to approve of? What then? Kif may be an infant, but he has a pretty mind of his own. You couldn't make him give her up just because she was given to baby-snatching, or whatever you suspect her of. What would you do?'

'What would I do? I'd have him in the guard-room or hospital, or Britain, or something, instead of mooning round writing silly rhymes on the backs of envelopes and not caring a dam' what anyone was doing.'

'*Touché!*' Barclay smiled. 'Very good, sergeant. I'll do my best to meet the lady, though how it is to be worked I don't quite see. As far as I know the damsel is most respectably hardworking, and her evenings as you know are rather occupied.'

'Who said anything about meeting her? It shouldn't be difficult to find out all about her if you wanted to. I thought every female in this town was ticketed like a cattle show until I . . . She must be very "also ran", 'cause no one seems to have heard of her.'

'Have *you* been making investigations then?'

"Course I wanted to know who the girl was! So ought you. That's what I'm telling you.'

55

Barclay broke into laughter. 'Heavens, Jimmy,' he said, 'if *you* can't find out what you want to know, a fat lot of good it is my going Sherlocking.'

'I haven't the time for Sherlocking, as you call it,' said Jimmy testily, 'but you're a gentleman of a private with nothing to do but amuse yourself.'

Barclay laughed again at this perversion, which was yet half a truth. He knew that it was the failure on the part of the watchful mothering Jimmy to keep track of Kif's doings himself that had brought his wrath down on the next responsible.

'Well, Jimmy,' he said, 'if no one knows anything about her it's a dam' good sign. In fact, it's so amazing that I have a sneaking feeling that we should be rescuing her from Kif.'

'That's right,' said Jimmy scornfully, 'get out of it somehow!'

And the argument dissolved into the friendly consumption of *vin rouge*.

And yet it was Marcelle who was the means of bringing Kif into his first trouble in the army. He had come back one evening in the cool dusk finding the world with its first pale stars a place of wonder. He had kissed Marcelle. And Marcelle had lifted her mouth gravely and sweetly to him as a child might. When they had come to the end of the path and she had given him her hand as always in good night greeting he had blurted 'Give me a kiss', and had known a moment of surprised horror at himself, for he had not meant to say it. The words had bubbled up of themselves. And then with her steady eyes on him she had lifted her chin without the smallest suspicion of coquetry, and Kif had kissed her blindly, almost blunderingly, in his surprise. But he had gone back to his billet treading the powdery white dust as if it were air. That embraceless kiss was at once a benediction and an intoxication. He was blessed beyond the common lot of man, a being apart, and the world was a beautiful place and his very own. He was unconscious of the tall purple trees patterned against the last washy primrose of the daylight sky, of the smell of the dust and the roses in the dew, of the way footsteps and voices melted into music on the magic evening air. But all of it helped to bring him to the fey-ness of his present mood.

And it was at this moment that he encountered Blyth as one slips up on a worm in the path. Blyth was a lance-corporal in Kif's company; efficient in his work, unattractive in his personality, and more immoral in speech if not in mind than most. As Kif came to the door of his billet he met Blyth, who, bursting with the officiousness engendered in him by the blue-and-crimson brassard, had just been shepherding stray lambs to their pen.

'You're late, Vicar,' he said. 'Get a move on.'

Kif took the rebuke mildly. He hardly heard it. He was moving on with the little group of last-comers at the billet door when Blyth was moved to further speech. He cocked a leering eye at Kif as he passed and half seriously made a proposition.

'When you don't want that girl . . .'

The blatancy of the suggestion was not the least infamous part of it.

Now since this history of Kif is a truthful one, with nothing mitigated and nothing touched up, it must be confessed that his attitude to Marcelle had in the beginning differed not one whit from his to Simone, which was by no means reverential. It was Marcelle who had made a difference, not Kif. If it had been a day previously even, any time before Marcelle had kissed him and made things wonderful, he might have passed into the house with a more or less careless 'Shut your mouth!' As it was the sentence caught him on the quick. His steps stopped with a queer jerk, the abrupt movement of one who has seen a step only just in time. His crystal world melted on the instant into such a wave of anger as he had never known. In the middle of a strange haze was the ruddy face of the corporal, solid, actual, mocking. Kif stepped forward and hit it with all his might and with indescribable satisfaction. Words were struggling within him, but rage barred their exit. All his pent eloquence was in that right fist.

There was no lack of words on the part of Corporal Blyth when he regained his feet; they poured from him in a turbid flood. Into the frothing spate of his obscenities cut the cool voice of Sergeant Layton, late of the Middle Temple.

'If you're wise, Blyth, you'll shut your rank mouth about the business. You deserved it.'

'Shut my mouth about it? Not —— likely! Do you think I'm going to be hit by a —— of a private and say nothing about it! Think turning the other cheek a suitable business for N.C.O.'s, do you? Well, I don't—see? He's for it, the ——, and I'll see that he gets his.'

'Don't be an idiot, man. You can't provoke a man and then get him into trouble when the inevitable happens. You apologise for the remark, and I've no doubt Vicar will apologise for his action.' He glanced to where Kif was standing, exhausted by his access of emotion, white and quick-breathing.

'Apologise! *Apologise!* You do make me laugh. Apologise to a —— private for remarking about a bit of skirt that——'

Barclay grabbed Kif's arm from behind just in time, while Layton moved forward till he stood in front of Blyth.

'Will you shut up,' he said slowly between his teeth.

'Yes, I'll shut up for now. But that complaint's going in. He's for it, I tell you. I'll talk at the proper time.'

'Well, I give you fair warning,' said Kif, finding words at last, 'that if you talk to that effect again I'll kill you.'

'Oh, threats is it, now?' said the corporal. 'You wait, my little man. You're for it, all right!' and he walked quickly away with his aide and disappeared round the corner of the house.

Barclay led Kif inside, and the audience—less than a dozen—stirred from their immobility, half regretful as one is at the fall of the curtain, half thankful as at a sermon's end. They regarded each other furtively, each eager to see how his neighbour was taking the incident. Then someone said, 'Well, Blyth asked for it,' and someone seconded with, 'There don't seem to be any call to make such a song about it, somehow', and discussion was deemed open. The sympathy of the meeting, it soon became evident, was very strongly in favour of Kif; not because he had stood up for his girl so vigorously—there was not one among the group

57

who in his secret heart did not think the boy a fool in his rating of the maiden—but because he was liked universally and the corporal was merely tolerated.

When the iniquity and unfairness of Blyth had been canvassed to a refrain of 'Exactly!' and 'Just my point!' and the luxury of discussion was gradually promoting Kif to the martyr's pinnacle, it occurred to a large heavy youth that the other side should have a hearing.

'Well, it do seem to me that he didn't ought to have hit his superior nohow,' he said.

Wigs, the little cockney, took his stub of cigarette from between his lips and spat accurately between a broken tile and a fragment of china.

'Your intelligence dazzles me,' he said.

And it seemed that the case for the prosecution was complete.

But in spite of the goodwill and the best efforts of Layton, who searched hastily but unsuccessfully for Blyth in the hope of persuading him as he cooled down to reconsider things, Kif spent that night in the guard-room under arrest for striking his superior in the execution of his duty.

While Jimmy swore and Barclay sorrowed and both slept, Kif watched the calm white square of moonlight travel round the white-washed walls. There were no bars to the window since the guard-room of the hour was merely a converted room in a former dwelling-house which was now used as army offices, and the light from it lay in an unbroken square so vivid that it seemed to Kif incredible that it was not a concrete thing that could be handled and lifted. He counted the hours as they were tolled out by the clock in the distant square. The chimes floated out into the silence with a sweet reasonableness that maddened him. The irrelevant calm of the night was a goad to the turmoil within him. The footsteps of the sentry, muffled in the dust, padded in time to the throb in his brain. Blyth, Blyth, Blyth. Blyth had done this to him and he was helpless. Blyth had insulted his girl, had hurled him from his pinnacle of happiness, and had caused him to spoil his army record.

It would be difficult to say which hurt him most acutely. The last was, of course, the gravest, the most permanent injury. In those campaigning days a man's army record was to him what business integrity or the cleanliness of his sports reputation had been to his civilian predecessor. But the murdering of his moment was probably a more heinous crime in Kif's eyes that night than the finger-mark on his record. His thoughts went back to Marcelle, sleeping somewhere almost within hail; so near that if he shouted with all his might into the still white night his voice would come to her as a far-away sound. The thought was vaguely comforting.

His rage, having exhausted both body and mind, died down for lack of fuel as a moor fire burns itself out at the edge of the heather, having nothing left in the black waste to feed on, and leaving behind the long-lasting unsuspected glow in the depths of the peaty turf that fools so often the feet of the alien and the too optimistic. Before four he fell asleep and was still asleep when breakfast was brought him by a facetious fellow-private of his own platoon.

'Cheer up, old top,' said that worthy, as his gay eyes met Kif's, sleep-sodden and lightless, in the midst of his badinage. 'It's Chicken on the bench. He'll just bleat "What'll I do now, sergeant?" and the sergeant will say "Give the —— the Iron Cross", and Chicken will say, "Amen. Put it down to the wine bill", and that'll be all.'

It was, in a measure, as the cheerful one had foretold. The company commander was on leave in Britain, and his place on the seat of judgment was taken by the second in command, a gentleman with a genius for the intricacies of indents and returns but without the normal capacities in other directions. With the unobtrusive help of his sergeant he disposed successfully of two routine cases, but boggled at Kif's, and referred the case to the commanding officer. Since the colonel was, in his turn, on leave, it fell to Murray Heaton to deal with the case.

Heaton's face looked more than ever like something carved out of teak as Kif and his escort appeared before him. His long eyes, masked by the folds of the upper lid and habitually veiled in expression, his salient nose, his expressionless mouth gave to his face an impassivity strange in so young a man. It had been said of his mouth by a subordinate that it looked as if it had not been opened for years and then only with difficulty.

He listened to the charge and to the case for the prosecution without 'batting an eye' as the orderly officer remarked afterwards. He watched Blyth unblinkingly as he gave his evidence until the corporal said, 'I said something in fun about his young lady, sir,' when he glanced at Kif for a fleeting second. When Blyth had finished his admirably concise account of the incident he asked:

'What did you say about his young lady, corporal?'

Blyth hesitated for the first time. 'I said he might pass her on to me when he was tired of her,' he said with an uneasy smile.

'I see. What have you to say, Vicar?'

Kif had had much to say in the long hours of the night, but in the official atmosphere of his commanding officer's presence his tongue deserted him. What had all this—documents, and people standing to attention, and all that—to do with the quarrel between him and Blyth, with what Blyth had said about Marcelle? What was there to say to Heaton—*Heaton*—about it all?

'He shouldn't have said what he did,' he said sullenly.

'You admit hitting Corporal Blyth?'

'Yes, sir.'

'You knew the seriousness of hitting your superior?'

'Yes, sir.'

'Then what induced you to forget yourself to that extent?'

'What he said, sir.'

'What did he say?'

Kif told him.

'Was that what you said?' Heaton asked the corporal.

'Not exactly, sir.'

But witnesses when called were unanimous in asserting that that was exactly what he had said.

Heaton accepted the evidence without remark. 'Anything else to say, Vicar?'

Kif was silent. Through Heaton's brain as the sulky dark eyes met his went the memory of a night of sleet and mud, cold and black and void as the beginning of time, when he and this boy had tumbled into a shell hole together, and the boy in the baleful light of a star-shell had removed his boots from Heaton's chest with a polite 'Sorry, sir, my fault.'

'You know that provocation is no defence whatever for what you have done?'

Kif was still silent. Then he blurted out: 'Can a corporal say anything he likes then?'

'No, he can't. But it is not for you to correct him. That is where your mistake lay. Do you understand that?'

'Yes, sir.'

'Anything else to say? . . . I want you to say it now if you have. Get it off your chest.'

'No, sir.'

'May I have his record again, sergeant?'

There was a little silence. A fly buzzed on the window-pane. Leather creaked as the lieutenant on duty stirred a boot which his batman had wrought to a chestnut brilliance with an artist's pride, another man's polish, and still another man's brushes.

'In consideration of your good record, Private Vicar, and because of that alone, I am going to deal as leniently with your offence as army regulations will allow me. I believe that you hit Corporal Blyth without malice aforethought, and I expect that you will behave decently in the future. You will have three days in the guard-room in which to contemplate your future good-conduct.'

There was a general stir of relief when the sentence ended. Heaton wondered why the prisoner did not look more relieved.

'Do you want to say something?'

'Can I speak to Private Barclay before I go back, sir?'

That being granted, Heaton said: 'That is all, then, sergeant. I want to speak to Corporal Blyth for a moment.'

Kif, whose thoughts had gone ahead, was the only man in the room whose heart did not leap with an unholy joy at the last sentence. As the escort filed out each of them cast an almost loving glance at the carefully unconcerned face of the corporal.

'Strewth,' said one, as the door closed behind them, 'I wouldn't be in his shoes with little Heaton all polite like that, not for a fortune I wouldn't.'

'He'll wish he were safe in a ruddy guard-room,' prophesied another.

And the sentiments of Corporal Blyth were not materially different. He braced himself for the 'telling-off' that was coming. Heaton had a reputation for few but scorching words; and his eyes were particularly nasty at the moment. Would it be better to take everything in silence or to defend himself?

60

'You box, I hear, corporal?'

Blyth stared and tried to pull his scattered ideas together.

'Yes, sir. Yes, I do a bit.' What the devil was he getting at? Was he going to suggest that he should have defended himself?

'What is your weight?'

'Just about eleven stone, sir.'

'Yes. I should like very much to meet you in the ring one of these days. I am not much over ten and a half, but I think I could give you quite a sporting bout. Will you meet me at the divisional tournament next month?'

'Can it be arranged, sir?' Blyth was trying to reconcile the conversational tones with something unpleasant in his officer's eyes.

'I shall see to that if you care to have the bout. It may not be much fun for you, of course. (Wouldn't it! thought Blyth. An uppercut to that chin would be his idea of earthly bliss.) You need not accept unless you like.'

'I should be very glad, sir.'

'Ten rounds?'

'If you like, sir.'

'Very good. I shall see that it comes off. Good morning, corporal.'

And a very puzzled corporal went out into the sunlight.

It may be said here that the bout was duly fought a fortnight later at the divisional tournament, of which it proved by far the most popular item. Fare of this piquancy had not been offered within service memory. No secrets can be kept in the army; it is too full of batmen for one thing, and too self-centred for another. And though the Half-and-Halfers, who had put two and two together and made a most satisfactory five long before Blyth had done violence to his arithmetic in the same problem, were once more in the line by the time the bout was fought there was not a man in the audience who was ignorant of the history of its initiation, nor was there a single feint or blow which was not faithfully reported to the eager absentees. Not that there was much to report. The referee stopped the contest in the third round and Blyth was excused duty for the two succeeding days.

When Tim came, still indignant but relieved at the leniency of the sentence, Kif said without preamble: 'Will you meet Marcelle for me to-night and tell her I'm on duty?'

'I'll certainly meet Marcelle if you want me to, but I'm blowed if I'll say you're on duty. Why this modesty? Don't you realise that you're the complete little hero of fiction who has defended the right and is now suffering martyrdom for it? Marcelle will adore you more than ever when she hears about it.'

'Oh, stop it,' said Kif wearily. 'It isn't a bit like that, and you know it.' In the revulsion of feeling that had succeeded his night of anger the very contemplation of the incident gave him a faint feeling of loathing. 'Jimmy'd go, but I thought you'd better, somehow.'

This was his way of saying that he thought Barclay the more understanding of the pair, and Tim relented.

'I'll do whatever you like, Kif. Instruct me.'

'Say I'm on duty and that I'll write her a letter.'

'That all?'

Kif hesitated. 'Make it clear to her somehow that I'm not just backing out.'

'I'll do that,' said Tim heartily. 'Where do I meet her?'

Kif told him. As he was departing Kif said: 'I say——' and as his friend turned he mumbled hastily: 'Don't tell your people about it, will you?'

And Tim promised.

But Marcelle knew all about the affair. She had collected linen that afternoon from the commanding officers' quarters, and Heaton's batman, Carey, a talkative worthy whose natural propensities suffered sore constriction in his daily intercourse with Heaton, took the heaven-sent occasion with both hands and did it justice. Marcelle's face as he unfolded the story was spur to his talents, and he embroidered his subject with an artistry worthy of such a tale of gallantry. After her first exclamation of dismay she stood quite still, listening to the man's chattering gesticulative cockney, her grave eyes on his bright careless ones, her basket still propped against her hip. When he had finished and she had learned the extent of Kif's punishment she said: 'Thank you for telling it to me all,' and turned to go.

Carey followed her admiringly with his eyes. He picked up the dubbin tin again and was regretfully about to resume his labours when he bethought him. Something in the situation was missing. Such a tale called for a *beau geste*.

'I say, miss, if you'd like some of us to beat up that little runt of a corporal, just say the word.'

When his meaning was plain she shook her head. 'No, no,' she said, 'there has enough happened,' and went away.

So Barclay did not find her at the rendezvous and had to seek her out. He ran her to earth in a cottage on the outskirts of the town, a cottage with lime-green shutters and a garden full of round tight heavy cabbage roses of a boiled-sweet pink and a scent that drove to wild indiscretions. It was her mother who came in answer to his knock—a tall woman with unexpectant eyes and a presence as fine as Marcelle's. Tim explained his errand and she received his explanation politely but with a subtle reserve, very much as a reigning sovereign might treat a man from a hostile country whose ambassadorial privileges made his entertainment a necessity. Marcelle, she said, was at the back of the cottage taking in the washing. And there Tim found her, her bare arms round a bundle of linen and her supple body bending and straightening as she picked the dried garments from the grass.

'Mademoiselle Fleureau,' he said, and she turned.

Tim was conscious even in that moment of amazement. So *this* was Kif's 'girl'! What he noticed at the time was the graciousness of her air; what he remembered afterwards was her fine eyebrows and the perfection of her grooming.

'Monsieur?'

Tim said that he was a friend of Kif's, and had come to explain his absence, but before he had time to commit himself further she said:

'I have heard. They told me at the commandant's. And ever since I think. All the afternoon I think. It would be of no good that I would go to the colonel and ask pardon for him?'

Barclay was afraid not.

'The colonel knows me—and my mother,' she added. 'Might he not listen?'

Barclay explained that the colonel was in Paris and that, in any case, Kif had received the lightest punishment that they could have hoped for, and that no good could come of interference. There had to be some kind of punishment for discipline's sake.

'Deescipline!' she said, with unutterable scorn. 'That is men's talk. That is of the war. Not real, made up—what do you say?—artifeecial, *non-sense*! One cannot have justice, one cannot have comfort, one cannot have pleasure. Be calm! It is the deescipline. . . . It is dreadful!'

She became conscious of Barclay's reality and looked at him deliberately for the first time. 'Are you Teem?' she asked:

'Yes.'

She put out her hand and shook his calmly. 'How do you do?' she said. She looked at him a moment longer. 'Did Keef ask you to come?'

'Yes.' He explained what Kif had wanted him to do and gave her his messages.

'And Jeemy? What does he do? . . . Jeemy is pairhaps "beatin' up" Mistair Blyth?' She smiled for the first time, and Tim wondered afresh at Kif's girl. 'You have met my mother? Please come in and have a sirop.'

Barclay thanked her and helped, unnecessarily, to carry the basket of clothes into the cool tiled kitchen. He stayed for nearly half an hour, being pleasant to Madame and watching Marcelle, none of them mentioning Kif. When he rose to go Marcelle went with him to the door.

'Tell Keef that I shall write to him. And I shall see him before you go away altogether. It will not be long now—three days? five days?—but I shall see him, and it will be all right.' She stood searching his face.

'You are a good friend of his?' It was a question, not a statement.

'I hope so. Kif is a good boy.'

'Yes.' She was not going to discuss Kif with him. 'Thank you for coming. I am very grateful.'

She did not ask him, as he had half hoped, to come again, nor did he ever speak to her again. He saw her only once more, a fleeting glimpse as the battalion marched out to the railway on their way up the line. But for years afterwards Marcelle Fleureau was a vivid and gracious memory to him.

Kif's farewell to her was almost as brief. The battalion left the town thirty-six hours earlier than had been anticipated, and two hours after Kif's release. Kif, almost frantic at the imminence of their departure, would have broken still more canons sired by 'deescipline' if he had not been forcibly restrained by Jimmy, who pointed out with fervour and brilliant blasphemy that any more 'quod' just now would be unthinkable.

So Kif said good-bye to Marcelle as they passed up the *pavé* road between the poplars towards the low blue, sweetly curving hills that hid the gaping horror beyond; and not a man of the company, witnessing the leave-taking, called a ribald word or sucked a suggestive breath.

'I'll come back, Marcelle. I'll come back,' stammered Kif, and pulling himself away ran to get his lost place in the ranks.

10

On July the first, as all the world knows, the Somme offensive started. The Half-and-Halfers went into action at La Boiselle through the morning mists under the lifting barrage. Kif had waited in the intolerable racket of that first colossal bombardment like a two-year-old at a starting-gate, nervous, panicky, heart-quickened. And inside him was that other quickening which had nothing to do with his clamorous heart and which made Danger for him a siren—loved and hated and sought again. Uncertainty had reached its apex. The whole of life swung poised like a bubble on the moment. And every moment from now on was to hold a bubble poised. Fear. Ecstasy.

Perception was sharpened to an incredible fineness. Every blade of grass was remarkable. His finger-tip where it lay resting on his rifle, a little pebble embedded in the chalk of the parapet, the feel of the mist on his cheek, the texture of his khaki sleeve, all were miracles. All were caught up into the wonder of that poised moment. The mists swung and eddied. The guns stormed. And presently . . . Even now . . .

Fear. Ecstasy.

Kif never remembered much about that attack. He was drunk with excitement, bloodlust and achievement. He had been 'over' before on many occasions, but none were like this. He remembered realising that the crumpled white mess of chalk, wire and wood at his feet was the enemy front line and wondering why there were no Boches to do in. He remembered Jimmy cheering like a maniac a few yards away and almost inaudible in the row. He remembered realising that the heavy rain was machine-gun bullets. He remembered stumbling over a steel hat on his way to the second line and realising that its owner's head was in it and that the owner was Wigs. Of the fighting in the second line he remembered nothing at all, except that he seemed to carry a pain about with him which gradually localised itself to his feet, and that on looking down to rid himself of

64

the hindrance he found that one puttee was red and soaking and already growing sticky. He remembered seeing Heaton, unwontedly flushed, a bomb in one hand and a revolver in the other, and wondering what he was doing there.

He had just come up from clearing out a dug-out, two dazed men at his bayonet's point, when a 5.9 burst at the end of the section. Something hit him on the shoulder and spun him round. His legs felt like cotton-wool and refused to move, and the ground came up and hit him.

But in that last moment of consciousness before he fell his eyes saw the picture he carried away with him of the torn wire of the enemy second line, and Jimmy Struthers hung across it like a wet rag, his brave career finished.

11

He realised that the thing above him was a far-away white ceiling. That he was in bed. That he was Kif. For a long time now—he could not tell how long—he had been aware of the world he had come back to, of hands and voices. But he had not known what the hands did; the voices had been meaningless. The body the hands had moved and tended had not been his, and he had had no interest in the wordless voices. But now he entered fully into possession of his identity. He was Kif. And he was in hospital presumably. He tried to turn his head that he might enlarge the view, but the pillow was deep and he gasped at the pain which tore him. In that dim other-world he had inhabited he had been conscious of pain far away, as he had been aware of the hands and voices. But now the pain was a localised and searing reality. He could not breathe. It seemed to him that to draw another of even these shallow and inadequate breaths was more than he could manage. The ceiling wavered and grew distant. If he lay very still perhaps he could cheat the pain a little. But there was this business of breathing. He had to breathe. You couldn't live without breathing. Well, he would rather die than have to suffer like this. If only he would die quickly and get it over.

Someone near at hand was moaning softly and continuously. A voice said: 'It's all right, sonny, we'll soon have you more comfortable.' He opened his eyes to see if the ceiling had grown steadier and found the nurse looking down at him. It was to him she was talking. Was it he who had been making the row? He tried to say something, but she forbade it. 'I know it's pretty bad, but it won't be long now.' She had a round jolly face and dark hair that frizzed out from under her cap. 'It's your turn next and then you can have a long sleep and feel like a new person.' And she went away. He tried to piece things together. It must be a long time since that attack. Was this Britain or France? And what had happened at La Boiselle?

Jimmy! He saw the picture clearly and cried aloud in his mind. The ceiling pressed suddenly down to crush him, and as suddenly retreated to an illimitable distance. And Tim. He didn't know what had happened to him. And he had such a thirst. Why hadn't he asked the nurse for a drink? If she couldn't stop this hellish pain at least she might give him some water. 'A cup of cold water.' Something out of the Bible. 'Inasmuch as ye have done it unto one of these.' She couldn't refuse him that. He was managing his breaths better now. You sneaked one in when the pain wasn't looking, as it were. As long as he didn't move he could just bear it. That fellow had stopped his row. Oh, no, of course, it had been himself. Funny. If only he could get a drink? Just a few drops of cold water on his tongue. The well on the moor road at Tarn had never gone dry, not even in summer. How had he ever chosen beer when he could have had water for the asking. Water. Cool clear stuff. God, why didn't someone give him some cold water. He knew now what the fellows in the Legion felt like. Only they didn't have this pain. Not always. Tim had been good lending him all those books. What had happened to him? Was he like Jimmy? Oh, Jimmy! Perhaps he was the only one left of them all. It was no good asking them here because of course they'd not know anything about it. All he could do was to wait. Lie still and try to dodge the pain. It was like stalking a Boche in the dark. You never knew where he was or the minute you were going to bump up against him. If only Heaton were here. He could work it in a minute. No, how silly of him. Heaton didn't know anything about doctor's business. Heaton knew all about . . .

Here was the nurse back and two orderlies with her. He managed to ask her for the drink. She shook her head and smiled at him just as if she had not taken away more than his hope of salvation. 'But I'll give you a real beauty when you come back,' she said. As the orderly insinuated a careful arm under his shoulders the pain came alive again: rampant, tearing, clutching. It was choking him. He couldn't bear it a second longer. Life at this price wasn't worth it. It wasn't worth it. Why did they fuss with him like this when he'd probably go west anyhow? It was just cruelty. They had put him down again. One of the orderlies said, 'Good man!' And the nurse was smiling at him again. That was the way with people. They thought it was their duty to torture you instead of putting you decently out of it as soon as they could. He remembered the first life he had ever taken. That rabbit he had jumped on unexpectedly coming over the fence by the low meadow. It had been in the grassy rut of the lane, lying doggo, and he had landed on it unawares. Well, he had not left it long in agony. Why couldn't they see that he'd rather . . .

A new ceiling now. One with windows in it. And another nurse. This one didn't smile, and she hadn't such pretty hair. At least her cap hid it all. If he could stick this perhaps a second or two longer they might find some way of stopping it.

A man's voice said: 'All right, Carter?'

66

Some one behind him held a little white cap above his face. A sickeningly sweet scent began to steal out from it. He realised what it was and gave himself up to it.

What a long time it was taking. He always thought anaesthetics . . .

His clenched hands relaxed.

12

There were daffodils round the slatted board at his feet, and a pale spring sky over his head. The wall at his back, covered with the meagre green of a budding pear-tree, reflected the warmth pleasantly. On his knees was a basket of mending wool which he was unravelling for the night sister, his big-jointed long-fingered hands, still smooth and thin from their months indoors, playing in and out among the tangle with the light sureness of a shuttle. And at the other end of the garden seat a fellow convalescent was sterterously engrossed in putting bead eyes in a bright woollen golliwog. Those were the days when a flood of golliwogs percolated out of the hospitals and inundated the country.

Now and then Kif let his eyes rest absently on the green perspective of the garden, but he did not see the flame of the tulips in the beds nor did he hear the riot of bird-song. What he saw was Hyde Park Corner with the first wash of green on the trees; what he heard was London traffic. Presently—when they were satisfied about his lung—he would go there. And it seemed to him that all the weariness and the pain of the last nine months was a little price to pay for the chance of nine days in London. It would almost be worth while going west afterwards—though he had no intention of going west if he could help it—if his death would ensure that London would go on being the London he knew.

Which is as near as Kif ever came to that form of exaltation known as dying for an idea.

'Did I see you getting a cup of tea from the pantry-maid this morning?' asked the little man at the end of the bench.

'You probably did if you were hanging around,' Kif said.

'Well, you keep off the grass, young fellow. That's my cup of tea, that is. And she's a very nice girl, even if she *is* a duke's daughter. I don't hold with titles as a rule, but with a cup of tea thrown in I'm not one to stick at trifles. She's a nice girl and we're great friends, so don't you try to come it over me.'

'Are you making that horror for her?' Kif asked, indicating the golliwog.

'Not so much of it!' said the outraged artist in coloured wools. 'This is my shay-doover, this is. It's on commission, like an 'ouse or a picture or what-not, for sister. Not Big Bertha. My one.' He handled the gaudy heap on his lap lovingly. 'What d'you think?' he said, dreamily contemplative. 'Seriously. Do you think yellow legs would look better with the red body and them green arms, or would you 'ave the purple? I 'aven't used any of the purple yet. Pretty colour, ain't it? Like the vi'lets outside Charing Cross. What d'you think? Would you carry out the scheme, as they say, or would you 'ave a little variety?'

'Oh, put 'em all in,' said Kif tolerantly, and watched in secret amusement while the gaudy object grew momentarily more gaudy. A large content possessed him. The present was good, the immediate future was better, and afterwards, when he was back in France, there would be Tim—Tim who was at present in hospital in Scotland. It was strange how his heart lightened at the thought of being with Tim again. In those first chaotic days in hospital it had been, not the missives from Golder's Green, but the first sight of Tim's neat small script on an envelope that had given him the most acute pleasure.

'I can't tell you what a relief it was,' Tim had written, 'to have the news of your whereabouts from home. The second line at La Boiselle was such a mess when I saw it last that I began to think I was the only one out of the bunch left. Jimmy has gone west. I saw him when they were bringing me down. Do you ever think what those early days at the depôt would have been without Jimmy? . . . They asked me, coming across, where I should like to be nursed back to health and strength, and I said: "Oh, thanks very much. It's awfully good of you to consider the matter. If it's all the same to you I should like to be as near London as possible." And much touched and comforted by such evidence of consideration for the feelings of a poor private I went to sleep. And I woke up in Aberdeen. At first I wasn't fit to speak to, but after a day or two I got over the shock, and now I am enjoying myself immensely. Buck up and get better, old boy, so that we can have another leave together in London. If you want books or food or anything, do ask Mother for them. She will be dying to do something for you and will be delighted to find an outlet for her energies.'

Golder's Green had indeed been prodigal in providing for his comfort, but the general hospital that housed him had been in Leeds, and he had consequently seen nothing of the Barclay family since he had stayed with them a year ago. Now, as he arranged the wools, he let his mind play pleasantly with the thought of seeing them all again.

'What an industrious pair!' said a quiet voice, and the commandant sat down beside them, restraining with a movement their embryonic effort to rise. She was a little elderly woman whose fine-boned face and hands belonged to an eighteenth-century miniature, and whose quiet talk was as full of modern slang as it was of raciness and point. The contrast between her appearance and her personality—only a little humorous twist of her small mouth gave the lie to her looks—gave her a piquancy that made her unique. To talk to her was like eating salt and sweet together, or finding a hot dish in the middle of an iced one. Her neat black clothes were tailored in Bond Street, and she was rumoured to be one of the four best judges of a horse in Britain. Her only child—a major in a line regiment—had been killed on the Aisne. At his death she had turned her home into an auxiliary hospital of which she was commandant. But it was characteristic of her that she was more often to be found talking to the patients than sitting in state in her office.

'I say it is for the good of my soul,' she would explain to inspecting colonels, 'but really it is a flight from the boredom of being a figure-head. Everyone of my staff knows more about nursing than I do, and my secretary knows more about the business side, and yet they will never talk to me as man to man. I am merely the awful object on the prow that they say their prayers to. So I sneak away where I can talk to my equals for a bit.'

She hardly ever talked to a man with whom she did not find something in common. To Kif she talked of horses and dogs, of London, of racing, of cabbages and kings. She liked the dark youth with the unhurried ways—Kif, even in the immobility of weakness, managed to convey more of quiet in his demeanour than did his fellows—and when occasionally his eyes slid laughing round to her after one of her remarks she had always a disproportionate sense of pleasure.

To her girl chauffeur she said one day: 'Why are privates so much more worth talking to than cabinet ministers?'

'Give it up,' said the girl, who was also her cousin. 'Perhaps it is because they haven't a microphone inside them,' and the old lady had laughed.

Kif was certainly not out to impress anyone. He was habitually unselfconscious and natural.

To-day she asked him what he proposed to do when the war was over. He was on the point of telling her what he had told Ann of his ideal occupation, but contented himself with:

'Something in London.'

'If you are so keen on horses, wouldn't you like to work in a racing stable?'

'Well, you see, I weigh nearly eleven stone, and I wouldn't like just to——' he hesitated.

'Yes, I see. There wouldn't be much hope of promotion for you. I had no idea that you were as heavy as that. You don't look it just now.'

'No, I'm a bantam weight at the moment.'

'Are you a boxer?'

'No. I've always wanted to learn, but I haven't had the chance so far. Perhaps it won't be too late when the war's over. Our captain—Heaton—was a nib.'

'Heaton?'

'Yes, the jockey, you know.'

'Good heavens! was Murray Heaton your captain? The really incredible minuteness of the world! And what was Murray like as a military despot? Very Prussian?'

'One of the best.'

'Oh? You liked him? . . . Did they all like him?' She was looking at him with a frank and amused curiosity.

'Yes,' said Kif simply; but he made a little movement with his head which emphasised the monosyllable to a superlative.

'Why? What was so fascinating about Murray?'

'I don't know,' said Kif, not having consciously looked for reasons for his captain's excellence. 'He never fussed, somehow, but he always got things done.'

'No,' she agreed. 'No, he wouldn't fuss. We used to tease him in the old days by saying that instead of a text above his bed he had the motto "You mind your business and I'll mind mine". I have known him ever since he was a small boy. His father and my brother were great friends, and Murray rode a lot for my brother before he started training for himself. . . . And so Murray is popular? And as stunningly efficient as ever, of course? Does he still look as if nothing in the world affected him, and then give the show away by fiddling with his hat?'

Kif watched a picture with his mind's eye for a moment.

'Yes,' he laughed, 'he takes it off a wee bit and settles it differently.'

'And then puts it back the way it was. *I* know. Well, he had a wonderful way with horses. Perhaps it is the same with humans—in spite of his alleged motto.'

Kif had a sudden desire to tell her the story of Heaton and the corporal—how she would delight in it!—but the presence of his fellow-convalescent restrained him. He would save it up for a time when he was talking to her alone.

'I think, you know,' she said later, when she was taking her departure, 'that even if he reached the cabinet, Murray Heaton might be worth talking to.' A remark which passed over Kif's head, since he was wondering at the queerness of the fact that someone who took Murray Heaton as a matter of course—almost!—should sit by his side and be chummy like that.

When she had gone his companion began immediately to patronise him, because in the piping times of peace he had seen Murray Heaton ride and Kif had not. But for each exploit of Heaton's on the racecourse Kif produced a more thrilling one in France, and this amiable competition was in full swing when a nurse came down the path to them with a letter in her hand.

'I think you must be the only two men who don't hang round the hall at post-times,' she said. 'Has your girl given you up, Knight?'

Knight, who, as everyone knew—he produced their photographs at the slightest provocation—had a buxom wife and four children, grinned and smoothed the finished golliwog approvingly, and the nurse handed the letter to Kif.

'If it had been a girl's writing I would have stuck it on the board and let you find it. You dance much too well for me to let you go without a struggle,' she said, and turned to receive the golliwog from the proud author.

Serenely diplomatic, she admired the motley atrocity, and as she turned to go her eye encountered Kif's with a sense of shock. So *this* was what that quiet boy was like.'

'He's sorry he hadn't any more colours, Sister, or he'd have put them in,' Kif said.

70

'You wait!' she said. 'To-morrow I shall say that your foot is not well enough for you to dance!'

The letter was from Tim.

'DEAR KIF' (he wrote), 'I came home last Friday night, free at last from their beastly electric baths and things. My leg is as good as ever it was. I can't even get up a limp that might wangle a longer leave for me. They probably wouldn't believe me, in any case. Unimpressionable collection of hard cases, army doctors! The mater has elected to take the whole family to the Isle of Wight for the duration of my leave. If you are out before we come back, and would like the place, follow on. But I am going down to Derbyshire to-morrow to see the grandmother, and I'm quite determined to do the extra journey and drop in at Laythwaite. Partly because I'm dying to see you and I have a sneaking suspicion that even if you are free in time the Isle of Wight wouldn't be your idea of a leave, but mostly because I want to have a good yarn with you. Expect me on Wednesday.'

Kif thumbed the hand-made paper thoughtfully. He could read quite distinctly the thing that was not written. Barclay was coming to say something that he could not write. What was it?

A little chilly wind scudded suddenly round the corner. It had an edge to it that mocked at the weak but valiant sun.

What was it that Tim had to say? He considered various possibilities. Perhaps he had got engaged. But he wouldn't come in person to tell him that. He would have been entirely off-hand about it. He had a queer feeling that it was going to be unwelcome to him, this that Tim was going to talk about. And having made up his mind on that point he quite characteristically dismissed the thing deliberately from his thoughts. There were still two days in which he could be blissfully ignorant. And anyhow he was going to see Tim again after many months, and nothing could alter the fact that he and Tim were very good friends. Whatever the thing was it was outside their relations to each other. And for the first time in his life Kif had come to set store by his relation with a fellow man.

But on the following night he dreamed vividly. He was lost in a strange waste place. Fear such as he had never known in waking moments, even in the tightest corners, strangled him. Tim was somewhere just out of sight but within hearing. He knew that. But when he called there was no reply. He knew that Barclay was there, quite near, listening. But he did not come. And the agony of his mortal fear was shot through with the new agony of grief at his friend's desertion. 'Tim!' he cried, 'where are you? Tim!' and woke sweating and breathless, his heart hammering.

He lay a long while awake before his nerves were lulled into indifference again, but he had forgotten all about it when he came face to face with the real Barclay.

'Heavens, Kif, you've actually grown!' was his unemotional greeting, but his handshake was eloquent, and the habitual smile was strong in his eyes and round the corners of his mouth. 'Where can we talk in this place?'

'Come into the garden,' Kif said. 'You're very posh,' he remarked as he led the way down a flagged path. Tim was in irreproachable mufti. His nondescript suit was so faultlessly tailored that one forgot it had been a piece of cloth, cut and seamed and pressed and padded; it was an integral part of its wearer. It was impossible that it had ever looked new and it was highly unlikely that it would ever look old. Kif, who had a real appreciation of good clothes, gazed a trifle wistfully at it. Even in the days when his wardrobe consisted of his working clothes—cast-off and colourless—and his Sunday suit—stiff and angular and navy blue and too tight everywhere—he had hankered after sartorial beauty. He would not have known how to produce it, but he recognised it when he saw it.

'Pre-war,' said Tim, holding the ends of his coat out between finger and thumb. 'And it's dam' good to be individual again. I feel positively god-like because I can choose a tie. It amazes me that I ever thought choosing anything a bore. I used to stay in bed till the last minute and then grab the first tie that came to hand. Now I have the whole stock out and dawdle over them. It seems that I never appreciated my privileges. You're still a bit lame?'

'Only in the mornings. It wears off. I can dance all right by night-time.'

'Having a good time then? It's a ripping place. It must be glorious in summer.'

Kif agreed. 'There's a fine view at the other side of the plantation. Let's go there.'

The path lay through the wood and ended abruptly at the other side, where a four-barred gate led into a field of pasture. From their feet the country sloped away in a wide valley of grass and plough and rose on the far side to distant moors, bluish in the pale sunlight. Tim sighed appreciatively and propped himself against the gate. Kif pulled himself up to the flat top of the side-post, swung his legs over and sat there. For a little they talked of their experiences since they had parted—'Funny to think that the last time I saw you was in a trench at La Boiselle,' Tim said—and much of Jimmy. It was amazing how vivid Jimmy still was to them. It seemed to them both that at any moment he might appear out of the still spring morning as out of one of his own abstractions, to bully, contradict and protect. The atmosphere as they dropped their reminiscent phrases was alive with his personality, and their hearts were warm at the thought of him.

Presently a little silence fell. 'Now, it's coming,' thought Kif.

'They've recommended me for a commission, Kif.'

Kif's heart turned over. So that was it! He thought Tim had definitely given up that.

'Good for you!' he said heartily. 'Good for you!' he repeated, because other words would not come. He turned to find Barclay's eyes watching him unsmilingly. 'It'll be rotten without you,' he added cheerfully.

Barclay was still watching him. Damn it, why didn't he take his eyes away for a moment till a fellow got his breath.

'I haven't taken it yet,' said Tim. 'That's what I came to talk to you about.'

'What are you hesitating about?'

'Well, you know I always said I wouldn't have one. I hated the thought of responsibility. I still hate it. I was born that way. But I hate the thought of going back there as a Tommy even more than that. I'm telling you this because I want you to understand. I can't explain things to my people. They wouldn't understand, and I don't think I want them to. If I take this commission it will be for the most rankly selfish reasons. There isn't anything in me that will make the right kind of leader for the men. I know that quite well, because I'm under no delusions about myself. The recommendation has nothing to do with it. They'll recommend anyone who has been at a decent school nowadays, they're so hard up. Taking the chance—because that is what it amounts to—seems to me to be a deliberate going back on the men I've known. As a private I was as good as the next man. As an officer I'd be a wash-out. I don't mean I'd be incompetent. I've seen too much of the business for that. But when it really mattered I'd be one of the no-use kind. You know what I mean. I don't have to tell *you*. I always knew I'd be no use at the business, and I didn't even bother to think about it when it was suggested before. Now it has been shoved under my nose again, and I've sunk to the level of considering it. And I've told you why—because I'm funking the unpleasantness of being a poor bloody Tommy like the rest of the decent chaps. I've come to you to be bucked up and told that the dam' duckboards won't be half as bad once I'm back in France as they look from here. I don't *want* to take the commission. I'll regret it if I do. You've got to help me do the decent thing, Kif. Fire away. Hot and strong.'

Kif sat very quiet. He was looking past Barclay at a periwinkle growing at a tree's foot. A strange sad blue, it was, growing there in perpetual shade. He felt as if part of his inside were missing. But there was no question in his mind as to what he was to do. Fine shades of ethics did not exist for him. Tim had the chance of a commission and he would be a fool to refuse it. It was up to him to see that he accepted it.

'I think you're making a song about nothing,' he said. 'I'd have you for my officer any day, and I'm particular enough. You've just got wrong notions with having someone like Heaton so long in——'

'Damn you, Kif,' Barclay broke out, 'I didn't come to hear you say that. I want with all my soul to go back with you. Only the rotten bit of me is funking. I'm drowning and you won't help me.'

'You're nothing of the sort,' said Kif. 'You're only a bit sick on the crossing. Once you're over you'll be as right as rain.'

'I appreciate the metaphor,' said Tim drearily. 'You're a broken reed, Kif, and I thought you were a high tower. No,' he added instantly, 'that's nonsense. I've just been fooling myself, that's all. Everyone's got to do his own deciding. Yes, I shall talk in *clichés* and be-damned. But I swear if you'd only tipped me the other way I'd have fallen right. It's on your head, or at your door, or any other dam' thing you like. But you've done it.'

Kif grinned. His dark eyes twinkled at his disconsolate friend from the tilted peak of his service-cap. He put out his hand.

'Congratulations, Mr Barclay!'

Tim caught the hand without taking it, and brought it down on the gate, imprisoning it below his while he looked regretfully at the owner.

'You old rotter, Kif,' he said affectionately, 'I thought you'd *understand*.'

'I understand you'll make a jolly fine general some day.' Kif had adopted many of Barclay's habits of speech.

'Oh, *general*—yes! That's what I'm afraid of. Being the "general" type. All routine and no imagination. Look what I'd be responsible for!'

'You think too much about your ruddy responsibilities,' said Kif amiably. 'Have you got a watch?'

'A quarter to one.'

'Have to be getting back. Dinner is at one. Why won't you stay? They will give you a feed.'

'No, I must get back to town to-night. I'll have something to eat at the station. Where's Big Ben?' He referred to the loud-ticking gun-metal object that was wont to adorn Kif's wrist. He had bought it for half a crown from a man on whom the bestowal of a gold one by a besotted sweetheart had had a delirious effect.

'Lost it when I was wounded. . . . 'Member Jimmy telling me to take the ---- thing off before we went out wire-cutting that night or it would rouse the whole ——— front line?'

'Yes, his language always got thick when there was a job on.'

And the talk went back to Jimmy.

Tim reclaimed his coat in the hall and they said good-bye on the steps.

'You'll come to us for your leave,' he said, making a statement of it, but glancing anxiously at Kif.

'Thanks very much,' said Kif, and Tim ran down the steps as the dinner-bell rang.

Kif went down the stairs to the basement dining-room rather sorrowfully. He did not feel that the world was coming to an end because Barclay was going out of his life. He had too great a faith in the good world in front of him for that. But to have lost both Jimmy and Tim was certainly going to make a difference. He had the feeling one has when the party is over; to-morrow may be full of promise, but the moment is desolate. He had the hump. Nothing more heroic than that.

What he could not be expected to know was the fact that it was the scales of his own life, not Barclay's, that he had tipped out there where the periwinkles grew.

13

Tim, in view of his coming promotion, had extended leave, and the Barclays were still in the Isle of Wight when Kif left Laythwaite. They wrote urging him if he would not come to them to use the Golder's Green house where Alison still remained, but Kif was not yet sufficiently accustomed to the usages of polite society to use a house in the owner's absence. It savoured to him of cheek to go and stay there alone, as if he owned the place. He wrote instead a stiffly polite little note, stiff not from intention but because of the baldness of its phrasing. Kif had naturally none of the epistolary arts. He did not, it is true, use the meaningless stereotyped sentences so beloved of his class. He said straightforwardly what he wanted to say and left it at that. They were his own words, not a peculiar form of English used solely for letter-writing. But he had not the knowledge to make what he wanted to say graceful. Mrs Barclay handed the flimsy indelible-pencilled pages over the breakfast table to Ann, with a little deprecating smile.

'Dear boy,' she said.

Ann found something peculiarly offensive in the tone of her mother's remark. There was patronage, of course, and a kindly excusing of short-comings, but there was something more: a sort of regulating and emphasising of her own position of patroness in view of the deplorably obvious lack of the graces on the part of her protégé. So Ann felt; but Ann had probably not risen on the proper side that morning. She read the backhand lines—Kif wrote a schoolboy hand, but the letters did not sprawl or lie up against each other in the usual fashion of the little educated—in a black rage. She had a disgraceful desire to hit her kindly always-in-the-right mother. Just because he doesn't spend six pages being clever, or telling her how wonderful she is, she thought savagely. Why, he's the only boy of his sort we've known who wrote an individual letter. But she wouldn't see that, of course. She never thought how he would have stuck out of the herd if he had had the right sort of upbringing. Why, the very words on the paper had more personality than nine out of ten of the would-be clever ones she was so pleased with.

The mere sight of the stubborn, unflourishing handwriting brought the boy so vividly before her that it was as if he had been personally snubbed by her mother's remark.

'Please don't worry about me. I'm all right. I can look out for myself.' No, of course her mother wouldn't revel in that sort of stuff. She was piqued, that's what it was. So she had to condone the crudity to show she wasn't. Ugh! If it had been a girl she wouldn't have bothered about her at all.

What she might have said in her black mood was prevented by the tardy arrival of her brother. He kissed his mother, who was gathering up her letters preparatory to leaving the room to answer them—or previous ones. It was typical of Margaret Barclay that, with time her own, she spent the most wonderful hour of the most wonderful days being animated on hand-made paper with her back to the window. Ann, with whom he had already had an argument over the tenancy of the bathroom, he greeted with cheerful opprobrium, and in his sunny presence she relaxed and blossomed. For weeks he had been a being she did not know; moody, distrait, independable. Looking at him now, rummaging among the dishes on the sideboard to the accompaniment of a running commentary on their merits, one would say he had not a care in the world. Only to the being who knew him best the difference was visible. The lazy acceptance had gone from his eyes; they had a lost, half-afraid look sometimes that it hurt her to see.

'*And* kedgeree!' he said. 'That's the third morning running. There must be an unlimited supply of stale fish in the neighbourhood.'

'You're growing very particular,' said Ann. 'Who are you that you should look a boarding-house dish in the mouth?'

'True, O Queen! Live for ever. But I cannot pretend to illusions that I am bereft of. I have seen so many wheels go round in the last two years that I mistrust mechanics. If you don't call that mechanics,' he held up a lingering spoonful of the glutinous mess, 'I'd like to know—'

'Be quiet and get on with it. It's a glorious morning, and it will be half over before you are at toast and marmalade if you don't hurry.'

'Hurry? Nothing doing. That's another thing I've lost.'

'What?'

'My capacity for hurrying. No one hurries in the army. Come in to Ventnor with me,' he added as he sat down with a plate of bacon and eggs.

'Wouldn't you rather walk the other way? It's a dream of a day for March.'

'I would, but I want to shop.'

'Oh, Lord! Not more ties!'

'No, it isn't for myself—don't look so surprised, it isn't tactful—I just feel moved to buy someone a present this fair day. And you need not look so expectant either. You don't enter into it except as secretary of the advisory committee. Honorary.'

'Oh, well. As long as I am allowed to hang over the counter and say Oo. Who is it for, and what is it?'

'I must have notice of the question.'

'Oh, all right, keep it to yourself if you want to. I am that rarest of birds, an incurious woman.'

'Myth,' said her brother indistinctly through a large mouthful.

'No—phenomenon. There's a letter from Kif.'

Tim laid down his knife and fork and put out his hand for it. For a little there was silence. Ann sat finishing her coffee and watching the wistful look come back to her brother's eyes. Was it just the war, she wondered? Just the strain and awfulness of things. Or was there a girl? He had never mentioned a girl, which meant that if she existed she wasn't the right sort. How terrible! Her Tim. She was beginning to incline to the girl theory. There was this business of the present. And he couldn't possibly have worried so much merely about taking a commission—a thing that all his friends had done long ago. Of course he had said he didn't want to, but that was just his old lack of self-confidence. He had always been like that, letting other people do things while he looked on. There must be another explanation, and the only explanation was a girl. Perhaps her presence at the buying of the gift was to give him his opportunity to introduce the subject. If so, then she must be decent about it and try to understand. She wouldn't be one of those harpies whose talons are fixed for ever in their male belongings so that they are dragged unwillingly at their chariot wheels. Terribly mixed metaphor. Harpies and chariots.

Tim finished the short letter without remark and was absent-minded for the rest of breakfast. As they walked into the town they were still silent. It was a still high blue morning that in summer would have been pleasantly appropriate, but which in this leafless March seemed a God-given thing of wonder. Something in the man and the girl, both so susceptible to impression, responded to the atmosphere of the day as a cat stretches itself in the sun; and deep in them both was the aching regret that a wholly beautiful thing rouses in those who appreciate it. Even in the broad stability of the days before the war they would have been victims of that ache; now, when all human experience was thistledown before a wind, the poignancy in beauty was very near the surface. So they walked in silence until the streets of the town roused them to friendly trivialities.

Tim led Ann into a watchmaker's and Ann followed, thinking: 'If only he'll tell me about her! I wouldn't mind what she was like if only he'll tell me.'

She could and would not ask questions. Ever since their nursery days they had respected each other's reserves, a habit which had the effect of giving value to their confidences and in some queer way reducing these reserves to a minimum. There is in human nature a perverse desire to give a confidence which we know will be well received but never asked for. Much of the complete understanding and good-fellowship which existed between Tim and Ann was due to their mutual light-rein methods.

Ann heard Tim say: 'I want to see some men's wrist watches—silver.'

In her surprise she blurted, 'Is it for a man?'

Tim, who was inspecting the display under the glass of the counter, took a second to assimilate this, then he turned his head in quick surprise to look at her, and his eyes were the laughing mischievous eyes of her brother of nursery days, the small boy who had found her out. 'A mere man,' was all he said, but as the assistant approached with the watches he added: 'I'll give you due warning of the other kind. And I won't take you with me to the buying thereof.'

Ann was so filled with relief at the revelation and annoyance at her unwonted betrayal of herself that Tim had made his choice before she came out of her abstraction to ask: 'Who is it for, Tim?'

'It's for Kif. Do you think he'd hate a square one? It's by far the nicest.'

'I shouldn't think so. Kif is no conservative. In fact I should think the most original shape ever invented wouldn't he too original for him. What has happened to Big Ben? He was rather attached to it, wasn't he?'

'Yes, but he has lost it.'

'Well, this should comfort him! Is it his birthday?'

'Not that I know of.'

'It's rather nice of you, Tim.'

'Nice of me!' His pleasant mouth twisted in what was nearly a sneer. 'This is the merest conscience money—and paltry at that. Let's go and have coffee.'

'But you've only just had breakfast.'

'Art criticism is thirsty work. I haven't considered the rival beauties of Swiss and British for nearly twenty minutes without developing that sinking sensation. We will have coffee—with cream in it.'

Over the coffee and the small hard cakes which were all that a war-time establishment could supply they dawdled until nearly noon. A slant of sunlight fell across the clothless table and drew a heady acrid scent from the four daffodils stuck mathematically into a glass vase at the table's centre. In the drowsy warmth both achieved a measure of happiness. There is no girl, Ann was thinking. No girl. I've been a fool. Meeting trouble halfway. A fool. He isn't that sort. Dear Tim.

The result of Tim's meditations was to make him bring out the little white packet and unwrap it. Together they eyed the watch in a mesmeric quiet. When Tim had turned it over several times Ann put out her hand for it, and she in turn fingered it absently; laid it on her wrist, dangled it from a first finger, held it in an embracing palm, gazed at its shrewd elongated face. Tim's hand came out for it again, and she surrendered it wordlessly. He laid it gently in its wrappings and thoughtfully and with infinite care parcelled it up. With as much deliberation as if it were for a mistress, Ann thought, watching the lingering fingers. No, as though he were burying something, she thought abruptly as he put the lid on. Laying a ghost. What made her think of that? Horrid thought.

Tim asked for the bill and together they went out into the sunshine.

14

From April 1917 until November 1918, Kif was in France; an insignificant private of a battalion with an enviable reputation, moved back and fore, careless and acquiescent, across the old battlefields until their very familiarity bred a bastard kind of affection in him, and the disappearance of a gable here or a tree there was a matter for amused concern on his return. He was led up the uncurving roads, *pavé* or rutted, trundled over the country in railway trucks, bucketed about in motor lorries, ignorant always of his destination and nearly always indifferent. The important things of life were whether his supply of cigarettes would hold out until next day; whether the Q.M.S. would agree that his boots were not what they had been; whether there would be a letter or a parcel for him; who would win the hundred yards; whether the sector they were taking over would be cushy or otherwise, and if otherwise which were the 'unhealthy' places. But the only really important thing which happened to him in all that time occurred just after he returned from England and hospital.

The battalion were out of the line. It was a chill mournful evening with a Scotch mist that wavered damply about the billets and made one think of firesides and hot toast, toast dripping with butter and generously overlaid with marmalade—the mushy kind, full of gleaming peel. But there were no fires. With luck there would be a stove somewhere. The new draft inspected, the Sergeant Major said: 'You'll find most of the company over in the Y.M. Your billet's the third door down on the left.' Kif dumped his kit thankfully in the dim deserted house, full of the ghostliness that personal belongings have in their owners' absence, and made for the Y.M.C.A. hut.

A thin golden line drew a square round the blind of each window and a pleasant hubbub came from within. Kif pushed open the door and savoured it all gratefully: the stove, the lights, the voices, the tobacco smoke, the click of billiard balls, the jigging of a mouth-organ, the flags, the evergreens belying their reputation. 'Hullo, Vicar,' said someone, and he crossed to the far corner and subsided among a group who might bring him up-to-date in regimental history. While they talked his eye wandered over the hut in search of old cronies, but there were none. He knew less than a dozen faces in all that crowded hut and of these only three had a name in his mind. Jimmy dead and Tim gone; it was going to be a dud time. He knew the back of the chap playing billiards, but he couldn't remember his name. He watched the fair head with its upstanding hair and the sloping muscular shoulders idly first and then with attention. Who *was* that? And where had he seen him last? He wished the fellow would turn round. Every time he moved a picture swam into his mind and broke before it became a whole. The unknown straightened himself abruptly and the picture rushed together until just as he was on the point of recognising it, it faded. It was connected with something exciting, unusual. Had it been a scrap somewhere? Kif took the cigarette from his mouth and with narrowed eyes concentrated his attention on the problem. But into no picture of a trench mix-up did the supple smooth-moving figure fit.

The unknown laid down his cue and turned round, his game finished. He was a complete stranger. No, he wasn't, then. He was—he was—he was the boxer who had knocked out the 'curry-comb' that night at Salisbury!

The fair boy came easily towards them, feeling in his tunic pocket for his cigarettes. And that is how Kif met Thomas Carroll, commonly known as

Angel, partly because of his beautiful colouring, partly owing to the suggestion of his name.

It was a month before Kif was admitted into even the outer courts of Carroll's friendship, and much longer before they reached the stage of boon-companionship. It was not that Carroll put any premium on his value as an acquaintance. When Kif told him that he had seen his triumph in the ring he seemed unimpressed; Kif could read not the faintest gratification in his face. And when Kif mentioned the fact of Carroll's prowess to others he found that the company had up till now been unaware of it. It was not from any sense of superiority, then, that Carroll kept Kif at arm's length. His withholding seemed to be due rather to a queer caution and reserve which was noticeable in all his dealings with people and was completely lacking in his dealings with things. Even when intimacy had been established Kif was often conscious that the comfortable quality which had distinguished his friendship with Jimmy and Barclay was missing. You could never bet on what Carroll was thinking or feeling as you had been able to with the others. He was to all appearances frank, he was good-natured, he could be very amusing both in private conversation and for public delectation (his most popular moments were those in which he 'did' the various officers for the benefit of whoever had the luck to be present); he was, as might be expected, a good man in a scrap, he was a good friend—that is to say he saw that no one pinched your share of the food when you were busied elsewhere, and if part of your equipment was missing at a critical moment he lent you his and pinched someone else's until the crisis was past. But he was incalculable. In spite of everything he remained an unknown quantity. And the comfortable sensation was lacking.

Carroll had enlisted the week after the Salisbury tournament and had been in France for six months when Kif rejoined the battalion.

'You weren't a professional?' said Kif, remembering that the bout he had witnessed had been an amateur one.

'No, but I would have been if I hadn't joined when I did. I was just going to be.'

'What was your real job?'

Carroll cast him a swift glance. 'An agent,' he said. He did not volunteer any further information and Kif shied away from the subject. 'A bookie's tout or something,' he thought. This conclusion was strengthened by the fact of Carroll's intimate and extensive knowledge of racing. That and boxing constituted two strong ties of common interest between them, and though Carroll asked frankly when the spirit moved him about Kif's previous mode of life Kif left it to him to proffer details of his own; and that Carroll never did.

His biggest concession was to give way to Kif's importunity and to teach him the rudiments of the game of his heart. Whenever they came out of the line he and Kif would retire to some approximately deserted place and he would put Kif through it. After six months of such stolen moments he was moved to rare expression of approval. 'You're not half bad,' he said. And Kif could have fallen on his neck.

In the early spring of 1918 they spent a leave together in Paris and made the gilt tawdriness of it sheer gold with their youth. The dreary sand-bagged Paris of war-time did nothing to shake the throne that London held in Kif's heart, but there were moments when, the pale spring sunlight falling suddenly from the wide Parisian sky across the squares and the bridges, he paused approvingly in the ploy of the moment, awakened to a half-realisation of the beauty of this war-haggard queen. 'A bonza place,' he said, still using Travenna's phrase as the superlative of praise.

They went back from waywardness and exuberance to bitter fighting and retreat. By the time that the British army had found a wall to set its back against and had drawn breath for recoil the incident of his Paris leave had faded from the surface of Kif's mind.

One day at the beginning of April, Carroll, who had been reading a letter from home—that home which he never talked about—handed an enclosure over to Kif and said: 'Want to back something?' Kif took the type-written slip and found that it was a bookmaker's list of prices for the Guineas.

'I wish I were going to see them,' he said wistfully, and read down the lists with attention. There had been no racing either during his leave with the Barclays or during his leave after discharge from hospital, which he had spent alone in London; and he longed unutterably to taste again the glow and satisfaction of it.

'What are you backing?' he asked.

'I'm having Gainsborough for the Two Thousand and My Dear for the Thousand. If you want to have something on I'll send it with mine, if you like.'

'Yes, I'm having one bet. I'm going to back a filly called Ferry for the Thousand.'

'Think again!' said Carroll.

'No. Ferry is the place I know best on earth—Wypers always barred—in fact, it's the place where I was born, and I'm putting a pound on it. How many francs make a pound to-day?'

Carroll again pointed out that it was a pitiful mistake to back outsiders at a hundred-to-one, especially in a classic race, where form was well known. 'You're worse than a girl,' he said disgustedly. 'They back a thing because it has the same colours as the dress they're wearing. Take a free tip and back My Dear!'

Kif smiled lazily at him and remained unmoved. And that is how he came to be possessed of a hundred pounds sterling and a bank book. Ferry won the Thousand Guineas at the starting price of fifty-to-one.

When Carroll, amused and congratulatory, asked him what should be done with his fortune, he decided that he would have it banked and the bank-book sent to Mrs Clamp, who had put him up on his last leave and to whom he wrote more or less regularly. He thought for a moment of asking the Barclays to take

81

charge of the money for him—Carroll did not offer that service—but though he still heard regularly and often from Tim, letters from Golder's Green had grown so infrequent as almost to have ceased. Ann still wrote to him at longish intervals, and her letters were still events which made a whole day vivid for him when they occurred, but he was shy of introducing the subject of money affairs into the correspondence. So he gave Carroll Mrs Clamp's address, saying happily: 'That will cure the old lady! She says no good ever came out of racing. Now she'll have documents to prove the contrary!'

A fortnight before the armistice Kif developed pleurisy. He was sent down to the base cursing feverishly, since the rumour of peace had been insistent for the last two weeks, and the bitterness of being out of the show now that the great moment had come was insupportable. Ten days later he was in hospital at Eastbourne and the Half-and-Halfers went into Germany without him.

He would have been mildly bored by his second dose of hospital life, since he knew all that was to be known about it, if the prospect of his imminent discharge had not given him a never-failing source of speculation. In his walks along the deserted front with the grey winter sea thick and still as if on the point of freezing, and Beachy Head very clear and near; to the sound of the falling cards as he played with his fellow patients; in bed at night when the night sister's lamp made a warm pool among the shadows and the breathings and stirrings of his neighbours filled the darkness: always the thought was with him. Free! His own master, with money in his pocket and the world to choose from. There was nothing he might not do. He played with possibilities as a child with coloured balls, tossing them up one by one and watching them spin and glitter and change colour as they turned, throwing up another before the last had come to rest in his hand. There was all abroad to be considered—America, Arizona, Oklahoma. The reality mightn't be as fine as the shining names, but there was nothing to hinder his going to see. He might go and punch cows till he had enough money to have a ranch of his own. The life had too decided a resemblance to the one at Tarn, and he would toss up another ball. New York, the home of the self-made. He didn't know anything about office work, but then neither did half the men who had made millions. And anyhow he didn't want to make millions. To go and do and see things while he was young—that was better than making a mint of money. And someday to have enough to take a taxi without counting his loose change; and to own a thoroughbred, bay with black points. But even while the balls rose and twisted and gleamed, deep down in his consciousness, unacknowledged but strong, was the realisation that he was only playing; that the American plains and the South Seas and New York and New Zealand were but foils to one thing, and his consideration of them but sops to his pride. I could do this and this, he boasted to himself, knowing full well that he never would. That he was caught. That once he stepped out of Charing Cross into the Strand again coral islands and cattle plains would be meaningless for him.

They gave him his discharge in January. 'You are sound now,' the doctor said as he passed him, 'but you will have to be careful for a year or two. No colds and no over-exertion. Good luck!'

'Ay, ay,' said the master tailor at the depot, 'so ye're through with it! I mind the day ye went out o' barracks with all yer bonnie white kit-bags and the pride o' the deil. . . . Ay! . . . . Well, good luck!'

The old lady in the tuck-shop at the gate remembered him. 'You were the boy who used to come for three tuppenny pies every evening. I'm very glad to see you safe. And your two friends? . . . Ah! . . . Well, good luck!'

So Kif came to London possessed of a hundred pounds, his gratuity—the tip a soldier received for dodging death for four years—and a light heart, and clothed by a grateful government in a suit which, thanks to a timely lubrication of an appropriate palm, was one which very nearly fitted him. He decided that he would find a *pied-à-terre* with Mrs Clamp while he looked for a temporary job which would keep him until he decided upon an investment for his fortune. But Mrs Clamp, loquacious and cheerfully reminiscent, had, for the first time in ten years as she explained, her husband and two of her sons home together, and consequently had no room to spare. She dragged the reluctant Kif into her kitchen and presented him to two of the world-wanderers, clear-eyed taciturn men with wind-bitten faces. They clutched pipes in a nervous silence while their wife and mother trotted back and fore in the preparation of the fatted calf for Kif, and translated for the visitor's benefit their lightest word, their most embryonic gesture, their very silences, into an exhaustive commentary on the world's affairs. She played showman to them very much as she had played the part to their empty garments on Kif's first leave. As they drew in their chairs for the consumption of the calf—fried eggs and sausage—Mr Clamp said to Kif:

'Looking for a job?'

'Yes.'

'Know what you want?'

'Well, I'll recognise it when I see it. But I'm taking anything to begin with.'

'Know anything about the sea?'

'Only enough to keep off it.' Kif grinned.

'Well, well, perhaps it's just as well. Lots of chaps coming out of navy service. Overcrowding. No prospects. Eh, Bert?'

Bert, secure in the possession of a first engineer's 'ticket', believed that that was so. And Mrs Clamp took hold of the conversation again. She was not, it appeared, going to turn him into the street unaided. Her sister's daughter's husband had a sister who let rooms. She lived in a mews near the far end of Tottenham Court Road and if she had a room vacant would do for Kif right willingly, Mrs Clamp was sure. So Kif, primed with the fat of what was then a lean land, armed with the address of his haven written in pencil on the back of a bill-head, and with a warm feeling under his government suit too high in situation and too potent in effect to be due wholly to eggs and sausage, went out into the street, his hand still glowing from articulation with the hands of the inarticulate mariners.

When next he went to pay his respects to his benefactor, some weeks later, he found her gone. Mr Clamp had been given a shore job, a neighbour informed him, and they had gone to live at Southampton.

At 5A Fitzmaurice Lane Kif set up his household gods. His landlady, a pathetic little wisp of a woman with mouse-coloured hair and a subdued manner, had been made a widow by the battle of Arras and supported herself and her child—a girl of five—by letting her rooms and by taking in fine washing. There was sometimes on her kitchen sink, in queer contrast to the rough crockery and the poor room, a foam of lace as delicate and lovely as happy dreams, frail beautiful mockery. Kif, coming into the kitchen one morning to clean his boots, paused at the white heap on the scrubbed spotless wood and touched it with a tentative finger. The stuff fell across his finger-tip with no more friction than would a cobweb.

'Do people really wear that?' he asked.

'That they do,' Mrs Connor said. 'Pretty, isn't it? Made by hand every bit of it.' There was vicarious pride in her voice.

'How do they keep warm?'

'Oh, that kind live in heated houses, and when they go out they have furs to put on.' Again there was no malice in her tone.

'Don't you envy them?' asked Kif, who envied no one on earth, but could understand a woman resenting other women's fripperies.

'If they didn't have them there would be no work for me,' she said.

It seemed to Kif that there was something wrong with the reasoning, but it was not the kind of thing he bothered his head about. As long as his little landlady was content it was all right. There were times when her eyes were so unhappy, hopelessly unhappy like a dog that has been beaten and, knowing no future, touches the nadir of despair, that he was uncomfortable. He had seen war in being, but he had not till now been brought into contact with the backwash. He had gone through the mill and come out and was free of it. This woman was caught; hopelessly and irretrievably caught. The insane thing was going on grinding her to pieces long after the need for it was over. Kif tried in various ways to show his sympathy and she made it obvious that she appreciated his unspoken goodwill by the thought she gave to his comfort, mental and physical; the garnishing of a dish at supper or a vase of flowers in his room. Hetty, the small girl, fell in love with him and, being at that refreshing age of maidenhood when reticence is not, made no attempt to hide her passion. She would waylay him on the stairs with a brazenness which was disarming, and if an invitation was not forthcoming would invite herself to his room with a mixture of determination and charm which Kif found difficult to resist.

'Are you going to your room?'

'Yes.'

'Are you going to do anything speshul?'

'No, I don't think so.'

'Because if you were doing anything speshul Mother said I wasn't to bother you.'

'Oh, did she?'

'Shall I come and talk to you for a little?'

'What will you talk about?'

Pause. 'Me.'

She would sit on the edge of his bed, her small thin legs swaying gently back and fore, the movement varied every now and then by a click of the shabby heels. Before he had been many days with them she had catechised him on his birth, parents, beliefs, war experiences, and had passed an opinion on most of his belongings.

'Why haven't you a tex'?' she asked one day, her round blue eyes on his bare walls.

Kif didn't know.

'How many tex' do you know?' she pursued suspiciously.

'Oh, thousands,' said her victim, trying a big bluff.

'Well, say one.'

Bluff called. "Fraid I can't remember any at the moment. Haven't used many lately. Only King's Regulations.'

'That's not a very good one.'

'Well, you say one.'

'God is a ghost,' she said promptly.

'That doesn't sound quite right.'

'It's *quite* right. And if you don't know any how can you tell? Shall I give you a butterfly kiss?'

'Will it hurt?'

'No-o! It's just a little tickle-ickle. Has no one ever given you one before?'

'Don't think so.'

'Poor Mr Vicar!' She pulled the boy down beside her and wound her skinny arms round his neck. She laid her creamy cheek alongside his and, her breath tightly held, brushed his cheek with her long lashes. 'There!' she said, thankfully expelling the pent air from her lungs, 'that's a butterfly kiss. Did you like it?'

'Rather!'

'You can have one every day if you like.'

'Thank you.' Kif gave the slight little body in the curve of his arm a gentle hug and lifted her to the floor. 'You'd better go to Mummy now. I'm going to wash.'

'*Must* you wash?'

'Don't you?'

'Oh yes. But I shan't when I'm your age. Are you fond of washing?'

'Love it.'

'Would you like to bath me? To-morrow's my night.'

'Don't think I'd be any good at that.'

'I'll teach you. Please bath me! Please!'

85

But this time Kif was firm—until next evening, when, on his way upstairs, he heard soft heart-broken crying from the kitchen and Mrs Connor's patient protesting voice. He leaned over the balusters and said 'Hetty in trouble?' and learned that it was his delinquency in the matter of superintending her ablutions that was the cause of her sorrow. He came slowly and shyly back down the stairs and into the warm kitchen full of steam and the faintly carbolic smell of soap. In an oval zinc bath before the fire sat the infant, her soapy shoulders jerking convulsively to her sobs, her fair hair screwed into a quaint knot at the top of her head.

'You said you wouldn't come,' she said accusingly, at once defending her lapse by making him responsible and preventing any criticism of her conduct by carrying the war into the enemy's country.

'Well, I've changed my mind,' said Kif humbly. 'Have you been soaped enough?'

On every bath night after that he not only assisted at the ceremony but carried her up to bed on his shoulder, a small bundle of satisfaction, half crowing baby, half Cleopatra on her royal barge. Upstairs she reverted wholly to baby and Kif tossed her three times and then tucked her up. He was slightly ashamed of his own enjoyment of these moments, and was glad that no one but Hetty's mother could see him. But he never willingly missed one.

At 8.30 every morning Kif went round the corner to the little newsagent's and came back with two daily papers. These he studied and clipped in the quiet of his attic bedroom until, about ten o'clock, he sallied forth in all the glory of a made-to-measure suit of the brown he had once coveted on Travenna. Between five and six he came back, tired, and each day a little more disillusioned. He had climbed stairs, penetrated into yards and warehouses, waited in queues, and had been interviewed by all sorts of men who had yet this in common, that they looked at him with one of two expressions: hostility or a pitying contempt. It is an old tale now, that reluctance on the part of the home front's defenders to employ men out of the army, but Kif had to find it all out for himself. Incredulous at first, later in a dull rage that ate up his vitality like a furnace, he pursued the search for a job, *any* job that would keep him from spending his precious fortune before he had chance to invest it.

'What did you do before?' asked the foreman in a contractor's yard where they wanted labourers.

'A farm servant.'

'You look it, I must say!' said the man, with a glance at Kif's clothes.

After that Kif went job-hunting in his government 'tweed'. But the results were no better.

It was significant that no one asked his age. Kif at nineteen gave no impression of immaturity. Though not so tall for a man as he had been for his age at fifteen he was yet fairly tall, and, as always, well put together. The army had abstracted the drawl from his step and there was nothing left of the countryman either in his appearance or his manner. He carried himself well and spoke easily. Even his accent, thanks to his imitative faculty and Barclay's long proximity, was less rugged. He had presentability, he had a man's strength, and he had the goodwill to work; but no one wanted him.

So used had he become to rejection that he was almost shocked when he found himself employed as assistant to a greengrocer in Camden Town. Until he had been two days there he could not rid himself of the apprehension that he had been engaged by mistake. Since this relief promised to be merely temporary— his predecessor was 'off with appendicitis'—he continued to live at Fitzmaurice Lane, and studied advertisements in the intervals of enticing carrots and turnips into the packed baskets of Mr Grabham's customers. On his first day he had wrapped up a cauliflower—yea, in fair white paper—and it took him a week to live down his mistake, and to reinstate himself in the good graces of his employer.

'Paper!' Mr Grabham had shrieked. 'No paper, you great fool!'

'Don't you wrap up anything, then?' asked Kif humbly.

'Certainly not. Nothing's been wrapped up for the last two years.'

'And what's that for?' asked Kif, pointing to the pile of virgin sheets.

'That? That's just to show that we're a firm that knows what's what, even if we don't do it. And don't ask so many questions. I bet you didn't ask your sergeant questions.'

Kif's dark eyes rested sardonically on the fussy meagre man with his cockatoo crest of thin grey hair. He had a picture of the mighty chest and withering glance of Mullins, company-sergeant-major. What did this little . . .

'I didn't,' he said good-humouredly. 'He usually got in first.'

I do not think Mr Grabham found Kif a bad assistant. He was at least strictly honest, which, as Mr Grabham remarked in camera to his wife, was a pleasant change from the last five bar one. But when the appendicitic one came back two months later he returned to unemployment with a feeling of emancipation which was as welcome as he recognised it to be illogical. Sometimes among the barrels of apples and the vegetable baskets even in these eight weeks he had had waves of that bitter impatience which he had not known since he left Tarn. Now he was free to pursue the search. The search for what? He was not quite sure. The search, anyhow.

If the labour market had been overcrowded in January, in March it was infinitely worse. The days passed barren and workless, and Kif rationed himself to two meals a day—and these he censored—in his desire to keep that precious sum in the bank intact. He felt that if he tapped it even to the extent of ten shillings the magic would somehow have gone from it and he would not be able to resist further inroads. He no longer bought papers. Mrs Connor pointed out that there was no need to buy a paper just to look at advertisements; you could see all the papers you wanted in a public library. So Kif made one of the eddying impatient crowd round the green baize supports in a murky reading-room whose very atmosphere breathed despair. A railway waiting-room may be the abomination of desolation, but there is a smug certainty on the faces of the jetsam who occupy for a little its penitential benches; trains are inevitable as night and day, and the tide that washed them up on so forlorn a shore will take them out at the appointed time, or thereabouts. But a London reading-room at ten o'clock of a working morning is hung with a gloom shot with malice and despair. In 1919 it was the mouth of the pit. Each individual in the crowd round the daily papers pushed and squeezed so that they might not be the one to be forced over the yawning edge. Every day they jotted down on the backs of envelopes or in little notebooks the precious addresses and hurried out so that they might be in the first flight, and always on the morrow they were back, their roughened fingers clutching the much-licked stub of pencil, their eyes searching the columns again. Except for their hands, and the set of their shoulders, and the look in their eyes they had outwardly as little in common as that first gathering that flooded the barracks on the outbreak of war. In mufti they had once more reverted to type, this to spats and this to a muffler. The time had not yet come when spats were to disappear in favour of the bare necessities of clothing. At present their only common attribute was the stamp of their service, and their need; their urgent need. Some of them, it is true, tried to camouflage the urgency under a mask of indifference; but it deceived no one. The man to whom a job is a matter of indifference does not consult the daily press in a public reading-room at ten of a morning.

'I say, mister,' said a small man in a government suit and a rubber collar to Kif one morning, 'what's a fly-tyer?'

Kif could not help him.

'Oh well, it don't matter. I'll have a shot at it.'

'Good luck!' said Kif, grinning at him; the man's cheerful remark was less suggestive of present need than of the old army motto: Apply for everything, just in case. Kif never saw him again, so he was never enlightened on the mysteries of fly-tying.

The odd spasmodic scraps of work which eventually came Kif's way were thrown in his path by blind chance, not obtained by any effort or premeditation on his part, and none of them offered more than a short breathing space in the battle. He was going despondently down the stairs of some Strand offices one afternoon when a wild clattering announced the descent of someone in a hurry, and a small fat man shot past him, arrested himself several steps down by dint of a grab at the railing, and, evidently overcome by a sudden idea, said to Kif:

'Not looking for a job, by any chance, are you?'

'Oh no,' said Kif bitterly, 'trailing up and down stairs is just my amusement.'

'C'mon!' said the small man, laying a plump pointed hand on Kif's arm and urging him upwards again. He propelled him into a cigar-thick office lined entirely with photographs, and said triumphantly to the man who was tearing his hair at the desk: 'I've got one, Sol. Ain't he a beaut!'

'Keep them in a pocket or what?' grunted the other.

'No, I got this one on the stairs.'

That night and for fourteen nights after, Kif, chocolate brown all over except for the necessary apron demanded by a grandmotherly censor, held a flaming torch (electric) up stage centre in act two of a new production with an Eastern motif. The new production flopped severely, and Kif ended his stage career without having found a substitute for it.

And then came the great idea.

In a paper one morning he read 'Wanted, a gentleman with capital (£100-£150) as partner in bookmaking business, working or sleeping.' Kif answered the advertisement and by return received a letter asking him to call at an address in Charing Cross Road. He exchanged his now disreputable tweed for the carefully preserved brown suit. As he drew the trousers from their resting-place below the mattress he whistled. Walking through the spring streets he whistled soft tuneless phrases under his breath. Climbing the dark stairs in Charing Cross Road he was still whistling. He was climbing the road to fortune. His luck had turned. He knew it.

It was too dark on the landing to read the white card on the door, but he knocked confidently, and a voice roared a cheerful 'Come in!' and Kif went. At a large square table furnished simply with a telephone sat a pallid little man with dead eyes and a peevish mouth. He had the complete colourlessness of something that has grown under a stone. If Kif's spirits were dashed by the sight of so unattractive an individual he was reassured when his gaze met the merry blue eyes of the man who was lounging in the window. This was the owner of the voice undoubtedly, a ruddy person of forty or so.

'Hough and Collins?' he said.

'I'm Collins,' said the pallid man. 'This is Mr Hough.'

'I'm Vicar, come to talk business.'

'Pleased to meet you, Mr Vicar,' said the pallid man with an airy gesture to his forehead. Hough came forward and shook hands.

'Just out of the army?' he asked, and Kif had the feeling that it was not merely a conventional or business query.

'Not just. Last January.'

'Beat me by a month. France, was it? . . . Carnshires. I was in Egypt most of the time with the —— Yeomanry. Horses have always been rather in my line. Before I joined the army I helped my father in a "silver ring" business. And now that I'm out of it I'd like to go back to the old job, with a little promotion. Mr Collins here knows the business from A to Z.'

It did not require any perspicuity on Kif's part to realise that Mr Collins, though Hough's junior by nearly ten years, had not had sufficient love of horses to draw him into any yeomanry. No army had owned the wan-skinned thing at the table. How had he managed to escape service? In what way could this spineless object have been indispensable? He was answered almost immediately when Collins rose and crossed to a cupboard. The man was so undersized in every way that even a bantam battalion would have looked askance at him. A shade of pity mingled with Kif's contempt until he wondered suddenly in what capacity Mr Collins had learned the business from A to Z. A stable lad or a jockey? Not a jockey certainly; his shoulders were ill-developed and narrow. Nor did he look like a bookmaker's clerk. He was more like a tout. There was about him that subtle suggestion of having no legal standing in the universe, of being perpetually ready to run. Kif's glance went back to the glowing solidity of Hough, who was setting out chairs. Hough caught the look and smiled rubicundly. 'Expect you're looking for a billet for your gratuity, same as me,' he said. Kif assented absent-mindedly. He was wondering how he was to test the apparent frankness of Collins' partner. He certainly had every appearance of having seen service in Egypt, but how was he to know? And then he remembered a boy who had come one night to dance at the Barclays, a trooper in the 2nd ——, a pleasant youth with a devastating stammer.

'Which battalion of the —— were you in?' he asked casually.

'The 2nd.'

'Ever met a fellow called Heseltine?'

'You b-b-bet your b-b-boots,' laughed Hough. 'Shared a blanket with him often.'

So *that* was all right.

'Have a drink, Mr Vicar,' said Collins, proffering the bottle he had taken from the cupboard. Kif refused.

'Perhaps you're right,' Collins said in his thin creaking voice. 'Never drink before a business discussion.' And Kif took the indicated seat by the table.

Collins talked, with occasional appeals to Hough for corroboration. He had, it appeared, been a partner in a small bookmaking business before the war. He had not attended the meetings, but had looked after the town end of the business. For the last two years he had been making munitions and had spent even with decent living only half of what he had made. With the other half he now proposed to start business. Hough, who was coming in as junior partner, would do the outside work, attending the meetings—'He has a daisy of a voice!'—and Collins would look after the office side. If Kif was able to do clerk's work he was to be roped in as Hough's second on the course. If not, he could be a sleeping partner and a clerk would be engaged. But their original idea was to have the third partner as clerk.

He produced ample proofs of all his statements and Kif was satisfied.

Kif explained that he had always been interested in racing, and that he would like to do the clerk's work if it were possible to pick it up. Figures were the only kind of learning he had ever received praise for.

In the end it was agreed that a clerk should be engaged for the first weeks and Kif could attend and learn the business until he was able to take his place. 'I don't expect that business will be so brisk to begin with that anyone will be killed in the crush,' Collins said.

And that is how Kif became a part of Hough & Collins, the Firm You Know, The Sure Payers. He proved a good pupil and made a smart enough clerk because he liked the life. The shifting situations in the day's work were what he had always sought. For no two consecutive minutes was the outlook the same; the unexpected became the usual. And what would have been mechanical work in an employee became a never-ceasing interest for him since he was part of the firm. It was *his* fortune that was being made or lost. It was his tragedy when Bog Oak, the favourite, fell lame on the way to the gate and made the race an easy for Old Sinner which had stood at fives in their book. It was his good luck when Mealybags, which no one had ever heard of, pipped the well-backed Musical Evening on the post. And he liked the changing scene of their fortunes; here to-day and there to-morrow. He liked the coming and the going; the leisurely arrival in the high-light of noon, the dawdling setting-out of their paraphernalia, the atmosphere of expectant waiting, of shared jests; the hasty last paying-out, the hurried packing and rush for the trains. But most of all he liked the period of stress between.

He still kept the attic at Fitzmaurice Lane, but had two rooms instead of one. Occasionally Hough took him back for a meal with his wife, a little dark woman, pretty and bird-like, in their rooms in Fulham, and they went to theatres together. And once or twice he went by invitation to visit Collins, who was a bachelor and lived a lonely and apparently misanthropic existence in a small flat on the floor above their office. Mrs Hough introduced him to her 'crowd', which was limited, good-hearted, and a queer mixture of extravagance and hardheadedness. Kif liked them mildly, and did not regret them when he was away from them. He was still to a large extent self-sufficient. He danced expertly if unenthusiastically with the wives and sisters of the Hough circle and remained heart-whole in the midst of their by no means limited attractions, and apparently unimpressed by their approval of him. Mrs Hough's sister, especially, a little Dresden beauty who had enjoyed the war and found it difficult nowadays to put the necessary 'pep' into existence, made no secret of her preference for him.

'What can you see in him?' asked her best friend of the moment. 'He's ugly. And he hasn't a word to say for himself. I thought you liked them snappy.'

'So I do. But he's a heavenly dancer.'

'Lord, since when have you fallen for a man's feet?'

'Not his feet, his figure. He's got a divine figure, you'll have to admit, Kitty Farrant'

'Yes, his figure's good enough, I suppose.'

'You suppose! And his eyes just make me weak. They're so dark, and sort of lazy and not taking any notice of anything, and then they wake up all of a sudden and tease you, sort of.'

'Huh! You've got it all right. But that doesn't alter the fact that he's plain. Nice and all that, but plain.'

'You're jealous, that's what it is.'

'So far I haven't anything to be jealous about. He isn't exactly pining away for you, is he?'

This being only too true, the infatuated one acknowledged it and changed the subject. Kif infinitely preferred an evening in unalloyed male company to playing cavalier. His happiest nights were with Hough at the Ring. As a spectacle boxing never lost its first fascination for him; indeed the understanding of the game which his sparring with Carroll had brought him had added rather than detracted from its allurement. He sat literally and metaphorically at the feet of the combatants, his eyes eager, his brain retentive. And afterwards, alone in the attic, he would rehearse feint and parry with his shadow on the wall, and would go to bed with a glowing body and a speculative mind. Carroll had said he was good. Presently he would get someone to give him lessons. After all, he was only twenty.

He was entirely happy.

And then one Saturday night he decided to do what he had been meaning to do as soon as he had found a job. He would not go to Golder's Green as an out-of-work nobody, a suppliant for favours. But as a partner in Hough & Collins he could go with a free mind. Early on Sunday afternoon he departed from Fitzmaurice Lane, radiant, rather nervous, full of reminiscence. The thought of the Barclays had lain at the back of his mind all those months like a promise—a promise to himself—so that they had come to be associated in his thoughts With his graduation, his promotion to fortune and recognition. In the bus going up Baker Street he remembered how he and Tim had walked from Victoria in the dark; how uncertainly he had stood in the damp garden, afraid of his reception, afraid of life among these people, whose ways and thoughts he did not know. And there had been nothing to be afraid of after all. And never would be again.

He had heard regularly from Tim at intervals of about a month until the armistice, when Tim went into Germany with the army of occupation. Since he had been in Eastbourne he had had no word, but that was in accordance with the general slackening of effort which overtook everyone when the strain relaxed and safety had once more become the birthright of the humblest private. Kif wondered if Ann would be at home. Perhaps she had found her job; or perhaps she had got married in the last year. She had not been engaged before the armistice or Tim would have told him. It was strange: he had started out primarily to see Tim, but it was Ann who came and went in his thoughts. He got off the bus at the stop with a slight quickening of heart and an approving glance at the boots he had taken such pains with that morning. If grooming alone was a passport to society then Kif was qualified to attend a levée.

He went down the path under the pergola of red ramblers hoping intensely that everyone was out. There was no immediate answer to his ring, and he was consumed with a fear that there was no one at home. And then Alison opened the door.

He was just about to say 'Hullo, Alison!' when her unrecognising glance gave him pause. He asked for Mrs Barclay. At the sound of his voice she looked at him again, puzzled. 'Yes,' she said. 'What name, please?'

'Vicar,' said Kif.

She swung round from opening the drawing-room door. 'Bless us!' she said. 'Goad bless us! Well, I give thanks this day.'

Kif put out his hand, and Alison, with a totally unnecessary wipe of her palm on the hip of her spotless apron, shook it warmly and long, and with a 'Sit ye down' she fled to announce him.

There were new cretonne loose-covers on the chairs, but otherwise the drawing-room was as he had known it. There was a crystal jar of iceland poppies on the mantelpiece. He wondered if Ann had arranged them. And on Mrs Barclay's desk . . . He crossed the room carefully, lightly, and looked at the photograph. Yes, it was Ann; the level brows, the curved chin, the small laughing eyes, and the uncompromising manner he had known; the Ann who had welcomed him that night in the black-and-gold thing and had taken him so beautifully for granted.

There was a stir at the door, and he turned as it opened.

'My dear boy,' said Mrs Barclay, 'my dear boy, this is nice of you.'

She greeted him kindly and waved him to a seat. 'I am so glad to see you looking so well. Tell me all about yourself. You have left the army, of course. And you have found something to do. Something congenial, I hope?'

Kif had been ready, though he did not know it, to give her by degrees the whole of his Odyssey; the greengrocer's, the Egyptian with the torch—all of it. Instead he said: 'Yes, I have a share in a bookmaking business.'

'Racing.' It was impossible to tell whether the word was a question, a statement, or an exclamation; her deliberate voice was habitually unaccented. 'And you like that?'

'Well, it's as near perfection as I expect to get. Yes, I like it.'

'I am so glad. You are lucky to find your *métier* so easily.'

'Oh, I did a lot of things first. But I'm settled for a while now. How is Tim?'

'Tim went back to the city a month ago and does not seem to be hating it as much as he prophesied he would. He brings home a new tie every day. He says it emphasises the freedom of the citizen or something of the sort. You may understand him; I don't.' She smiled her charming smile at him and arched her brows. 'Ann is poultry farming near Ticehurst in Sussex with two other occupation-mad young people. At the moment she is upstairs engaged in what she calls "poshing up". They take turn about in having the week-ends off, so we see her one week-end out of three. And not very much of that. She is going out to tea now as soon as her hat is at the proper angle. Tim is in Birmingham on business. That *is* a pity.'

Well, he wasn't going to miss her after all. In a minute or two she would come in at that door. Or—awful thought!—would she go out without coming in? Perhaps she did not know that he was there.

'Is your work office work? Mrs Barclay was saying. 'You must find that trying after the open air life in the army.'

'Oh no, I'm out in all weathers. I'm the clerk and book the bets. One of the other partners does the shouting.'

What Mrs Barclay's mind said was 'Good Heavens!' What her voice said was 'But what a wearing life! And in this climate!'

'Oh no,' said Kif. 'Oh no!' He was struggling against a dawning feeling of—not quite disappointment, but of being done out of something; a feeling that there was something wrong somewhere. Mrs Barclay had turned the tap labelled 'Gracious small-talk.' Kif knew only the mixture as delivered by the taps 'Chumminess' and 'Motherliness'. He was looking for familiar signposts and had not yet realised that he was in the wrong landscape. The homeless Tommy had been a very different proposition in Margaret Barclay's eyes from this uninteresting nobody in a suit of too obvious a cut. Ann had once said—not to Kif—that her mother would excuse a muffler, but not a collar of the wrong kind. Not that Kif wore the wrong kind of collar—he saw too many of the right kind in the course of his day's work to make that kind of social mistake—but . . . The 'but', from Mrs Barclay's point of view, was a very big one. She would be nice to him, poor dear. That went without saying. Margaret Barclay was never not nice to anyone. Of *course* she would be nice to him.

'Are you quite strong again? You were in hospital with—pneumonia, was it?'

'Pleurisy. Yes, I'm all right again, thanks,'

A little silence.

In Mrs Barclay's mind: 'Quite attractive in a way, but of course not possible.'

In Kif's: 'She couldn't have gone out, or I'd have heard the door.'

The door opened and Ann's voice said: 'You know, Mother, I think it would be better if I took Lavender's——' Kif had got to his feet, and she stopped, looking calmly at him.

'Why, good lord, it's Kif,' she said suddenly, and went over to him smiling with her hand outstretched. 'Good Lord!' she said again.

He grinned down at her wordlessly. He had not remembered her as so small. But all the rest was the same: the vividness, the directness, the taking him for granted. She was even dressed as she had been that last night in some dull-surfaced stuff of a clear green. Nothing shone about her but her eyes and the hair under the hat.

'And what are you doing now?' she asked, resting on the arm of a chair. 'Found the ideal job?'

So she had remembered that. 'Not quite, but very nearly. I'm a bookmaker's clerk with a stake in the firm.'

'Congratulations! I see you at thirty with a large watch-chain across your middle and a flat in—in Half Moon Street, let us say. If I come to your firm'—she did not ask the name of it—' will you give me a point over the odds?'

'We might. But don't mortgage the chickens.'

'Oh, you've heard about that? Well, it's not very nice on wet days, but it's heavenly on fine ones. Is bookmaking very exciting?'

'Fairly,' Kif admitted.

'Between you and me and the hen-house door, it's more than chicken farming is. But then, *noblesse oblige*, back to the land, a stake in the country, justifying one's existence!' She laughed. 'Well, I must fly. I'm awfully glad to see you looking so full of beans. No more trouble here?' She tapped his chest lightly. 'That's good. Good-bye. It's rotten luck that Tim's away. You'll look us up again, won't you? I wish I hadn't to go out.' She made the characteristic little gesture with her hand from the door and was gone.

'Yes, it really is bad luck that Tim should be away.' Kif came back to the realisation of Mrs Barclay. 'But you will stay and have tea, won't you?'

'No, thank you. I—I've got to meet a chap.'

'I really don't want to keep you, my dear boy, if you must go, but I should be delighted if you could wait. Alison won't be long in bringing it.'

'No, really, thanks very much.' He must get out of the house. Out into the air.

'Well, you must come again when Tim will be at home.' She went with him to the hall door. 'He will be very disappointed at missing you. Stop. You had better let me have your address.'

Kif gave her his business card.

'Good-bye, my dear boy. I am sorry you won't stay. But I am delighted to see you again and looking so well and prosperous.' She patted his arm and waited at the door smiling as he went up the path under the red ramblers to the gate.

Two hours later he threw away the butt of his twentieth cigarette and kicked himself mentally.

'Don't be a fool! Don't be a fool! They're not worth it.'

'Ann,' said his other half.

'But you're only one in a hundred to her. What did you expect? She was very nice.'

'Well, Mrs Barclay. Was all that kindness just bunk? How could it be bunk?'

'Just bunk. It was all eyewash. They're not worth bothering about. Just you wait, and you'll show them. You're just as good as they are.'

'But, Good God! I didn't want to hang on to them! I only wanted to see them all again.'

'Yes, but how were they to know that? They were afraid you were going to. They simply choked you off.'

'Tim wouldn't have been like that.'

'Wouldn't he?'

'No, he wouldn't! he wouldn't!' his mind cried out. 'He wouldn't. Tim's not like that.'

'Well, just wait and see if Tim comes.'

So with a mind half protesting half leering Kif went back to supper alone at Fitzmaurice Lane. And far beneath his arguing mind was a sore spot that no argument reached.

15

For the next few months Kif was busy. When he remembered the Barclays a dull rage swept him—Tim had not come—but otherwise he was completely happy. He liked Hough and had developed a reluctant respect for the shrewd brain that was Collins. Collins was the most single-minded man he had ever met; nothing but business—his business, of course—existed for him. Hough was a normal man who liked his wife, and theatres, and a drink, and good company, and other pages of the penny press besides the sporting one; but none of these things existed for Collins. And then, towards autumn, business, which had been surprisingly good for the first year of racing after the war, began to stagger. The volume of betting was unchanged, but several of their clients had lucky coups which it took all the firm's resources to pay. Only the coolness and resource of Collins saved them once or twice.

'It's a hell of a nuisance,' grumbled Hough in the train one day. 'Wonder what that chap Fotheringham in Leeds does. Something to do with a stable, I'll be bound. He couldn't know all about these eight-to-ones and ten-to-ones unless he was on the inside. Wish he hadn't picked on us just when we wanted to earn our winter keep.'

'But he's been a client of ours all along,' Kif pointed out. 'We've had some of his.'

'Well, he's having the devil's own luck now. If Collins weren't so keen, to get some of it back he'd close his account.'

It was the end of October, and for the last fortnight things had been better. Kif whistled as he climbed to the office on a Tuesday morning to meet Hough. Monday had been a blank day with no racing, and he felt already the itch to be back in the excitement of work. He had spent the week-end with cousins of Mrs Hough's at Brighton, and nothing in the last two days had pleased him like the prospect of his work this morning. He hoped anxiously that the fog would prove to be lighter in the country than it gave promise of being in London. Still whistling, he turned the handle of the door and found it locked. Strange. Hough might not have arrived, but Collins, if he were out, would not leave the office without even the office boy to answer the telephone. Perhaps he hadn't arrived, and the office boy was ill. Perhaps . . . His key turned in the lock and he went in.

The office was quite deserted. A loose-leaved calendar on the mantelpiece waved with the wind of his entrance and subsided. The table was clear of papers as he had seen it on his first visit, except for an envelope lying mathematically in the middle of it. Kif's heart missed a beat at sight of it as if he had come on a bomb. He walked round to the front of the table and regarded it without picking it up. On it was written in Hough's writing 'Vicar'. With a mind suddenly blank of surmise and a faintly unsteady hand he opened it.

'DEAR VICAR,

Collins has gone. Lit out. I came up here this morning to arrange things for to-morrow and found him gone and of course everything gone with him. There was ten pounds left in the bank—in case of questions, I suppose. No money has been paid out for a fortnight. He had the nerve to leave the accounts ready. There is nothing to do but clear out. Even if we got Collins it wouldn't help. We're done for. I have managed to cash the £10, and with what I can borrow that will take Ethel and me out of this damned country. I am leaving you in the lurch quite deliberately. If anyone had told me yesterday that I would do that I would have knocked him down. Now I can't think of anyone but Ethel. You are alone and can look after yourself. If she asks about you I shall say we went fifty-fifty in what was left. There is a pound note in the left-hand drawer in case you are on the rocks. If we ever meet again you can kill me, but don't tell Ethel why.

H
E
N
R
Y
H
O
U
G
H.

P.S.—Collins was Fotheringham. There is no such person known in Leeds. What bloody fools we've been.'

Kif put down the note and drew Collins' chair from the knee-hole of the table. He sat down in it stumblingly. His knees were trembling and he felt sick and shaky. He put his elbows on the table and rested his head on his hands, but his arms were shaking so that they were no support, and he withdrew them and sat with a blank mind, drawing a hand over his forehead, which was cold and damp. Presently he picked up the letter and re-read it absently, as one reads an advertisement in the Tube. But before he had come to the end for the second time he had come alive again, and feeling poured through him agonisingly, as blood through a frozen limb. Collins! He would find Collins if he had to work his way round the world to do it, and when he found him he would kill him. He would put his sinewy hands on that mean neck and throttle the life out of him. He would beat him into unrecognisability. Hough he hardly thought about, and it never occurred to him to doubt Hough's honesty. Hough had been wronged too, ruined. Ruined! He was ruined. His money gone. Hopelessly gone. All his plans gone. He was left with a pound note and . . . He snatched out his pocket-book. He had a ten-shilling note in his pocket-book and five and threepence halfpenny in loose change in his pocket. He opened the top left drawer and found the note. One pound fifteen and threepence ha'penny. And he paid his landlady on a Wednesday. That was to-morrow. He would have to look for a job, of course. Any kind of a job that would keep body and soul together. Never any more the happiness of taking a job 'until'. He was a beggar. A year ago he might have faced the fact with the courage of ignorance. Now he knew what the chances of success were. It would be a body-and-soul job for ever. The realisation was too bitter to be borne. For the first time since he was thirteen Kif broke down. He laid his head on his arms and sobbed—hard dry tearless sobs that hurt him and brought no relief. When they ceased from exhaustion he stayed as he was, despairingly indifferent. The light came and went as the wisps of fog passed between the window and the opposite chimneys. Footsteps came and went on the stairs. The rumble of traffic came through the closed window in a steady monotone. Kif lay motionless.

It was nearly an hour later that he lifted his head. The first thing that his eyes lighted on was the watch on his wrist. Good heavens, he would miss his train! And then he remembered. It was finished. Even the racecourse was closed to him for some time to come. He sat up and pushed his fingers through his thick disordered hair; his gaze wandered round the office. Collins had made a pretty tidy job of it. Or was it Hough? No, Collins, probably; it would be like him. He drew out the wastepaper basket; it contained the accounts for the previous week made out by Collins and torn across by Hough. One by one he opened the drawers and ran a sensitive hand into the further ends of them. He had no definite purpose; at the back of his mind was a faint hope that something of value had been overlooked. But there was nothing. Once his finger-nail caught in something and he drew out a square of pasteboard. A visiting card. He turned it over. 'Timothy R. Barclay.'

So Tim had come!

It did not seem to matter very much at the moment somehow. It wasn't his relations with anyone that mattered. It was life and himself. He, Kif, was what counted, and he was being overwhelmed, drowned. Quite unconsciously he put the card into his pocket; but it was as a souvenir, not as a gage for the future. He finished his examination of the drawers, picked up his hat from the chair on which he had dropped it at his entrance, cast a last glance round the office and went out, slamming the door behind him.

Only poets and martyrs greet calamity without seeking that fortification of the common man, a drink. Kif had a large whisky in a bar in Leicester Square. He did not like whisky—beer was his habit—and he could not afford it, but both seemed somehow excellent reasons for indulging in it. He waited hopefully, staring at the lettered mirrors, for the transformation which should ensue, but the drink had no effect, mental or physical, beyond eliminating the queer empty feeling that had settled below his heart. Disgusted, he went out into the grey streets again and walked to Fitzmaurice Lane. He must tell his landlady that one room would have to suffice from now on. And he would have another look at this morning's paper, which he had skimmed so light-heartedly such a short time ago. It already seemed long ago that he had opened that letter in the office. Years. Time had nothing to do with a clock ticking, it appeared. He had lived years since he set out from Fitzmaurice Lane this morning, and yet the race-trains were not yet at their destination; the day's work had not started.

He told Mrs Connor simply that the firm had gone to blazes, snatched the paper which he saw lying among the wreckage on the kitchen table, and went abruptly upstairs out of the range of her anxious eyes and tentative sympathy. He wanted no one's sympathy. What he wanted was Collins' blood. His impotence made his anger a living thing that mauled him in spasms which left him weak and sick. He found it easier not to think of Collins; the searing agony of his helpless rage was unbearable. He shut the bedroom door behind him, stood a moment looking incredulously at the quiet room, and then, flinging the paper on to the bed, he crossed slowly to the fireplace and with arms propped on the mantelpiece surveyed the row of photographs as if he had never seen them before. There were several army groups, one of Tim, Jimmy and himself in the early days of training, a studio portrait of a little Parisienne who had lightened the leave he and Carroll had spent in Paris, one of a hospital sister, and in the middle, slightly in front of the rest, Marcelle. It was a snapshot taken before he had met her, but it represented her as he always thought of her. Her smooth head was bare and the eyes looked straight at him, gravely smiling in sympathy with her gravely smiling mouth. A wind blew her full skirt to her and lifted a single tendril of hair from her centre parting. Kif had never seen the Samothrace Victory and might not have liked it if he had, but he was intensely aware of the living beauty of that photograph of Marcelle.

'Marcelle,' he said. He had always liked the sound of it. A lovely name. He took the photograph up after a little and sat down with it on the edge of the bed. He had gone to look for Marcelle on the first possible occasion after his return to France from hospital, but he had not found her. She and her mother had gone to Paris, he was told. No one knew their address. In those days of flux no one knew anything. The *bel-soeur* of Madame, it was said, kept a *blanchisserie* in the Raspail district; that was all they could tell him. Kif accepted the inevitable, and Marcelle stayed with him as an unspoilt memory, without sting and without regret. In Paris, it is true, he had inveigled his companion into spending nearly a whole morning among the streets between the Boulevards Raspail and Montparnasse. He had even penetrated into a small laundry on the Boulevard Montparnasse under the pretext of asking his way. When Carroll showed signs of impatience he was assured that he was seeing the Latin quarter—a thing which everyone did. But when at last Carroll's desire for the Place de l'Opéra grew too insistent to be comfortably ignored, Kif went away from the district that somewhere held Marcelle, with a regret that was more sentimental than poignant.

Now he sat moving her photograph gently from side to side so that the eyes followed him. Occasionally he bent forward and scrutinised it more closely. Slowly the strain in his face relaxed, the murder faded from his eyes.

He propped the photograph on top of the pillow, and opened the paper at Advertisements.

16

It was the end of December. The wave of hysteria which descends on the city at Christmas time had passed. The crowds had the spent disgruntled look of those who have worked themselves up to a crisis which has eluded them. Goodwill was at a premium; and the weather was bitter.

A squall of thin sleet tore on an east wind up Oxford Street. The water spouted from the shop-fronts and sluiced across the pavements in a thick ripple. The gutters were the beds of evil-looking streams. A baleful pale light lay on the street under the black sky. There was comfort neither in heaven nor earth. Kif, sheltering in a doorway, looked at his leaking sodden boots and cursed. He remembered suddenly the doctor's injunction of nearly a year ago. No colds! He uttered a short stifled laugh. A young woman who was finding temporary refuge in the same doorway glanced at him hastily and opening her umbrella went out into the storm. Kif was aware neither of her presence nor of her departure. He felt ill, and it was not always easy to tell what was real and what was not. If he were to be really ill, that might end in a hospital and warmth and comfort, even if he pegged out afterwards. But there probably wouldn't be any such luck. It was only that he was short of a meal. Old soldiers never die, and all the rest of it. Only it would be dissolving to-day; not fading. He laughed again. A man coming abruptly round the corner of the doorway with his head down cannoned into him and apologised breathlessly as he turned down his collar and shook the wet from himself.

'It's the kind of day——' he said, straightening himself. 'Well, I'm damned. . . ! Well, I'm damned!' he repeated, rallentando.

'Carroll!' said Kif.

'A bull,' said Carroll, beaming on him.

'I suppose you are real?' said Kif and laughed.

'You bet! And what are you doing now, chum? This *is* luck. I lost your address down a German drain.'

'L'm see. I don't remember what I did last. Yes, I do. The day before yesterday it was. Watched a car for a fat gentleman in spats. Very heavy day's work.' He laughed again.

Carroll's blue eyes scanned him searchingly for a moment; they came to rest on his friend's boots and then slid away.

'That the way? Well, I'm on the way to eat and you'll come along. There's a lot to talk about. It's my turn anyhow,' he added casually. 'You stood me that last blow-out in Amiens.'

100

'It's all right,' said Kif. 'Don't apologise. There's only two men on earth I wouldn't take a meal from just now, and you're neither of them.'

The sleet thinned suddenly to drizzle. Carroll propelled Kif out of the doorway and down a side street into Soho Square. At a restaurant in Old Compton Street they ate, satisfyingly. At first Carroll talked—the old Carroll talk, infinitely amusing and infinitesimally informative—while he watched the dark face opposite in furtive solicitude. As Kif ate, the world slid back to cold reality, and he ceased to find things amusing. At the apple-tart stage, Carroll fell silent and let him unburden himself, and Kif in his bitterness talked unreservedly.

At the mention of Collins, something leaped in Carroll's eyes.

'Know him?' asked Kif.

'Know *of* him,' amended the other.

'I'm going to kill him some day,' said Kif, as one announces a golfing appointment.

'You have my blessing,' said Carroll. 'There will be no wreaths.'

And Kif took up the tale again. He told everything except his visit to the Barclays; that was not for Carroll; and Tim had come, even if he had found out too late. He told of the jobs he had got and those he had not got. He made no comment as he went along, but bitterness dripped from his curt phrases like blood.

'My landlady put me up for a fortnight after I was broke, and I still owe her for that. Even when her rooms were let she used to give me a meal in the evenings. Five or six nights she did that, till I refused to go back. She's hard enough up herself. For the last nine or ten days I've been sleeping in models or wherever I had enough money for.'

'What about that chap who got a commission? Haven't you seen anything of him?'

'Barclay? He came to the office one day I was out, and they forgot to tell me. I only found it out when things had gone bust.'

'You wouldn't look him up now?'

'What do you think,' said Kif. It was not a question.

'Well, I don't know,' said Carroll, mendaciously considering. 'You were very good pals, weren't you? And——'

'Shut up,' said Kif. 'If I didn't before I'm not going to now.'

'I was only going to point out that he would probably be fed up if he thought you didn't. Besides, Pa was something in the city, wasn't he? And——'

'*Shut up!*'

'All right, all right,' Carroll said amiably. 'Have some more coffee?'

Kif shook his head and took one of the cigarettes from the case Carroll was offering him.

'Are you a pro. yet?' he asked.

'No. I've given that up. Haven't the energy to start training again. The army spoils you for that, somehow. My Dad has a newsagent's shop and I'm in the business now.'

'Good for you! Well, it's lucky for me you came along when you did. I was just wondering whether I had the nerve to break a window and spend a night in quod. Funny, isn't it? but I hadn't.'

Carroll smiled his angelic smile. 'Never found you lacking in that way,' he remarked. 'Well, listen. There's a bed vacant at home. It's only one degree removed from prison—the chap who occupied it is there now—but it's a dashed sight more comfortable, and you can go out when you like. Are you on?'

Kif hesitated painfully. 'It's awfully decent of you.' (Shade of Tim!) 'I haven't a bean, you know. What will they say if you bring in a——'

'It's my room,' said Carroll succinctly. 'Besides, they're not used to introductions. Not the social kind anyhow. We're not a bit a Sunday-school crowd, but that's no reason you shouldn't take the bed till something turns up.'

'I'll take it,' said Kif; and Carroll pressed the butt of his cigarette down on the ash-tray.

As Kif was getting into his sodden overcoat Carroll asked if he had belongings anywhere. They were with his landlady, Kif said. 'Well, you can send for them later on. We'll go home now. It'll be good to see a fire.'

When their bus came it was full inside and as the rain had stopped they climbed to the top rather than wait on the wet pavements. As they sat down Carroll laid Kif's pocket-book gently on his knees with a 'Yours, I think.'

'How did I drop it?' asked Kif, amazed. 'It was in my inside pocket.'

'You didn't. A chap took it from you when we were getting on to the bus, and I took it from him. That's all. He'll be a very surprised little fellow at this moment' In answer to Kif's questioning look he added: 'I've been able to do that since I was eight, but I haven't indulged since I was about thirteen. Dad beat it out of me. It isn't in his line. But I did it a darn sight better than that chap. He *was* an amateur.' And he smiled in unregenerate satisfaction.

Kif was very much more interested than shocked. But Carroll relapsed to his habitual bright superficiality and Kif devoted the rest of the journey to the difficult task of believing he was warm.

Carroll lived in a terrace of narrow, three-storied houses in Wandsworth. About a hundred yards away was a block of business premises; the usual semi-suburban collection of butcher, baker, grocer and tobacconist-newsagent. 'The shop's down there,' Carroll informed him, and led him through a spick-and-span doorway into a spick-and-span passage. A bright green carpet, cheap and hard, but gay, covered the middle of the stairs, and the woodwork was painted white. Very conscious of his muddy boots he followed Carroll to the second floor, on which were two minute bedrooms. 'Here's yours,' said Carroll, and opened the door of the back one.

The abode of vice consisted of an irregularly shaped attic hung with a cream-and-roses paper and furnished with a black iron bedstead, a crazy basket chair cushioned in turkey-red, a grey-painted washstand with most of the paint worn off round the basin, a brown-painted chest of drawers, and a board with a row of hooks nailed to the wall. On the floor was a very shiny linoleum patterned with brown-red cabbage roses on a green ground, and at the bed a strip of violet carpeting. Everything was gleaming and clean, and to Kif at the moment it looked like heaven.

'Sammy won't be wanting it for two years, so you're quite safe,' said Carroll. 'It doesn't look so bad on a fine day.'

'It looks all right to me! What is Sammy in for?'

'Burglary.'

Kif whistled.

"M,' agreed Carroll. 'Used to be a swell at it, but he's lost the knack in the army. Joined up of his own accord, too. Awful luck. My room is next door.' He had turned to lead the way when there were footsteps outside, and a woman's voice said: 'Is that you, Tommy?'

'Hullo, Baba, I was just going to look for you. Come here. This is Vicar, who was my pal in France. My sister—christened Barbara.'

It seemed that sunshine had come into the grey room of a sudden. The girl who stood looking at him had all her brother's fairness, but her hair, instead of being straw-coloured as his was, stood round her head in a fine golden cloud that glowed as if illuminated from within. Kif had never seen hair like it. Her face was slav-like in its smooth pallor, and the curve of cheek and chin bones, and her wide grey eyes were outlined with dark lashes. Her mouth was full and pale; her hands short and broad with stubby fingers and ugly thumbs. She gave him her hand now and smiled at him. Carroll was explaining that he was going to stay for a few days until he got a job.

'You can stay as long as you like,' she said. 'Can you dry dishes?'

'You bet!' said Kif.

'In that case you can stay for ever,' she laughed. 'This room will look better when the bed is made up. I'll put the things on presently. Come down now and get warm. It's freezing up here. Bring your coat to the kitchen. And you, too, Angel.' And Kif followed her down to warmth and comfort with his eyes on her glowing misty hair.

Kif went to bed that night in the little back room filled with a mild amaze at the unexpectedness of life, and a deep thankfulness for the security of a friendly roof. To-morrow there would be breakfast as a matter of course, and dry clothes, and no immediate need to turn out in the pitiless weather to look for work. Carroll senior had made him welcome as a friend of his son, and had said, 'Stay as long as you like, my boy', as if he had meant it. There had been no discussion of his financial position, but Kif had felt that when he retired to the kitchen to wash up with Baba after the abundant high-tea Carroll had told his father all about him. In that he guessed correctly.

'Your chum in low water, Angel?' his father had asked him.

'Yes. Birdie Collins did him down.' He recounted what Kif had told him, and said heatedly: 'Fancy a —— swine like that never having seen the inside in all his days, and a good chap like Sammy gets put away first go-off!'

'Distressing,' said Mr Carroll. He was a mild pink little man with his son's blue eyes and a gentle manner. His phraseology was so restrained that on occasions it was disconcertingly like sarcasm until one became used to it. He never swore, but on the other hand he never appeared pained when others exploited their vocabularies in his presence. His abstention was due to inability rather than conviction, it seemed. It was a long time before Kif discovered that Mr Carroll's gentleness could be infinitely more intimidating than any thunderings of wrath.

In the kitchen Baba had fallen suddenly from animation to a busy abstraction. She treated Kif as if he were not there, swilling cups and plates diligently before slipping them into the hot water. Kif dried expertly and watched her hair and her profile; but in a little it annoyed him that she should find him so negligible. The Kif who had been full of gladness that Ann should take him for granted did not in the least want to be taken for granted in the eyes of Baba Carroll. Ann's acceptance of him had been promotion; Baba's was depreciation. He made a few polite and tentative remarks—after all she was his hostess—but she answered them absently. Kif was piqued. Was she regretting perhaps that she had seconded her brother's invitation so warmly? That roused a slight panic in him.

'Do you do all the work of this house yourself?' he ventured.

'No, a girl comes in for three hours in the mornings and a char once a week. But for the rest I do like to have the house to myself.'

'Well, I won't be round much during the day,' said Kif, half in fun, half in earnest.

At that she smiled. 'Funny!' she mocked.

And Kif went to sleep wondering whether she were lovelier smiling or serious.

17

It was Angel who woke Kif next morning as he put a tray of breakfast down on the chest of drawers. He was fully dressed and very good to look upon in the morning sunlight. 'Eleven o'clock, sir,' he said, and hung Kif's trousers dry, cleaned and pressed, over the back of the chair. 'Shall I turn on your bath?'

'Who did that?' asked Kif with a jerk of the head to the trousers.

'Well, it was a sort of company affair. I took them out of your room last night when you were sleeping sound enough to be safe, and Baba did the rest. She rather fancies herself as a tailoress. It's the only thing she'll ever do for me— press my pants. She makes an edge you could shave with—so that it hurts to sit down.'

But Kif was not listening. His long muscular arm was groping agonisedly on the floor. 'My boots!' he said.

Angel laughed at the dismay in his face. 'It's all right,' he said, 'I did these with my own. They're outside the door. And you needn't be so scared of Baba. She's not at all perishable goods. Her label's, "No matches to be lit in the vicinity of this package". They wouldn't take her in the post. She'd have to go by rail. I'm off out. There's no hurry to get up. Have a holiday. I'll be back to dinner. See you then. S'long.'

Kif, eating the ample breakfast, pondered Carroll's apparently meaningless remarks. This was the first time he had heard him make a comment on any possession of his own. It was not in accordance with the Carroll he knew. Was it just that he treated Kif as being inside the family circle now and therefore privileged? Or was there a note of warning?

'Oh, rot!' he thought, swinging his legs to the floor. 'You're going balmy. Nerves.'

Half an hour later he presented himself before Baba in the kitchen. She was baking, and a bright green cretonne apron covered her entirely. She looked like some exotic flower. 'Sleep well?' she asked, casting him a glance and going on with her work.

Kif thanked her and asked if there was anything he could do for her before he went out.

'You're not going job-hunting to-day? Have a rest.'

Kif shook his head. 'There are two places in this morning's paper that I must go after. It's rather late in the day to get a good place in the queue, but you never know. I look so smart this morning that someone may be impressed.'

'Well,' she said, not smiling as he had hoped, 'if you don't get them come right back. I'll keep some dinner hot for you.' She propped herself for a moment on the rolling-pin, and looking straight at him said matter-of-factly: 'Have you got enough cash for bus fares? If not, I can lend you some.'

'Oh yes, thanks,' said Kif, 'I can just manage that.' He had eightpence ha'penny in his pocket.

When he had gone she finished the pie she had been making, put it into the oven, tidied the table, and went upstairs humming a music-hall song and breaking into the words at intervals. With a duster and a mop she went into Kif's room and her song ceased. The bed was faultlessly made, the corners folded on the slant and turned in hospital-wise, the top cover level as a billiard table. The room was tidy and—yes, shining. She swept a swift and experienced finger over the top of the chest of drawers and examined it. Yes, it had been dusted.

'Would you look at this!' she said to the small maid who had followed her up to ask some question. The maid looked round with the air of one to whom no event which might occur in a world like this would occasion shock.

'I know,' she said. 'I was doin' the landin' 'ere when he comes up from the baffroom. "Wot's yer nime?" 'e ses. "Pinkie," I ses. An' 'e smiles (That was bad of Kif, but excusable; there was nothing pink about Pinkie except the rims of her eyelids), an' 'e ses, "Lend me yer duster just a tick." So I give 'im the good one, an' 'e give it to me back when 'e went dahnstairs. *Fowlded*, if y' please.' She surveyed the room again. 'Brought 'em up well in the army, didn't they? 'Orspital, I suppose.'

'I wish to God Tommy'd had a dose of it! Oh *yes*, use the methylated, and buzz off.' As the clatter of the maid's footsteps died into the lower regions Baba crossed to the small case which had been rescued from Fitzmaurice Lane the previous evening and was now lying by the fireplace, and lifted the lock with a tentative finger. It was not locked. She raised the lid and propped it carefully against the wall. Squatting on her heels she let her eyes wander over the contents. Nothing was visible except Kif's army uniform, which the pawnshops had presumably refused, and in one corner, half-hidden under a fold of the tunic, a worn pocket-book. Gingerly, as though it had been red-hot, she lifted the fold and abstracted the wallet. It contained all the photographs that Kif had collected in the last five years. She did not disturb them, but viewed them all satisfactorily by squeezing the pliable leather at top and bottom so as to form a cavity. There were no letters; Kif kept none. She paused over the trio at the depôt, over a group taken at a picnic during his Golder's Green leave, and at the Parisian Nymph; but Marcelle she did not see. Her photograph Kif carried along with his army papers in the pocket-book which Carroll had rescued on the bus step. When she replaced the wallet in its original resting-place not a millimetre's deviation was visible to shout a warning to the most suspicious eye. Her stubby fingers sought again under the folds, but there was nothing there. She replaced the lid, mopped the floor hastily but comprehensively, and betook herself with mop and duster to her brother's room.

Kif did not come back until six o'clock. He was still workless and damp—it had been very wet all the afternoon—but cheerful withal. He had eighteen and sixpence in his pocket, and had very much the feeling and attitude of a financier who has made a quarter of a million in five minutes. He had been coming along Conduit Street in the rain and had offered to get a taxi for a very immaculately dressed man who was standing in a doorway looking as if the rain were a direct insult to himself. The offer had been cheerfully accepted, and when Kif came back with the taxi, the immaculate one—he had Brigade of Guards written all over him, Kif said—had asked 'Ex-service?' Kif had said, 'Yes, 5th Carnshires,' and the man had handed him a pound note. When Kif tried to thank him as he shut him in, the man had said: 'My dear chap, you don't understand. You've saved my life. If I had been late I should have had to buy her a tiara, and if I had arrived wet she'd have called the whole thing off. Saved my life—absolutely.'

Kif told them the tale, his eyes bright with laughter, as they sat round the table consuming fried fish and mashed potatoes. There was a new-comer in the gathering to-night—a small round-shouldered man who might have been anything from twenty to thirty, thin and swarthy, with a pouting lower lip, high cheek-bones, and fine dead-black hair which he wore without oil, so that it had a matt surface and hung straight and free like a child's. He was introduced as

Danny Anderson, but that was the last time that Kif ever heard his surname mentioned; he was known to all his world, he found, as Danny the Dago or Dago Danny. Not that there was any dago in his blood. His grandfather had been a Highland ghillie who knew the ways of red deer and cock and grouse, but nothing of the world. The ghillie's youngest son had come to London to make his fortune and had married a domestic servant from Cornwall whose knowledge of the world was too extensive. The mixture of Cornish and Highland Cel had produced Danny, who looked like an assassin and who earned his living as a barber's assistant. I have met Danny once, and have always thought that the men who sat calmly in a chair while Danny flourished a razor were either extraordinarily brave or extraordinarily unimaginative.

Baba was wearing a black frock and a string of green beads. She had touched her full mouth with lip-stick, which added vividness if not beauty to her triangular face. Kif noticed that Danny, who took no special interest in her while she sat at table, followed her with his eyes each time she rose to fetch or take away. He was unconscious that Angel's indifferent blue glance remarked not only Danny's preoccupation, but his own discovery of the fact. Baba was once more animated. It would not be true to say she chattered; her talk was not continuous enough for that. She tossed the ball of conversation from one to another of the four men as cleverly and with as little effort as any ambassador's lady at a political dinner. She had a real flair for the provocative.

And yet later, when Kif accompanied her to the kitchen, followed unseen but suspected by a malevolent glance from Danny, she did not bother to make conversation for him and seemed little interested in his thoughts and opinions. She made a few inquiries about his day's perambulation and made a few practical suggestions for the future; but she did not follow up any of his tentative leads. 'Damn,' he thought, 'what's the matter? Doesn't she like me? Doesn't she like me being here?' He watched her white neck as it turned to and fro from basin to rack. The strap of a green rubber apron made a vivid line across it, and just above it melted into the glory of her hair. The silence grew thick suddenly; thick and suffocating. He must say something. Something everyday and ordinary. The uninterrupted clatter of the dishes seemed to come from a great distance.

'Green's your colour, isn't it?' he heard himself say, which was not at all the kind of remark he had intended to make. But even in his slight dismay he was aware that it had broken the spell.

'That's right,' she said. 'It's my lucky colour, too. And thirteen's my lucky number. What's yours?'

'Haven't got one,' said Kif, still conscious of escape from something unknown.

'Oh, nonsense, everyone's got one. It's only that you haven't found it out yet.'

'Well, I should think running into your brother was the luckiest thing that ever happened to me. What was yesterday?'

'The twenty-eighth.'

'Well, twenty-eight is my lucky number. It's my birthday date too.'

'There, you see, I told you!' She squeezed out the dish-mop, waggled it vigorously to separate the strands, and propped it in a wooden frame.

'I'm not superstitious,' he said, hoping to provoke her to argument.

'No? Would you light three cigarettes with the same match?' She laughed at his hesitation. 'You lose,' she said; she polished her nails hurriedly on the towel and led the way back to the living-room.

The four men played cards while Baba sat by the fire with some mending, and just before ten o'clock Angel went out to lock up the shop and relieve the boy who on half-holidays ran both the newspaper and the tobacco sides of the business from six o'clock onwards. And Kif went to bed, leaving Danny in possession. But before Angel came back Danny and Mr Carroll had departed together. Baba saw them off at the door and said 'Good-night. Be careful, old sporty. Good-night, Danny. Good luck!' When Angel came back she was once more sitting by the hearth with her work. It had been lying in her lap until she heard her brother's key in the door, when she recommenced it with an air of industrious abstraction.

Angel came in rubbing his hands in cheerful protest at the cold, but when he saw his sister his hands slid into his trouser pockets and he came slowly over to the fire.

'Look here, Baba,' he said, 'hands off!'

Her wide eyes looked up at him, and dropped more hastily than she had intended. It was not her brother who occupied the hearth-rug, but Saint Michael on the war-path.

'Don't be so deep,' she said wearily.

'Oh, you know quite well what I mean. And you've got to keep off the grass.'

'If you show me what I'm doing wrong I'll be delighted to oblige.'

'Come off it, Baba. Kif's my pal, and I'm not going to stand by and see you do for him.'

'You *are* complimentary. Have I lifted a finger to do for him, as you call it?'

'Of course you haven't. Don't I know it! It's the old game—keeping him guessing. You want him to stay here. Well, I don't—much. Sammy was different. He was in the game. But now it's hands off, see?'

'And just because you have a nasty jealous mind am I to——'

'Oh, carry on! I'd a sight rather you had your knife into me than your claws into him.' He paused. 'Baba,' he said, 'be a sport and let up!'

Her eyes were very cold. 'If you'll explain exactly what I'm to let up about I'll oblige, as I said before.'

He stood looking down at her in silence. 'I wish I could beat you,' he said suddenly with venom. 'I don't know why Sammy never did it.'

Her smile was like sunlight on arctic wastes.

Baffled, he flung himself into the opposite chair. 'Well, you can clear out now. I want the room to myself for a while.'

'I'm not ready to——' She met his eyes. They were not noticeably angry, but she said sulkily 'Oh, *all* right!' She folded up her work deliberately, putting away pins and needles with elaborate care. As she went to the door she said: 'And if you leave your bedroom in as untidy a mess to-morrow as you did this morning I won't touch it. So now you know!'

She went slowly upstairs, her face heavy and dark with anger, but on the first landing she paused, teased the carpet with a considering toe for a little, and then threw back her head in a silent laugh.

18

Kif came back from the hunt for work next day still unsuccessful but comparatively happy in the reflected glow of yesterday's windfall. He went upstairs two at a time without seeing anyone, elated at the thought that in a few moments he would be face to face with Baba. He swung into his room and stopped short. A man stood with his back to him inspecting the contents of his suitcase. The bed had been turned up so that the mattress showed and the drawers were half opened.

'What the——' he began. The man swung round, and at the surprised shock in his face Kif leaped. Taken aback, the man fell backwards across the bed with Kif on top of him, his hands groping blindly for Kif's throat, while Kif with his left elbow under the unknown's chin was hitting him wholeheartedly with his right. As they rolled over Kif's left arm slipped, and the man, his throat free for the moment, shouted 'Richards! Richards!' before another roll brought Kif on top once more, and both Kif's sinewy hands on his neck. Kif was shaking him as a terrier shakes a rat, heedless of the wild blows the unknown was raining on him, when a hand plucked him backwards, and he was dragged to his feet by one of the largest men he had ever seen. Sheer amazement kept him from struggling.

His victim sat up, trying to adjust a collar which was hopelessly wrecked, and said: 'That's right, hold him there a minute. Bright boy, isn't he!' He glared malevolently at Kif.

'Who the devil are you?' demanded Kif.

'Well, *we'd* like a little information first if you don't mind. Who are *you*?'

'And what——' Kif was beginning, when Baba appeared.

'What's the row, sergeant?' she asked, looking, Kif thought, very faintly dismayed.

'Who's this?' growled the man on the bed, waving a hand at Kif, who was still standing mildly in the grip of the huge man.

'That's Vicar, an army friend of my brother's. What's your first name, Kif?'

'Archibald.'

'Archibald Vicar. May I introduce Sergeant Wilkins of the Metropolitan Police. And Constable—er——'

'Richards,' supplied the huge man, grinning amiably.

'Constable Richards. Did you do that to the sergeant?' she asked Kif. 'My goodness, what a mess!'

But the sergeant did not appear to find the comfort that her sympathetic tones might be supposed to convey. And there was that in his subordinate's eye every time it came in contact with the mangled collar that made magnanimity impossible.

Kif now began to stammer out apologies and to feel a complete fool. 'How was I to know?' he said. 'I just came in and found him with my things, and there was no one about. How was I to know?' Most of his apology seemed, strangely enough, to be addressed to Baba. He was consumed by a fear that what he had done might reflect on her or her household.

'Well,' she said, 'perhaps the sergeant will fine you a collar and call it quits. Eh, sergeant?'

The sergeant growled without looking at her. 'How long have you been here?'

'I came the day before yesterday.'

'And before that?'

Kif gave him a brief *résumé* of his doings.

He then demanded a detailed account of his actions during the day, which the constable noted in a little book. That done, the sergeant heaved himself off the bed, adjusted his clothes and hair at the mirror on the chest of drawers, and was moving to the door when Kif, desperately anxious to effect a reconciliation said: 'I'm frightfully sorry, sergeant. Really I am!'

The Barclay adverb did not add to the sergeant's goodwill, but he had to keep up appearances. 'So am I, young fellow,' he said, turning round and smiling not at all pleasantly at Kif. '*Frightfully!* But we'll say it was a mistake—this time. Finished, Richards? Aw right. All clear, Miss Carroll. We're going now. Don't bother to come down.'

Baba went out to the landing and watched them stump their way down and then came back to Kif, who was adding two and two together in an attempt to make four.

'What did they want?' he asked.

'Father and Danny did a job last night, and they were looking for the stuff. I forgot to warn them that you were here. I *am* sorry.'

Kif was more anxious about her welfare than dismayed at his association with the Law's suspects. 'But your father—is he—how did they know?'

'Oh, there are no flies on the police. Besides, Father is so good at the game that they would recognise his work. He's all right though. He hasn't been "inside" since I was little. He's in the shop right now, selling Navy Cut and *Evening Standards*. And he'll go on selling them. Father wasn't born yesterday.'

The pride in her voice arrested his attention. So that was the kind of man she admired. Did she think him a sissy?

'Does Angel——' he hesitated.

'Oh yes, Angel will be as good as Father some day. Only a month ago he and Danny—— But that's telling. Perhaps I'm a fool to be telling you anything. You'll be going away one of these days, and who knows?' She turned her great grey eyes on him in appeal. 'You wouldn't give us away, though, would you?'

'What do you think!' said Kif. 'After you taking me in when I hadn't a bean? You don't really think that. Besides, I'm not going away if you'll let me stay. I'll get a job soon, and you can have me as a lodger. Will you?'

She seemed to consider. '*I* wouldn't mind, but I don't think it would be good for you to stay. I'm sorry. You see, it was different with Sammy.'

'Did Sammy work with the rest, or did he—do jobs alone?'

'Oh, he worked with the rest usually.'

'Well, I'm coming in in Sammy's place.'

She laughed outright, a low gurgle of amusement. 'Nonsense. You don't know what you're talking about. You don't know anything about it.' She was indulgently scornful.

'Well, I'll make a very good apprentice, you see if I don't. There's nothing I'd like better than to relieve some well-to-do folk of their cash.'

She smiled at him and sighed a little. 'It isn't for me to say, anyhow, is it? Get tidy now and come down to tea. The others will be in presently.'

'You're not angry with me for kicking up that row?'

'Angry with you? With Wilkins' collar looking like that? Why, I love you! Don't be long. It's sausage.'

While Kif pulled his tie straight he whistled gently under his breath. It was not a sign of any real elation on his part; it was what a groom does to quiet a restive horse. He was, quite unconsciously, whistling to the unquiet, eager stirring in his heart. Something had come awake there—the faint delicious excitement before battle—and for once he wanted to ignore it, to pretend that the possibilities ahead were of no great moment. There was something about the prospect that did not bear close examination, and his mind slid away from the contemplation.

He found only Mr Carroll in the living-room—Angel was to come home as soon as his father relieved him at business—and it was impossible to tell from his manner whether he knew of the occurrence or not. He asked interestedly about Kif's luck during the day, and seemed genuinely sympathetic over his lack of success. As Baba came in with a steaming tray, however, he said:

'I am sorry you should have been put to inconvenience over your room. We occasionally have these inspections, and have to put up with them as best we can. But it is rather hard for a visitor to be subjected to the same treatment. We feel we owe you an apology.'

Kif was not sure whether the 'we' was collective, editorial, or royal, but he had, vaguely, the feeling of watching greatness unbend. He again apologised, if not quite so heartily, for his hastiness in action, and Mr Carroll smiled.

111

'Well, well, youth always hits first and asks questions afterwards. It is no bad thing to be what our American friends call quick on the draw. Though personally, I am a man of peace.'

Kif examined the man of peace curiously as he portioned out the dish of sausages in front of him. A burglar! It was ludicrous. Smooth pink face and smooth pinky-fair hair growing a little thin on the top, bland blue eyes and a contemplative manner. A crook! In Kif's early literature crooks were all swarthy, black-eyed and vaguely sinister; rather like Danny on a bigger scale; and though five years of rubbing elbows with all the world had modified his ideas on most things he still unconsciously pictured Crime as the Knave of Spades. And Mr Carroll upset his ideas with some violence.

His eyes turned to Baba, pouring out tea at the other end of the table. The steam rose in slow waves round her like the smoke of incense. Serenely aloof she sat there among the instruments of her rites, a votary, a goddess, incalculable, unapproachable. Kif had a spasm of despair. Who was he to aspire? And then she handed him his teacup and her eyes rested on him for a moment; what he read in them made his replies to Mr Carroll's conversation border on the incoherent. But when she joined the conversation and Kif dared to look at her again her manner was matter-of-fact and her eyes impersonal. And Kif cursed himself for a fool that he should imagine vain things. She refused, later, to let him help her in the kitchen. 'You're tired,' she said. 'Sit down and rest.' And Kif felt as though a benediction had been said over him.

He was hunting through a collection of 'sevenpennys' hung in a two-shelved bracket on the wall by the fireplace for something to read when Angel came in.

'So you've been beating up Wilkins, I hear,' he said lightly, but the eyes above the beautiful laughing mouth were not laughing.

Kif turned slowly from the sevenpennys. 'Do you mind?' he asked.

'Not I, but I'm afraid Wilkins will. Turning the other cheek isn't Wilkins' strong point.'

'Well, I licked his boots till there couldn't have been any blacking left.'

'That should have soothed him. He can stand any amount of that. Got indigestion now?' He surveyed Kif half whimsically, half shrewdly.

'Not exactly. But I don't like being a neutral. If I offered you my services, would you have them?'

Baba came in from the kitchen with fresh tea, and Angel was silent until she had gone again. He pulled in his chair to the table, but instead of eating he propped his head on his fists and looked long at Kif.

'You're a real sport, Kif,' he said, 'but I'd much rather you didn't. You'd probably like it at first, but you'd probably get fed with it in a little. And it's a darn sight easier to get into than out of. I'd feel sort of responsible too for taking you here. You weren't born to it, like me.'

'You think I'd be no use to you, that's it, isn't it?'

'Not a bit of it. It's that I think you'd probably get disgusted with it, and be sorry you started that sort of life.'

'Well, but that's my look-out, isn't it? Of course your father——' he hesitated.

'Oh, my father mightn't say anything against it.'

'In that case the only reason against it is that I might wish I hadn't. And you might say that of anything.'

'Yes—but—— Well, you see, it isn't like starting a business, or something like that. It's more like entering a ruddy convent. You're not one of the crowd any more.'

'Well, I'm not so stuck on the crowd.' Kif's voice was bitter.

Angel considered him again. 'Well, don't decide yet anyhow. There's heaps of time in front of you.' He started to eat as Baba came back.

She cast a suspicious glance at the two men, which Kif did not see, and Angel ignored. 'Looking for a book?' she said.

'Yes, what would you recommend?'

'I'd recommend you not to,' she said. 'I never read a line myself, except the papers. What do you see in it? It's all lies. What's the good of reading a lot of lies? What you read in the papers is true—mostly. But *that*!' She waved a hand at the red rows. 'And at school we used to have to write exams on what a person who had never lived *thought*. Can you beat it? Crazy!'

Kif considered this new point of view with some amazement. 'But if you had a very dull life you'd want something to make it exciting even if it was only pretending.'

'Pretending wouldn't excite me. I wouldn't need to pretend, anyhow. I'd make my own excitement.'

'Well, perhaps it's different for a girl like you.' Kif said it sincerely, and without any flirtatious motive. 'But I bet if you were stuck on a farm miles from anywhere even you would take to reading.'

'I'd take to drugs first.'

'Well, reading's a sort of drug,' Kif admitted with a grin.

'Oh, let's go to the pictures,' she said, dismissing the argument. 'Will you, Angel?'

'Righto,' said her brother, his eyes on his food.

'I thought you didn't like things that weren't true?' said Kif.

She made a little moue. 'But they are true,' she said. 'They really happened.'

This exhibition of feminine logic left Kif speechless. He smiled at her, his eyes alight with laughter. 'Oh, kamarad!' he said, and left it there.

They went to the local cinema, and Baba sat between her brother and Kif. She sat erect and still in the middle of her chair, exhibiting none of the droopiness and tentative *rapprochement* which Kif had come to associate with the young female patron of the cinema. Her whole attention seemed to be given to the story unfolding its hackneyed length on the screen. And yet she appeared to be quite unmoved by the misfortunes of the shadow world. She shed no tear in sympathy with the wild grief of the heroine when the hero, as is the way of screen and opera heroes, jumped to the worst conclusion immediately on finding her in a mildly compromising situation and departed in (presumed) sound and fury. The

113

beautiful impassive face in the flickering light showed no softening when the accident happened, and the heroine, taking it for granted without attempting anything so mundane as first-aid that the hero was dead, forgave him beautifully for the injustice she had suffered. Kif forgot the shadows entirely in watching her. He had played so long with shadows, and she was so wonderful, this intoxicating reality beside him; the fine small nose, the tilted chin, the turned-back mouth like a flower. Her eyes he could not see; her hat hid them. But he could picture them. And he pictured wonders for himself more miraculous even than those being told on the screen. But when the hero, recovering with a celerity which in any other world would have laid him open to a charge of malingering, had enclosed the heroine in a last apologetic embrace, and a farce—intentional—followed, Kif resolutely wrenched his attention back to the film; and since it was funny he was soon laughing unselfconsciously.

And then when the fun was at its height he suddenly became aware of Baba as he had not been aware of her before. The laughter fell from him like a garment. He was conscious of her presence as something so potent as to be intimidating, and he was defenceless and half afraid. He could not turn his head to look at her. He wanted to take her violently in his hands and shake the magic out of her and the fright out of himself at the same time. The jigging four-four time of the piano and the pale haze of the tobacco smoke fused suddenly to make the air suffocating. He wanted to call out; to break something; or to say something reassuringly casual. With a deliberate effort he took out the case which held his last two cigarettes. His hands shook slightly, but the feel of the cigarette between his lips—standby in many tight corners—was somehow comforting. He sat breathing quick shallow breaths like a hunted thing. His eyes watched the pails of whitewash and the custard pies missing their destination. He would not think of her. And he would not sit next her again until—until——

The lights went up. She turned to him with a cool small smile. 'Funny, wasn't it?' she said casually, and to her brother: 'There are the Higgs, two seats down.'

'God!' he thought, 'God! is it just me?'

19

At the beginning of the year Kif found work as traveller for a small firm of soap manufacturers in North London, his beat being in outer London and the suburbs. The work was exhausting and the recompense meagre in the extreme. His salary was sufficient to pay for his room and board with the Carrolls, and no more. And if chemists and grocers found Messrs. Vidor & Pratt's representative

114

irresistibly persuasive it was because of Kif's urgent need of a margin which would make life tolerable. But it was rarely that his commission on sales was sufficient to warrant his having an evening out with Baba; and his ambition in life had narrowed down to simply that. He became more and more obsessed by the thought of her. Everything he did was done in relation to her. And yet he saw very little of her. After the six o'clock tea she went out usually with one or another of the 'crowd' who were always willing to act cavalier at the slightest hint of her willingness. When she stayed at home there was the probability of Mr Carroll being present too. Unless Kif took her out there was little chance of their acquaintance progressing as Kif ached to have it progress. And so he badgered and cajoled and bluffed unwilling customers into making trial of Crimson Rambler soaps, bending his stiff tongue into slickness, and subduing the loathing the work roused in him, for the sake of the few extra coins that made the difference between Heaven and Hell.

And he never ceased to sift the papers for a more congenial way of making a living; and clerks or cashiers or office-boys would be mildly astonished when, just as they were preparing to shut up shop for the night, a tallish man, very carefully brushed and rather tired about the eyes, would present himself as candidate for the vacancy which had been filled six hours ago. Occasionally in desperation Kif filched an hour from his legitimate business so that he might come somewhere at the head of the queue. But his luck was no better.

And then three months later he stepped over the border line without a backward glance. His first essay in crime was not a particularly difficult one. He stood for an hour one night in the shrubbery of a suburban villa while the laurels rattled suspiciously and the rain dripped down the back of his neck, until the constable on the beat had passed. When that had happened—and the officer had hesitated at the gate long enough to give Kif a thrill which cancelled the discomforts of the wait and made his mind leap to find excuses for his presence were it discovered—Kif, according to plan, walked down the street loudly whistling a music-hall tune. When he reached the end of the street he came back without melody, and, the street being reassuringly dark and empty, gave vent to a long low whistle on one note. The lack of variation in pitch made the sound, in spite of its carrying quality, quite unarresting to one who was not waiting for it. In a moment or two Carroll *père* stepped out of the gate carrying an attaché case, and Kif without looking at him and without greeting walked away in the opposite direction. He crept to bed in the dark house and was asleep before his partner returned. Three days later Mr Carroll handed him ten pounds in treasury notes. 'Slept well?' Mr Carroll had said at breakfast on the morning after their adventure, and Kif, taking his cue, had said 'Yes, and you?' and had asked no questions. He was not going to spoil his chances of further enlightenment by an ill-timed curiosity as to the ways and means. It was enough that Carroll was pleased with him.

With this windfall he redeemed his watch—the one that Tim had given him—which had been the last article to go to the pawnshop, and took Baba to dinner and theatre in the West End. He had never seen Baba in what she called war-paint before, but it did not need the tribute of turning heads and murmuring to tell him that his estimate of her beauty was a true one. Her frock had been her father's present to her, and Baba had chosen it with an intuition which would have made her fortune in the dress-making world. It was incredible that any other woman, by paying the price of it, could have worn it. It was as if a piece of exquisite cloth had been draped on her half-casually by a master; and she wore no ornaments except the jewelled clasp at her hip which was part of her frock. She was running over with happiness and the love of life. She jested and mocked and criticised the world of their inhabiting until Kif could have sought her for her tongue alone, and not for her arms and her hair and her eyes. He had long forgotten his spasm of nerves in the picture-house, and to-night he was nearer happiness than he had been since he had walked into the Charing Cross office that foggy morning and found it empty. He never thought about that if he could possibly help it. In his dreams—those post-war dreams of confused nightmare struggle—it was always Collins he was killing; but in his waking moments he had a queer feeling of emancipation, a queer conviction that nothing he would ever meet in life again would hurt him as that had hurt; he would never suffer like that again. If he ever met Collins he would beat him up, of course; that went without saying. In the meantime he did his best to forget about it. No one at Northey Terrace had ever heard him talk about his bad luck—partly because Kif was no talker, partly because it did not bear talking about.

'Can you dance?' she asked as they stood on the steps of the theatre after the show.

'Yes,' said Kif, a sudden light in his face.

'Well, let's go somewhere to supper where we can dance.'

They went to a semi-suburban dance-hall and Kif spent the time in the taxi trying to keep his emotions in decent check. In ten minutes—five minutes—he would have Baba in his arms.

'I didn't know you could dance like this,' she said when the orchestra stopped for the first time.

'Well, you know now,' said Kif, uttering words but having no knowledge of or interest in their meaning. The music started again and his arms went out for her.

Shortly after two o'clock they came home. Baba, who had been quiet and half-asleep in the taxi, went upstairs first, and Kif put out the light which had been left for them in the lobby and came up in the dark. She was waiting for him on the landing and he took her into his arms without warning and kissed her again and again while she stood acquiescent.

'Good night, Baba, good night,' he said huskily and dropped his arms. Her hand slid lingeringly from his as he moved away, but he went without pause up the last flight to his room. He sank on the edge of his bed breathing quickly as if he had been running, his head propped in his hands.

Baba in the room below turned on the light, flung her bag on to the bed and said in a fierce whisper 'Hell and Damn!' She moved over to the mirror scowling. Slowly the scowl faded. Gradually she smiled, one corner of her mouth higher than the other. Her reflection smiled back at her knowingly. Rapt in contemplation of herself she stood there, breathing gently, her head propped on her hands.

20

Kif learned that Angel and Danny habitually worked together, and that the unfortunate Sammy had been the partner of the elder Carroll, except on the occasion on which he was pulled, when he had elected in the face of much good advice to do a job alone. Mr Carroll seemed quite willing to use Kif if Kif were usable, and Kif did his best to qualify. Twice he was entrusted with the task of obtaining the layout of a house. The results of these were so good—Kif had included in his report the habits of every member of the respective households—that Mr Carroll beamed on him and signified his approval by introducing Kif to his most precious possession—his tools. These were, amazing as it may seem, kept in the house, and though ultimately Kif learned to his intense admiration and amusement their hiding-place it is not to be recorded here. Carroll is still in business, and I have no doubt is using the same tools. Kif handled them curiously and reverently as another might have examined the emblems of priestcraft, and Carroll lectured on them—jemmies and bits, nitro-glycerine, oxy-acetylene, torches, cylinders, queer contraptions of wire—explaining their uses, peculiarities, and some of their history with the enthusiasm of the specialist. And Kif listened and admired.

He spent no time in examining the morality of the situation. He was not even possessed of as positive a thing as a grudge against society. A way had opened for him and he liked the look of it; that was all. The way led to comfort—which he had had stolen from him and to which he felt vaguely that he had a right— and to what was much dearer, adventure. He accepted the chance as unquestioningly as he had joined the army at fifteen, ignoring the main issue since the incidentals were what he wanted. There was no one to keep him back; he had shed his acquaintances as he went along—his family (he knew the whereabouts of one brother who had heard from a sister three years ago but had lost the letter), the folk at Tarn, the Barclays, his army friends, Marcelle, Hough and his crowd—they had all melted into nothingness behind him; he was as

117

unattached now as he had been at fifteen. Only Carroll remained—Carroll and Baba. There was nothing to deter him.

So Kif, who would never have dreamed of taking possession of an object which was not his merely because he wanted it—with the exception of that 'winning' which all his fellows practised in France—became a professional at the job with no more self-examination than he would have had on entering the secret service. He kept his job with the soap manufacturers since, financial considerations apart, Mr Carroll explained, it was as well to have a perfectly good occupation to point to as the means of one's existence. So Kif sold just as many cakes of Crimson Rambler as satisfied Messrs. Vidor & Pratt and, remembering the days when he had sweated in agony in case the order he had fought for was not forthcoming, smiled smoothly at the manager when he said how kind of the firm it was to employ useless ex-service men, and devoted his interest and his energies to things nearer his liking.

For six months all that came his way was a succession of odd-jobs for Mr Carroll, all of them what he had known in the army as 'intelligence'. Mr Carroll found no fault with the results—indeed it would not be too much to say that Kif had done the work with love—and Kif found no fault with the payment. In that time he took his place in the queue of Baba's recognised retainers, with a slight lead of the others because he was her favourite dancing partner. His promotion paradoxically lessened the urgency of his passion for her; made it a more reasonable, a less devouring thing. Her treatment of him remained what it had been to begin with, silent and talkative by spasms superficially frank but always enigmatical. Now and then in their intercourse he was reminded forcibly of Angel as he had known him first. Mentally she was as difficult to 'get hold of' as her brother had been; she afflicted him with the same sense of impenetrability.

And then in August Mr Carroll looked up one morning from the patent food of a burnt sawdust appearance which was his breakfast—he was full of theories on diet and for six or eight weeks at a time would begin the day enthusiastically with the latest discovery, only to supersede it at a moment's notice—and said to Kif: 'Are you doing anything to-morrow night?'

Kif had been going to ask Baba to dance because it was pay-day, but he said immediately, 'No,' and waited.

'Well, I'm going to be busy. You could come along with me if you would care to.' Tableau: a benevolent old gentleman asking a young one to spend an evening at his club.

Kif nodded and turned over hastily in his mind the various commissions with which he had been entrusted lately. Which was it?

Mr Carroll went on: 'It's an easy business, and you might as well start easily,' and it dawned on Kif that he was on the threshold of his initiation. He felt as if a hand squeezed his heart. For a moment it seemed that Heaton had warned him for a wiring party or something of that sort. He was on the point of saying 'Very good, sir,' when he met Carroll's mild blue eyes, realised the placid, lower-middle-class breakfast table at which he was seated, and nodded again. There

118

was silence for a little; Angel was not down yet and they were alone. He became aware that Carroll, carefully masticating his unappetising granules at the other end of the table, was still regarding him with a dreamy gaze, and it occurred to him with a sense of shock that any 'dumb insolence' would be as impossible under these gentle blue orbs as in the presence of Heaton's cold grey eyes.

When he told Baba the next morning of the projected promotion she nodded indifferently. Neither the fact that he was going on a 'job' nor the necessity of missing the dancing which she must have expected made apparently any difference to her. He had hoped for either a smile of encouragement or an expression of regret, and when neither materialised was left wondering, as he so often was. After tea he watched her depart with Danny to the cinema.

'So long, you two. Good luck. Don't forget to leave the key.'

At half past ten—it was the end of the month and the days were short—they set out, Carroll carrying an attaché case and an umbrella. The umbrella was known in the family as Delilah—Danny had been responsible for the christening—because it led honest men astray. Carroll said that nothing soothed and impressed a doubtful constable like the presence of an umbrella. 'Sir' came to their lips as soon as their bull's-eye lighted on it. And since it was unmarked and of a pattern with ten thousand replicas it could be discarded, if in the way, without providing evidence of any value to the Law.

They went a short way by bus and then alighted and remained at the bus stop for nearly ten minutes, ostensibly waiting for a special number but in reality, as Kif knew very well, making sure that no one had followed them. Having strolled fifty yards in both directions they resumed their journey to a south-western suburb, and at half past eleven—an hour still not too late to make their presence in any way remarkable—they were walking down a retired road bordered by the railings of large gardens which rendered the houses invisible. Half way down Carroll paused, lit a match, and looked at his watch.

'Come, not so late!' he said in a cheerful well-fed-citizen voice. But the pause showed that they were alone on the road. Far away a late bus droned and a thick damp silence possessed the world. It had been raining in the afternoon, and the sharp smell of sweetbriar came cleanly through the mugginess from some invisible hedge. Kif drew in an abrupt breath.

'The gate is locked,' Carroll said, 'but it's quite easy to get over. I'll go first.' His citizen voice had gone and he was talking quietly though still not surreptitiously.

In the faint light from the nearest lamp they climbed over the gate and walked into the dripping blackness of the avenue.

'The house is shut up. Everyone away in Scotland until the end of September. Keep hold of me.' Carroll walked through the dark with the assured step of one who knew his way. They coasted the house to the back premises, where Carroll stopped. 'Scullery window,' he said. 'Nine-tenths of the scullery windows in London are open invitations.' He produced a pocket-knife and slid back the catch. With surprisingly little scraping or fumbling he climbed over the lowered sash and helped Kif after him. Kif felt his ankle held and his boot guided to a level resting-place. 'The edge of the sink,' explained Carroll. 'Don't go backwards. It's a drop behind.' Kif came safely to floor level and Carroll closed and bolted the window.

'Now in half an hour the policeman on the beat will arrive.' Mr Carroll never referred to a 'bobby', still less to a flatty, or any of the other more descriptive nicknames used by his kind. 'Until then we make ourselves as comfortable as circumstances will permit. No lights and no smoking.'

Kif grinned in the dark at the familiar prohibition and followed Carroll up a narrow passage, his hand on Carroll's shoulder and his feet moving as Carroll directed—'Three steps up' or 'Don't fall over the rug.' So familiar was the proceeding that he found himself waiting for the star-shell that would bring them to a halt. But the kitchen smell of water and stale food and dried cloths gave way to the smell of floor polish and varnish, and they moved unchallenged into a wider space and across it to a door which, as it was opened, emitted the stuffy warm chintzy smell of a living-room.

'Drawing-room,' said Carroll. 'Make yourself at home.'

Kif groped his way to a chair, cretonne-covered and very springy, took his hat off—yes, he wore a hat; Carroll insisted on that; caps, he said, were an object of suspicion to the force—and wiped his forehead.

'Why couldn't you use your presser?' he asked. 'That wouldn't show, surely?'

'Well, Sammy is "abroad" now because of his torchlight reflected from a brass door-knob shining through a key-hole. It does not sound very credible, does it? But it is always the incredible things that happen; don't forget that. I know a man who forgot as obvious a thing as a skylight. And a reflection did for him too. Don't use a light until you come to business and it's absolutely necessary.'

'You've been here before, of course?'

'Oh yes, I was here in daylight. Daylight's all right for reconnoitring, but no use for serious work. You are liable to be interrupted at any moment and that cramps your style. Don't talk any more.'

The stuffy quiet lapped them round and the quick prickings of excitement in Kif had died to a sleepy acquiescence when a round light flashed straight in his eyes. It took three heart-stopped seconds for him to realise that it was a light on the drawing-room blind. He watched it crawl over the fastenings, slide along the lower sashes, swerve back to the fastenings and disappear. From outside came the faint sound of movement and then silence. Kif remembered that the lawn at the side of the house grew close up to the drawing-room windows, and that even a policeman's steps would be inaudible on it. The quiet was so complete that it was difficult to realise that Carroll was within a few feet of him. He could not even hear him breathing. He resisted a desire to find out if he were really there, and sat still. And then, inside the house apparently and thunder-loud in the silence, came a shot-like sound. Kif sat still, his heart thumping, determined to make no move without a sign from Carroll. But the silence flowed back and nothing happened. He realised that the man had tried the kitchen door, and as it dutifully resisted had let the bolt fall back with a crash. And presently he heard, faint but unmistakable, the tread of footsteps on gravel. The front door shook. Several loud crunches on the gravel outside and the light moved over the front windows of the drawing-room, hesitated and went out. The footsteps died away. A small gurgle began above the window; it was raining again. Carroll made no movement and Kif waited. Endlessly he waited, motionless and determined. It was Carroll's move. At last Carroll said: '*That's* all right,' and got to his feet. Something in the tone conveyed to Kif more than the words said, and he felt happy. 'There are old shutters on the windows,' Carroll said, and Kif heard him moving them. There was a click and the green light of a reading-lamp broke the darkness.

Kif looked round him curiously—he had seen the interiors of so few homes that he had still a child's curiosity about other people's belongings—but Carroll was bent on business. He lifted the lamp from the low table on which it rested and placed it on a neighbouring secretaire, which stood against the wall between the fireplace and the large side-window.

'It took me a good hour to find the safe,' he said, 'and even then I would have missed it if it had not been for a finger-mark on the wall. Mrs Neuman was hot and flurried last time she put her jewels away. That is what makes me think they are here, and not in the bank where they ought to be. But I suppose having made a cache like this she is rather proud of it.' He was standing on a chair now, and, reaching up to the electric-light bracket on the wall, he detached a bulb and a length of cord, which he allowed to hang from where it entered the room immediately above the bracket, and swung the whole bracket sideways on an invisible hinge. 'See!' he said. 'That is exceedingly neat work. Observe that hinge. Observe the catch. Observe the way the cord lies in the groove. Nothing so crude as dummy lights. Delightful work!' He sighed with a craftsman's delight and came to earth, literally and metaphorically. 'You get another chair'— Kif had been standing on the edge of his—'and hold the light.'

Kif lifted another chair forward, unconsciously choosing the one which would be least damaged by his boots, and while he held the lamp watched steel and flame bite into the barrier between them and what they wanted. When Carroll at last stretched his hand into the hollow and drew forth a flat morocco box he uttered a gently deprecatory 'Oh, women, women!' As they looked at the double string of pearls Kif said: 'Are they real?'

'We shall know in a moment,' said Carroll, burrowing again.

The two boxes which he brought to light contained respectively an emerald pendant—six large stones set in diamonds—and a bracelet of alternate diamonds and sapphires. At the back of the safe, thrown casually in, were an uncrossed cheque for twenty pounds six shillings and twopence and a roll of notes which amounted to seventy-three pounds ten shillings.

'Women,' whispered Carroll again. He closed the safe, swung back the bracket, and replaced the cord painstakingly. Then he climbed down, removed the lamp to the floor and said: 'While I pack up these go upstairs to the first room on the right and bring me the ivory crucifix you'll find hanging above the bed. It is the only thing of value to us in the house. Don't use a torch more than you can help.'

Kif stepped from the lighted room, warm now with familiarity and habitation, into the chilly hall. He found the room without trouble, and swept it with a cautious but curious eye of light. It looked like a girl's room, somehow. There was a single bed, stripped now, but with pale mauve and pink hangings on the silver-grey wood. A large wardrobe of the same wood ran the whole length of one side of the room. Kif pushed back the sliding door and surveyed the contents. Frocks mostly, soft shining things that seemed queerly alive in the white light. He ran his big supple hand along them, lifting the folds of now one and then another consideringly. A faint sweet scent came out from them. 'Girl's things,' he thought. 'Queer!' It did not occur to him to think 'Less than a year ago when I was at starvation point this girl was buying frocks she had no need of.' It simply had nothing to do with him. He pulled the door to again, made a casual examination of the pictures—Medici reproductions of early Italian religious paintings—and took the crucifix from the wall. It was nearly eighteen inches long and beautifully carved. He considered the writhing figure dispassionately. He had seen many calvaries in France, but this one was more alive than any he had seen. 'Well,' he thought, 'lots of our chaps took far longer to die, and were a much nastier mess while they were doing it. And for far less reason.' His head went up at the sound of a drip-drip outside. It was still raining, damn it. Carroll would have some use for Delilah. Good old Delilah.

Carroll saw his teeth in the half-light as he came back to the drawing-room and asked what the joke was. He had packed away his tools and their reward, and was waiting for the crucifix. As he stood up from disposing of it he faced Kif and said:

'Have you taken anything on your own account?'

For a moment Kif felt as he would have felt six months ago if someone had accused him of stealing. His right hand was already clenched and lifting when he realised that he was about to be ridiculous.

'Not I,' he said.

'That's all right, then,' Carroll said. 'There isn't anything else in the house that is worth the risk its disposal would entail. We already have a destination for the crucifix in America. Otherwise it would be valueless. My agent,' he never said fence, 'would not touch it. And to try to get rid of an article through the pawnshops would mean disaster for all of us. Forgive my asking, but you will realise that it was important.'

They left the room as they had found it, and made their exit by the scullery window again. After a long pause in which there was no sound but the drip of the rain, Carroll put the case and umbrella into Kif's hand and said: 'Take these and wait for me near the gate. If you hear me call out get away as quickly as possible.' Surprised but obedient Kif went, the whole of the night's haul and all Carroll's tools in his possession. He marvelled, alone in the wet, until he heard the suck of footsteps growing gradually nearer and slower and Carroll's voice said his name.

It was nearly two o'clock as they went briskly down the gurgling street under Delilah's chaperonage. 'We have a considerable walk in front of us,' Carroll announced; and presently: 'You are no doubt wondering why I stayed behind. If that window were not fastened our little night's amusement would be discovered to-morrow by the constable on the beat. But if the screw I put in remains unnoticed, nothing will be found until the lady looks for her belongings a month hence.'

When they had walked for more than twenty minutes, judging by the quarter hours boomed from many steeples, Kif decided that they were not making for home. He revolved this a while and came to a conclusion. 'Going to get rid of it'—and he wondered what the agent would be like. But the method of getting rid of it was not his least surprise that night.

They were walking down a back street which, Carroll said, was a popular short cut between two great highways of traffic. On one side were high buildings—stores and garages—and on the other the back-garden walls of a series of smallish houses, each back gate marked on its right by the oblong iron covering of the coal shute. As he passed one of these, Carroll lifted the lid, and without pausing let his case drop into it. They had gone several steps past it before Kif realised what had happened and then he made no comment; he was still on probation.

They walked for another ten minutes until they came to a halt on a wide corner where there were shops—a local Piccadilly circus, black now and silent. They had not been there two minutes before a taxi slid up to them.

'Taxi, sir?' said the man, but Kif saw the grin under his drooping moustache.

The speed, the warmth, and the safety all conduced to make Kif sleepy, but it was a still wide-awake Carroll who pushed him out into the damp again when the taxi dropped them at the end of Northey Terrace. As they went up the street, the clocks of all the world, it seemed, ringing three, they met a tall slowly-moving figure.

'Good night, officer,' said Carroll cheerfully.

'Good night, Mr Carroll. Out late, aren't you?' said the tall man.

'Oh, a little, but one must keep young. Have you ever seen'—he mentioned a popular musical comedy of the moment. 'Well, don't miss it. Only if you go to the upper circle, don't take the third seat from the right in the third row. There's a pillar directly in front of it. Miserable!'

And Kif, ten minutes later, was ravenously devouring cold ham which Carroll carved with delicacy and precision, and being silently grateful for that coal shute in a back street and for Delilah.

21

Carroll's screw remained undiscovered, and no reports of a suburban burglary enlivened the press of the succeeding days. Kif received his portion of the night's takings a week afterwards, and at Baba's instigation bought himself some much-needed clothes. She had come into his room one evening in the process of distributing the contents of the laundry basket, and holding up a shirt for his inspection had said: 'The first thing you do with your next pay is to get yourself some new things. I don't mind sewing on a button for you occasionally, but I draw the line at trying to make this hold together.' So Kif refitted; and had his first serious difference with Baba over the choosing of his suits.

She came upon Angel and himself, their elbows on the table and the tea-things pushed back, contemplating samples of cloth in the large content born of well-fedness and a congenial occupation. They were turning over the patterns in a monastic calm, with none of the twitterings and head-leanings and eye-narrowing and advances and retreats which are part of a woman's method of conducting the business. Baba, on seeing their occupation, immediately became authoritative. She took possession of the situation and became the self-elected oracle on the subject of shade, texture, suitability and wearing capabilities. A slow surprise dawned in Kif at some of her pronouncements, but though Angel made what she called crushing remarks occasionally he said nothing, and she did not appeal to him. It became clear to him presently that she was seriously engaged in choosing a cloth for him. At last she said: 'That's the best', and turning back to where a white forefinger was inserted, 'and that's the next. Have this for everyday and that for meetings.' She put down the book and began to clear away the things.

Kif disapproved so wholeheartedly of her choice that he found it difficult to believe that she was in earnest. Baba! who dressed her own lovely body with such an exquisite suitability. Angel was whistling softly to himself while he turned over a second book, and Baba evidently considered the subject closed.

'Well,' Kif said, 'here's my choice.' And held it out to her. She did not take the book, but stood looking at him, her expression that of one who reads a direction-sign in a railway station. Then her glance came down to the pattern he was exhibiting, and the faint rare colour showed in her face.

'Much too dull for me to go out with,' she said, and lifting the tray carried it through the doorway he opened for her.

Angel lifted his head for the first time and grinned broadly.

When Baba came back from spending the evening with her only girl-friend—one Sally Myers, whose Jewish good looks were an excellent foil for her own—she found her brother alone with the last edition of the evening paper. He was occupying her own armchair, a fact which emphasised a feeling she had that their usual positions were reversed. There was amusement and malice in his eyes as he greeted her.

'You should take an interest in racing,' he said, waving the paper at her.

'So that more good money could be thrown away.'

'Ah, but think of the valuable lessons to be learned. The folly of betting on certainties. Miss Confidence lost to-day at Derby by five lengths. Terrible shock to all concerned.'

She was taking off her fur at the mirror over the fireplace and she looked sharply at her brother's reflection.

'You look all right in that coat,' he went on, in the under-statement which is fraternal commendation. 'Pity you don't approve of Kif's new suits. Saw them in the piece when we were being measured. They're going to look a whole heap better than your horrors would have done.'

She turned to him incredulously.

'Well, I'm glad I didn't take the odds on Miss Confidence.' He picked up the paper and met her glance over the top of it.

'Blast you,' she whispered, 'blast you!' and slashed him across the face with her fur. But he laughed delightedly from behind his upflung arm, and frustrated and beside herself she fled from the room.

So Kif was cast into outer darkness, and instead of spending what remained of his money on Baba found himself to his own amazement with a banking account. Since he had every intention of marrying Baba at the first opportunity he considered the sum in the bank as so much deferred bliss, and bore his exile from her good graces with an equanimity that disconcerted her not a little.

The direct result of his temporary loss of Baba was his discovery of Danny. As soon as it was apparent that Kif was in disgrace the little man had become unobtrusively friendly. Kif was unimpressed, until he one day used a phrase which Danny replied to with astonishing aptness. It was a minute or two before he realised that his phrase had been a quotation from a Kipling short story and that Danny had capped it. For the first time then he really considered the desperate-looking little fellow who was Angel's partner. Angel was at this time enamoured of a resting chorus-lady and was not available as a companion in the evenings, and so when Danny suggested that he should come round to his rooms for a book he went not unwillingly, and that was the beginning of many nights together.

Danny had two rooms at the top of a boarding-house, and he had furnished them himself with a success which was astonishing in an effort so wholly instinctive. The colour scheme was a warm purple combined with shades ranging from buff to amber; it was almost as if he had longed unconsciously for the moors and burns of his heritage which he had never seen, and which he would probably have hailed with opprobrium in reality. There were but three wooden pieces of furniture in the flat—a bed, a dressing-table, and a table which was half desk, half chest-of-drawers—and they were all of walnut, dark and beautiful. The books he had invited Kif to come and choose from filled the open wood shelves that ran round the room, and over-flowed on to the chairs and the floor; books of all sorts, from the little red pre-war sevenpenny's to expensive volumes of travel and biography, thrown together without order or arrangement. No library this, but the bare bones of things on which Danny had feasted. And Kif who had come to borrow a book stayed to find out about Danny.

And through the rest of that winter Kif was to be found at least two nights a week buried in an armchair at one side of Danny's hearth, his long legs stretched to the fire and his nose in a book, while Danny, almost invisible in the cigarette smoke, sat curled gnome-like opposite him and drew music from the fiddle tucked under his chin. Or Danny would argue passionately some entirely unimportant theory—against himself perforce, since Kif would lie, interested but wordless, contentedly smoking. The atmosphere of the place fed a part of him which was starved to atrophy at Northey Terrace. The warm beautiful colouring of the room, the music, the books, Danny's husky voice in its unexpected cockney—one always expected Danny to talk broken English— playing with abstractions, Kif lapped it eagerly. When he had a home of his own it would be something like this—a place to come back to after adventure.

The thought of Baba was a discord at Danny's, but Kif, unintrospective as always, did not pursue the thought to its logical conclusion.

'What do you believe in?' Danny asked one night, dropping the fiddle in the middle of a phrase.

'Prairie oyster and cloves,' said Kif.

'No, seriously. Have you any ideas on the hereafter, for instance?'

'Not I,' said Kif. 'Don't believe there is one.'

'Well, that's pretty good for someone who has no ideas on the subject.'

Kif grinned. 'I never thought about it, but I just don't see how there can be. I'd need a lot of persuading that there was.'

'Were you properly brought up?'

'I went to Sunday school, when I was a kid, and learned the usual things, I suppose.'

'Pearly gates and streets of gold?'

'Yes, that sort of thing.'

'And when did you stop believing in that?'

Kif thought. 'I don't think I ever really believed it.'

'No, I should think you probably didn't,' said Danny musingly. 'Bump of scepticism well developed, bump of superstition a hollow. It isn't a matter of upbringing at all really. It's a matter of mental equipment. My father was a Catholic and my mother "turned" when she married him, but it was she who believed that Saint Anthony'd find her thimble for her, same as she believed in peeling apples on Hallowe'en, and he didn't give a damn for all the archangels in the heavens.'

He took up his fiddle and played a little crying phrase over and over.

'So you don't believe that when I go west I'll get it in the neck for emptying the safes of bloated companies of ruddy profiteers?' he said.

126

'Oh, between then and now you can start a new slant. Give all you have to the poor and go round shaving people for nothing.'

'I think not. I'd have to start too soon, for one thing. You see, I can't make old bones. I've got it here.' He tapped his chest.

Kif, arrested in the middle of a search for the matches, said: 'Gas?' forgetting that Danny had not served in the army.

'No, I—— They wouldn't take me. That was why.'

'But it isn't bad, is it?' said Kif, unexpectedly moved. Swift death he knew and understood, but this carrying death round with you—it was horrible.

'Three years, four years, not more. If it's the matches you're looking for, you're sitting on them.'

'But good God, man, they can cure it! Why don't you go away somewhere where the air's good? Switzerland or somewhere.'

'I'd rather live till I die,' said the little barber's assistant dryly; and Kif, groping wordlessly for the matches, understood, and felt a flame of fellow-feeling spring up in him. If *he* had only a little time . . .

'I didn't mean to talk about that,' Danny went on. 'I was only finding out what you believe in. Isn't it amazing what a lot of people accept what they're told merely because they're told it? I suppose that if they were taught from infancy that the world was a big mushroom and the sky blue paper they'd feel bound to believe it. Especially if some kind of bible said so. That's typical of their spoonfedness—the reverence they have for a Bible. If I had thrown a Bible across the room my mother would have thought that I was a certainty for perdition. A Bible! Just an ordinary hotch-potch of a book—some history, and some myth, and some poetry, and some stud-book, and a sermon or two. Nothing that you can't pick up from the tuppenny box any day. Even the prophecies aren't as good as some Highland ones that you can buy in any bookseller's at three-and-six. The only thing in the book worth reverence is the English, and they never think of that. It's the reference book of the whole Christian religion, and you can prove anything from it. "Vengeance is mine, I will repay," and "The wicked flourish like the green bay tree," and so on.'

Kif turned his head at that. 'What would you do if a man robbed you of everything you had in the world and everything you were going to have, and you were told that?'

'What? "Vengeance is mine?" I would have a call to be the instrument of the Lord. When clergymen go to a better paid job they always have a "call". "A region of greater scope and activity." Ugh!' Danny flicked his slender fingers as if to rid them of something foul, and wandered into a dissertation on the iniquities of the priest caste and the unloveliness of its history. He had reached the Druids by the time Kif got up to go, with the inevitable book under his arm.

Kif had taken to reading in bed again, a habit he had lost during his life in the army, and he devoured print at the rate of a book every two nights. Baba silently resented these oblongs of red or blue or green which she recognised as a talisman against her charms. If it were not for them, she felt, he would have capitulated long before now, worn out, starved. She had cast him out originally in a blaze of anger, and she had continued to keep him there 'to teach him'. But he was not proving the apt pupil she had anticipated, and she wanted him.

It is difficult to imagine how the affair would have ended if it had not been for accident. A shriek from the kitchen one night brought him pell-mell there to find Baba struggling with a blazing window-curtain.

'Keep away,' he said, and with a wrench brought the curtains, pole and all, to the floor, where with considerable difficulty he smothered them with the hearthrug. Breathless and fey with excitement he took the white and shaking Baba into his arms.

He came to his senses to find that she was answering his kisses with utter abandon.

'Baba,' he whispered, drawing her down to a chair, 'marry me. Will you? Baba!'

He had not time to analyse the look in her eyes. Her arm was round his neck, pulling him to her. 'Kiss me,' she said. 'Kiss me again.' And Kif was nothing loth.

Presently though she sat up, pushing her shining hair away from her face, and said: 'Lummy, look at the mess! And I bought these curtains only three months ago!'

He did not glance at the ruin. 'When will you marry me?' he asked. 'Soon? I can keep you all right. How soon, Baba?'

'Don't let's talk of it just now,' she said. 'I'm all of a do-da.' And he let her go.

But when he returned to the subject the following night while they were dancing, she again evaded him, and a small cold trickle seeped into his exuberance. Was it possible she was going to say no? In a slowly growing panic he reviewed his possible rivals: Bennet, the theatrical agent, typical London Jew, sleek and dark and talkative; Denman, the 'cellist, almost as beautiful as Angel, his red-gold hair brushed high from a white forehead and cut in a short side-whisker on his cheek-bones; Cleland, the antique-dealer, whose acquaintance she had made at one of the innumerable auction sales which she attended as other people go to plays—tall, shy, stammering, young and rich; Barkis, the little ex-service man who had bought the tobacconist's business in the next street; Miller, who as Raoul ran a cabaret up West, and was reported to have made a fortune in six weeks. He could think of others, but these were in the first flight. And yet—there was last night in the kitchen.

In the dim intimacy of the taxi home he tried again to bring her to the point.

'What makes you so keen on marriage?' she said at last, and something like exasperation sounded in her voice. 'What d'you want out of it? Kids?'

'No, I don't want anything but you. We needn't have kids if you don't want them. It's only you I want.'

'Well, you can have me.'

'Baba!'

'Only let's hear a little less of the marriage business.'

His arm round her relaxed. 'What do you mean? Are you suggesting—what do you mean?'

'Exactly what I say.' Something in his tone gave hers a defiant twist.

'But, Baba, I don't want that! I want you for keeps.'

'You don't want much, do you! No one's ever going to have me for keeps.'

She sat silent in her corner while he remonstrated and entreated; but it was she who mocked and he who was sullen as she bade him good night on the stairs.

A fortnight later Baba announced to her family at the mid-day dinner—a meal at which Kif was rarely present—that that afternoon she was going room-hunting for Kif.

'Dear me,' said her father, 'is he thinking of leaving us?'

'Well, it's time he had a decent place of his own, like Danny's. That little back room is a miserable hole.' Her wide eyes rested easily on her father's face.

'That's true enough,' said Angel. 'And Sammy'll be wanting it very soon anyway.'

Baba's eyes were suddenly swords with which she stabbed her brother's hostile stare. 'Wrong for once, Mr Clever,' she said; 'Sammy's not coming back here.'

'Oh? Is he going into rooms too? Shouldn't have thought Sammy would see the necessity of it, somehow.'

'Oh, you know a hell of a lot, don't you!'

'Be quiet, both of you,' said Mr Carroll mildly, and there was quiet.

The rooms into which Kif migrated were not at all reminiscent of Danny's, but the landlady was a friend of Baba's; and Baba had done her best with new cretonnes to give them a cheerfulness which would make up for their undoubted ugliness. Danny, who was called in at the last moment, casually, to view them, had asked her why she hadn't offered to do up the rooms properly, 'so you could get rid of that'—pointing to the patterned wall-paper.

'I did suggest it, but she put her foot down, and I can't afford to offend her.'

'Well, make her take away the portrait gallery,' said Danny.

For two months Kif lived at 18 Dormer Street a life of such brilliant high-lights and such deep shadows as he had not yet known. He was hopelessly in love with Baba, but he felt that he possessed her only when she was with him, that his physical presence was the measure of her liking for him. She made no pretence of giving up her usual round of amusement in his favour; she continued to divide her evenings as she had always done among the more favoured of her train, her choice being regulated solely by what appealed to her most at the moment. She had never any compunction in throwing over a previous engagement if a momentarily more attractive one materialised at the last minute, and her edict was accepted by the unfortunate one in the resigned and unresentful spirit in which we accept natural phenomena—flood, fire and tempest. Who were they to grumble? Were they not made free of the sunlight at other times? But what Baba did give Kif, she gave royally, because it was what she herself wanted most at the time.

In that lay, I think, the secret of Baba's unholy charm. She was, thanks to her ruthlessness, almost invariably doing what pleased her, and the joy of it lit her beauty to a flame. Whatever she did she did wholeheartedly, since she did nothing through compulsion or on sufferance. And Kif, comforted by the knowledge that if Baba did not belong to him, at least he was favoured beyond all the others, used his natural capacity for living for the moment to make their hours together particular separate heavens with which to balance the purgatories of her absence.

His days continued to be devoted to the sale of soap, and his evenings when Baba was otherwise engaged were spent with Angel at a boxing-match, or billiards, or the theatre, or in Danny's flat. Neither Angel nor Danny spent much time at Dormer Street; Danny said the colour made him sea-sick, and a quiet evening by the fire did not appeal to Angel as an ideal amusement. But Danny's friendliness to Kif had not suffered a relapse when Baba had once more shown him favour, and Angel, whose chorus-lady was again on tour, was prodigal with invitations and suggestions for their mutual amusement.

His evenings with Baba began usually with dancing and ended at his rooms. There Baba would lie in one of the creaking basket-chairs whose decrepit ribs showed abruptly here and there through her brave cretonne, blowing smoke-rings with her short pale mouth, and discussing people and things—concrete things; Baba's conversation never soared into the realms of abstract speculation. She would weigh the pros and cons of Denman's accepting an offer to play at a West End picture-house, or she would recount an adventure of Sally Myers, or she would criticise in retrospect the appearance and manners of their fellow-dancers and speculate on their private lives, or she would discuss the best methods of making people who had no intention of buying Crimson Rambler soap change their minds. And Kif would sit in the opposite chair, watching her, and pretending to himself that they were married.

Going home one frosty night in January they met Danny, who stopped to tell them 'a good one on Angel', and without waiting to see the effect of his ribald tale went away, chuckling, into the dark.

Baba stood staring after him until Kif took her arm and urged her into a walk again.

'Why isn't Danny jealous?' she asked abruptly.

'Perhaps he is, poor devil,' said Kif. 'I don't blame him.'

'No, he isn't,' she said, and was absent-minded for the rest of the evening. Later she said: 'Do you know that Danny has what they call second sight? Scotchmen have it sometimes.'

Kif grinned. 'All the winners?' he asked.

'You needn't be so uppish. Even scientists say there's a lot in it. And I know a girl . . .'

Kif listened to the tale while he watched the way her lips alternately hid and revealed her short level teeth, and between two kisses promised that he would go with her to a famous crystal-gazer. He had forgotten the promise entirely

130

until he found himself, some days later, being conducted to a flat above some business premises that bordered the park where they had been dawdling. Laughing he tried to back out of it, but she said, 'Why, you promised!' and looked at him with wide grieved eyes.

Kif was quite prepared to find the door opened by a pseudo-slave of alleged Eastern origin, and the tall correct parlour-maid in her black-and-white disconcerted him.

'Have you an appointment, madam?'

'Yes,' said Baba astonishingly.

'Is the appointment for two, madam?'

It was Baba who looked disconcerted now. 'I just made an appointment,' she said.

'I'll inquire, madam,' said the maid. 'Will you take a seat?' In a moment she was back. 'Miss Fitzroy will see either the lady or the gentleman, but not both.'

'You go, then, Kif,' said Baba. 'Go on!' as he was preparing to argue. And Kif, partly from natural curiosity, partly from a masculine desire to avoid a discussion in public, suffered himself to be led away.

Miss Fitzroy was an aquiline lady, inclining now to embonpoint, but by no means the fat old gipsy Kif had unconsciously expected. She bade him good-day in a pleasant cultured voice and asked him to sit down.

'You want to know about the future, of course. I have one request to make. Will you please not interrupt till I have finished the sitting?' Kif, feeling decidedly foolish, gave his assurance. 'And another thing. It is not always possible to tell whether the vision is of something past or something to come. But if it is of the past you will recognise it, I expect.'

She bent forward to the crystal lying on its black cushion on the table, and there was a long silence. Kif sat in his habitual quiet, his bright eyes sliding curiously from one article of furnishing to another. He had so far assimilated the Carroll point of view as to wonder what kind of a 'job' this house might provide, and he had almost forgotten the prophetess in his speculations when she said:

'I see a small dark man in a room with two others. I think the room is an office. They are laughing and he is talking. I think they are laughing at him. He is trying to convince them of something. He is very much in earnest. I think he is distressed. He keeps pulling one hand through the other.'

Kif, inattentive till now, woke to a sudden interest. Danny did that—pulled one hand through the other—whenever he got excited. But then—vague!

Forgetting the prohibition he said: 'What does he do with his hands? Show me.'

'This,' she said, her eyes on the crystal, and gripping one hand with the other imitated Danny's action.

Kif sat looking at her very much as a horse looks at the object it is making up its mind to shy at, but she was silent now, absorbed in contemplation of the crystal. After a long interval she began again.

131

'There is a dimly lit place. A barn. No, a stable. Someone—I think it is you—is hanging a bridle on a nail, and there is another man there. It all began then.'

'What did?'

'I don't know. Now it is brighter. No, it is another place altogether. A kitchen full of shadows. You are there laughing with someone—a woman, I think. There is something on the table, but her shadow is over it. Yours is swinging about on the wall. Enormous. No, it's—it's—— *No!*'

The last negative was shot out so unexpectedly that it almost brought Kif to his feet. She was no longer looking at the crystal; she was gazing at him in a kind of incredulous horror.

'What's the matter?' he asked. 'I didn't mean to talk. I'm sorry.'

She was still staring at him. Really the woman must be dippy.

'Yes,' she said vaguely, 'you shouldn't have talked. I asked you not to.' But she did not appear to care greatly or even to know what she was saying.

'Go on,' said Kif, 'I won't interrupt again.' But she shook her head.

'No. I'm sorry, I can't do any more to-day. I—it isn't—it won't come to order, you understand. I'm sorry. You don't owe me anything.' Her eyes, which had been fluttering between her hands and the crystal, came back to his face and stayed there as if fascinated. As Kif got up to go she said: 'Will you tell me your name?'

'Archibald Vicar,' said Kif, seeing no reason why he should withhold it.

'Thank you.' She stood up and remained standing, still and silent, as he walked past her to the door. 'As if I were royalty,' he thought, irrelevantly, and went out feeling sold.

'Well?' said Baba as soon as the front door shut behind them. 'Well?'

'Oh, a washout. Absolutely. She threw a fit because I interrupted her, and wouldn't go on.'

'But what did she tell you before that?'

'She didn't tell me anything. She said she saw three men yarning in an office, but none of them seemed to be me. Tell me—who does this?' He drew one hand, palm facing him, slowly through the other.

'Wait a minute. Do it again.' She watched, and in few seconds she said: 'It's Danny, isn't it?'

Kif nodded, and she gripped his arm till her finger-tips bit into his flesh. 'Did she see Danny? Did she?'

'Well,' he admitted, 'one of her three men might have been Danny, and again might not.'

'What was he doing?'

'He was telling the tale to the other two men.'

'What were they like?'

'She didn't go into details.'

'And what else?'

'That was all, I think. No, she saw me in a stable. Considering the amount of stables I've been in in my life that isn't a great achievement.'

'What did you interrupt her about?'

'I don't remember now. Oh, she said something began in a stable, and I asked what, but she didn't know. And then she cut up rough.'

'What did you pay her?'

'Nothing. She wouldn't take anything. Said the power was off and the switch wouldn't work, or something of that sort.'

'D'you mean to say that she didn't charge you anything?' Baba seemed strangely impressed.

'Well, she couldn't very well. It was a washout, even if it was partly my fault.'

'You shouldn't have been such a fool. She's very famous. Why, admirals and generals used to go to her in the war to find out what was the best thing to do.'

Kif gave his rare shout of laughter. 'Strewth!' he said. 'They should have come to me. I didn't need any switches and things for that. And I wouldn't have charged them a cent.'

'We'll give her a month to cool off,' said Baba, 'and then we'll go back.'

'Not me,' said Kif. 'You can!'

But by that time Kif was in prison.

On a February night he helped Mr Carroll in a job at the offices of an insurance company off Cannon Street. Carroll had entered and emptied the safe with his usual precision and despatch, and they had spent the rest of the night in the deserted office, until the hour had become one at which two pedestrians could traverse Cannon Street with an air of virtue and early rising. Kif had preceded Carroll downstairs to the marble entrance hall which marked the centre of the ground floor, Carroll being a good flight and a half behind, when he became conscious with that sixth sense which the war had developed in him that there was someone besides themselves in the dark. He was halfway to the door when the knowledge came to him, and he stopped abruptly. Almost before his light went out a pair of arms clutched him from behind, and before he had started to struggle he had warned Carroll.

'Look out! Beat it!' he called, and wondered immediately whether he had done the right thing. There was no sound from above, but Kif was too thoroughly occupied to notice whether there was or not.

'You'd better come quietly,' panted his assailant in the dark; but what had been merely the desire for freedom had become in Kif the rage of the fighting animal, and he was slowly but surely getting the better of the encounter when he became aware that there were now two people beside him. For one glad moment he thought that Carroll had come to the rescue, and then he heard the voice in his ear say: 'Grab him, Tapper, till I get them on him.' That roused him to a blind fury.

It was two strenuous minutes later that Kif felt his wrists imprisoned and heard one of the men cross the hall to the electric switch while the other held his arms above the elbow from behind. The light, diffused from inverted bowls in a ceiling of a subtle oyster shade, shed an incongruously mild radiance on the three dishevelled men.

133

'It's the chicken!' said the man who had switched on the lights, surveying Kif disgustedly. 'But the old man's somewhere up above. We'll——'

The front door swung gently open in the draught and fell to again, thudding softly against its jamb.

'I thought——' began the man who held Kif. But the other had dashed to the open door. He came back expressing himself with a fluency which roused interest in Kif, who was feeling sick and dazed.

'Surely you could have heard him and warned me?' he finished.

'Me? Talk sense. I was much too busy trussing your damned chicken. If you hadn't given him that wallop we'd be still at it.' He dropped Kif's arms and came round to have a better look at the man who had put up such a resistance. 'Daisy, isn't he!' Then, with a sudden change of tone, he said: 'Feeling cheap, chum? Sit down for a minute.' He pushed Kif, whose knees were trembling, back on to a carved marble seat.

Tapper, still mouthing vain curses, went to the telephone, and Kif's captor sat down at the other end of the bench. Something ran down Kif's cheek and dropped on his hand. He looked at it uncomprehendingly and put his hands up to his wet hair. The detective smiled, not unkindly.

'You wouldn't come quietly, you know. You asked for it.'

Kif looked at the blood on his hands and nodded indifferently. 'Give me my handkerchief, will you?' he asked, and the detective searched for it, and having mopped Kif's head handed it over.

Kif was feeling better by the time Tapper came back, but Tapper favoured him with an unlovely stare. 'It's good your girl can't see you now,' he said.

This was gratuitous insult, and Kif roused himself.

'If it comes to that,' he said, 'you're no oil painting.' His eyes indicated a bluish-red swelling on Tapper's cheek-bone. 'And if I'd had a truncheon they'd have needed an identification parade to spot you.'

'Not so much lip,' said Tapper sourly. 'You'll learn not to be so free with your tongue before we've done with you—you and Carroll.'

'Who's Carroll?'

'Very clever, aren't you?' said the detective. But Kif merely looked vague.

At the station a fat and sleepy sergeant wrote in a book while a constable bound up Kif's head deftly and impersonally, very much as an habitual church-goer turns up the epistle to the Ephesians, and he was consigned to a clean little room which he supposed was a cell.

He was terribly, abysmally tired. There was nothing he wanted in all the world but to go to sleep. His freedom, Baba, his old life—last night seemed years away—were mere names to him, unattractive and without meaning. All he wanted was to sleep. And as soon as he lay down sleep deserted him, and he lay watching the dawn come, his head throbbing, and every aspect of his predicament growing steadily clearer with the growing light. But he pulled his mind resolutely away from the future. Things were only bearable in this life if you didn't think about them; he had found out that long ago at Tarn; so he turned, and turned again, wearily, in the grey light, busying himself with his physical discomfort lest his mind, already pulling on the leash like a too inquisitive dog, reach the thing he knew was there—the locked door and all it stood for.

When he was brought into court in the morning he looked round eagerly for a familiar face, but there was no one there. He listened as one at a play to Tapper giving evidence of his arrest, of the implements found in his pockets, of his abnormal violence, and found no reason why he should not be committed for trial. With another despairing glance round the court he departed to a new temporary home. Two weeks later he was sentenced in the presence of Angel, Baba and Danny and an indifferent crowd of some fifty idlers to twenty-one months' hard labour. The young and earnest lawyer who had been presented to him for his defence could in the circumstances confine himself merely to the plea for leniency. The forces of the Crown, however, while admitting that there was no previous conviction recorded against him, had incontrovertible evidence of the violence of his character; and Kif listened in amazement to an account of his attack on his superior officer while in the army, and of his obstructing a police-sergeant while in the execution of his duty in January of the previous year. Kif's counsel, after a consultation with him, explained the reasons for Kif's two attacks on authority, and made the most of his war record. But the impression remained, even in Kif's own mind, that he was a desperate character. His thoughts went back to an interview he had had with Tapper shortly after being committed for trial. Tapper had begun on the 'You be sensible and we'll see what can be done for you' tack, and had asked, 'What was Carroll going to do with the stuff he had that night?'

'What Carroll?' Kif had said again.

Tapper had adjured him not to be foolish; it wouldn't pay him to make enemies of the police; and it would probably make a difference to his sentence if the stuff was recovered. But Kif was not going to be led into any admission that Carroll had been his partner.

'I suppose you'll admit that you *know* Carroll?' asked the detective, exasperated and sarcastic.

'I know *a* Carroll,' Kif said. 'The tobacconist on the Walham road.' And Tapper had snorted and called him a fool.

And now the world called him a desperate character. A bad lot, in fact. It was quite a new idea to him.

The judge pointed out that a good war record was not in itself any mitigation of his offence; the fact that he had fought for his country in war did not make him free to rob his neighbours in peace. What would have been mitigation would have been any evidence that the crime was committed through the urge of need or distress; but there was no such evidence. This was, it was true, the accused's first essay in crime—that was to say it was the first occasion on which he had been arrested. In most cases of a first offence it was usual to give a light sentence. But there had been a wave of this type of crime lately, and it was very necessary that a salutary example should be made in order to prevent others embarking on that first all-important step. Moreover, the large haul of booty which had been obtained from the offices burgled by the accused and his confederates was still untraced, and the accused had shown no anxiety to assist in its recovery. They had evidence that the accused had a distinct bias towards violence. There was no doubt in his own mind that he was a danger to law-abiding citizens. In these circumstances he sentenced the accused to twenty-one months' hard labour.

Kif heard the sentence without realisation. The thing was over and he was 'for it'; that was all he knew. It was a queer mix-up, but he had undoubtedly asked for it, and it didn't bear thinking about.

With which muddled but true summing-up he turned to smile at Baba and left the dock.

22

Kif found prison not at all the place of half-grim half-picturesque incarceration he had unconsciously pictured. It was a place of iron routine and heart-searing monotony. It was like hospital without the companionship and good-humour. In some ways it reminded him of the army; the new-comer as in the army—as in most human communities—found himself doing the least bearable work; 'scrounging' and 'winning' were certainly not possible through lack of opportunity, but wangling was in full swing; and if he were particularly young and innocent, which did not apply in Kif's case, his mates took an unholy delight in opening the new-comer's eyes to the wickedness and hardship of the world. Kif bore the dull work and the incredibly dull food with philosophy; he had asked for it; he recognised that. Even if he were still puzzled by his arrival in that *galère*, he admitted that he was paying the inevitable penalty of bad luck and illegal practices. But the monotony ground his philosophy into dust and ashes. He did his best to avoid it by getting himself shifted from one kind of work to another as often as chance offered or could be manufactured; he had not had four years of army service in war-time without learning all that was to be known of self-preservation. But the monotony remained: smothering, maddening, indescribable. He had thought the hours of soap-selling monotonous, but he knew now that they represented the wildest excitement; there was all the world to look at and wonder about, all the crowding petty incident which he had never noticed and which made life bearable. He had rebelled at the moribund life at Tarn, but, even there, there had been the spice of variety; what he had thought of as a smooth sphere was a thing of many facets; a journey to town to-day, to-morrow shedding turnips, at the end of the week a dance; if there was nothing more there was the changing weather. Here there was the same work at the same time with the same faces, the same food, the same surroundings, and the same atmosphere—always. To-morrow and to-morrow and to-morrow. To Kif especially, that was unspeakable misery. He had bouts of cafard which expressed themselves only in an added quiet, but while they lasted warders would look at him a second time and thereafter appear aware of him; and Kif, always quick to notice atmosphere, became aware of their attitude; which was very bad for Kif. He was a bad lot, was he? And they were frightened of him? Well, that was a good jape. No one so far had ever feared him—his hand or his eye or his tongue. And Kif, good-natured, easy-going, not yet twenty-two, found some relief from the awful monotony in the thought that he counted as different from the herd, and in watching the warders watch him.

His biggest anchor to sanity and to his native good-humour he found in the books with which the chaplain supplied him. (Visitors other than the padre he resolutely refused to have, either 'outside' or 'prison'.) They did for him now what they had done at Tarn—created a coloured world in a drab one. The padre was a cheerful Christian with a high ideal of brotherly love and a habit of not listening to what was said to him. He approved of Kif, and though their tastes in literature lay far apart—the chaplain's ideal would have been a mixture of Mrs Hemans and R. M. Ballantyne, and Kif preferred a dash of reality in his mixture—he nevertheless took considerable pains to bring to him what he called 'the nearest to specification'. And Kif approved of him to that extent. He listened politely on the few occasions on which the clergyman was moved to 'say his little piece', as Kif put it mentally; that was his job. The chaplain had been through the war—at Rouen—and liked to think that he understood 'the men'. But he knew nothing about things really, thought Kif. Black was black and white was white to him. He didn't understand things. He wouldn't see—even if he would listen while he was told—that Angel and Danny were decenter really than some of the fat rotters who came to his church, and who had never seen the inside of a cell in their lives, and never would because the things they did weren't punishable by law.

So the padre said his little piece about going straight, and making a new start, and virtue being its own reward (he did not put that last quite so blatantly—even to his intelligence it needed wrapping up), and was never told anything about Collins, or Angel, or—Baba.

Baba! She was as potent in absence as ever her shining aloof presence had been. It was she who defeated Kif's policy of not thinking of things. At nights her pale triangular face hung against the dark, and swam under the closed eyes pressed into his pillow. Baba with her pale turned-back mouth and her white neck, her infinite variety, her givings and withholdings, her boon-companionship; she was a torture to him. He would not think of her! And even while his mind protested, he was remembering for the thousandth time the men he had left with a fair field. They were seeing her, talking with her, dancing with her; and he had not the flimsiest hold over her. Two years. Oh God! What might not happen in two years!

And Kif would fall asleep, worn out, an hour before reveillé, and would start the day in despairing quiet. And the warders would cast that second glance, and Kif would be sardonically amused.

He earned his full remission of sentence, however, belying his reputation. The last three months were almost easy, so wonderful was it to have something to look forward to. Baba had written to him, and Kif had read her characteristically non-committal sentences until he had them by heart; and over his work would shred them carefully phrase by phrase, turn the phrases inside out and shake them for hidden meanings, fit possibilities to them, search behind them, make them new by changing the accented word. There was nothing to tell him what he wanted to know.

His final interview with the governor found him in no mood to listen to sane advice. He was about to be free—free to walk down a road, and smoke a cigarette, and talk to people, and have a drink, and do any blame' thing he liked. The nightmare was behind him, and he'd come out of it well, and he'd take jolly good care he never went back. He had learned a tip or two in his stretch. He would never be so easy again.

'You have behaved very well indeed, Vicar,' the governor said.

He was not in reality at all impressed by Kif's good behaviour. All the hopeless cases behaved exemplarily; it paid them to. He was merely agreeably surprised; they had not expected to find him tractable. Kif had been the subject of no complaints, and had himself complained only once, when the complaint had proved justified. 'I don't know what your plans are, but I want to say that if you find a decent job you will have no trouble from the police. This is your first offence, and there is no reason why it should not be your last.' Kif was admiring the way he clipped out his phrases without waste or preamble. Like Heaton. He rather liked the governor. 'There's the address of people who will help you to a job if you want it. Good-day and good luck!'

At eight o'clock the next morning the gate shut behind Kif's tall figure in a rather creased brown suit, and he stepped into the deserted sunny street half fearful, half expectant.

23

The sunlight fell about him like a garment, and the warm air was a benediction. A July morning and he was free. But he was afraid suddenly. And then he saw the only other occupant of the street. The clothes were unfamiliar and it was a moment before he recognised Angel.

Angel met him with a very little more demonstration than usual, but that little was, in him, significant. His eyes were very blue, and he had *in excelsis* his usual air of having bathed in celestial dew; a true son of the morning.

'Baba's making breakfast,' was all he said. 'I expect you can do with it.'

They sat on a bus-top in the sun, and while Kif watched the vans, the drays, the stray taxis, and the buses of the early morning traffic, Angel sketched the history of the last eighteen months. They had all had influenza; that seemed to be the most important event. And Carroll senior had done two more jobs, and Kif's share was waiting for him; one of them had been a really good one—a jeweller's. And Carroll had disapproved of the percentages he had been given on the last occasions by the fence, and had tried to send the jeweller's stuff straight to Holland. And the ways they had tried and the way that had succeeded. And of course Sammy was out a long time ago, but he was working with a man he had met in prison. He wasn't staying with them.

This last item was a crumb of comfort which sustained Kif through the desert of suspense and inarticulate questioning that lay between him and his meeting with Baba.

The house was cool and empty as they passed through the open door from the already hot street, and there was a faint sizzle of cooking from the kitchen.

'Baba's through there,' said her brother. 'I'll be down in two shakes,' and he disappeared up the stairs.

Kif opened the door of the kitchen with a thumping heart. Baba was standing with her back to him at the frying-pan, rapt in the process of bringing the contents to perfection. She had not heard him, but a second later she turned, wiping a thumb in a long sweep down her green apron, and their eyes met. Kif felt as if he were being hung over a bottomless pit by a piece of gossamer; his throat was dry and his palms were wet. And then her arms were round his neck and he was saying her name unintelligibly into her hair. He forgot his shabbiness—which had worried him when dressing that morning—his doubts, his lack of standing with her, the eighteen months he had been away, everything but the fact that she had welcomed him, and that he had her in his arms. Everything was all right.

'Oh, the fish!' she said suddenly, and drawing herself away from him clutched the pan.

Together they dished the golden fillets, but Kif's teeth did not water at the sight of them. He was occupied in remembering how the tip of her ear curved forward, and being foolishly amazed to find it still so. And the strand of hair that always crept down from the right side of her forehead, it was still there.

Breakfast was a gala meal. The windows were set wide to the street, and a warm air streamed into the cool room over a bowl of sweet peas, moving them gently in its progress, and bearing with it some of their delicate sweetness and the bitter fresh smell of new-sprinkled dust. Kif sniffed it appreciatively. It had some happy association for him, that smell of hot damp dust, but he could not remember what. He ate whatever was put before him—Baba had rolls hot from the oven to mark the occasion—and listened while they talked, answering their questions, and becoming more and more conscious of a subtle difference in their manner, of which they themselves seemed totally unaware. For the first time they were utterly unreserved in his presence, and their welcome to him was a welcome to one of themselves, not to any outsider, however good his standing with them. Mr Carroll had patted him on the shoulder and said: 'Well, my boy, it is very nice to have you back. I have business to talk with you, but that can wait. It is good business.' And he had chuckled bronchially and patted Kif's back again with an affectionate hand. They all lingered over the meal as though nothing in the day mattered but Kif's return. 'The boy' was opening the shop, it seemed. When eventually Mr Carroll departed, Angel remained, smoking placidly and feeding Kif with scraps of information as they happened to come to the surface of his thoughts.

'Danny said to tell you he'd blow in here after six. You don't need to go round to Dormer Street until after tea to-night.'

When Kif had mentioned his rooms Baba had said: 'Oh, Mrs Campany has yours waiting for you.'

'Yes, I must. I must change my clothes. Look at me. Come round with me now. You don't have to go to business just yet.'

'No, but——' Angel looked at his sister. She was extinguishing a cigarette end carefully in the ash-tray (Baba allowed no one to 'muck up the things' with cigarette ash) and as if conscious of the glance she said without looking up:

'Yes, you go along with him.'

Angel still hesitated, but seeing the dawning surprise on Kif's face said: 'All right. But Baba'll come along too. The house can wait for one morning.'

'Yes, but the dinner can't. And Pinkie'll never be cook at the Ritz. You take him along and see he's back sharp at one.'

'Oh, come along, Baba!' Kif said; but she would not be persuaded. She gave him a fleeting kiss as he passed behind her to follow Angel, and pushed him away from her.

'If you're later than one you needn't come back at all,' she said.

'Dance with me to-night?' he asked from the doorway. And she nodded.

As they debouched from Northey Terrace the dizzying racket of the main street staggered Kif. For eighteen months that racket had come to him as a far-away hum. He had listened so often to the low monotone—symbol of all that he was missing—that he had forgotten the mad cacophony of the reality. He felt that he needed the shelter of a dug-out from some incredible barrage, and it was more than ten minutes before he could walk along without being conscious of the row.

Mrs Campany—a tight-mouthed shrunken creature who had 'had misfortunes', and who wore habitually shirt blouses of aggressive stripes which looked still more aggressive on her meagre frame—smiled on Kif with as jubilant an air as her features permitted. She remarked on his look of health, and was going to conduct the returned exile personally into his kingdom when Angel engaged her in talk, so that Kif went alone into the room he had left expecting to come back to one evening more than a year ago.

When Angel followed him he was standing, hat in hand, just inside the door.

'Who is responsible?' he asked, without turning round.

'For goodness' sake say you like it,' said Angel. 'It'll be an awful come-down for them if you don't.'

Kif looked again at the cream walls, the four deep chairs covered in golden-brown loose-covers, the hanging bookshelves filled with books, the three framed prints of thoroughbreds in action done in pastel by a famous sporting artist, the folding oak table with its bowl of yellow roses. He remembered the grey-and-green patterned walls, the bilious tiles in the fireplace—they were fawn now—the mirrored wall-brackets, the unsightly ornaments, the improbable floral carpet which had mocked in its ugliness Baba's gay cretonnes.

'Who did it?' he asked again.

'Well, I think it was Dago's idea originally, but Baba did all the chivvying about what was necessary—and if you'd believe her, there was a whole lot. There were times when I was sort of sorry for the workmen.' Angel smiled his beautiful smile. 'And Dago'd come and say what was wrong, you see, and Baba'd repeat it next day to the folk responsible. It looks all right to me. What do you think?'

Kif put his hat on the table and sat down slowly in one of the round swelling armchairs. 'It's a lot too good to be true,' he said. 'There must be a snag somewhere.'

'Not that I know of. May I smoke in this palace? We owe you much more than this. It's thanks to you the old man got away that night. (The stretch you got was a bit of a shock to him, by the way.) He'll settle up with you for that. But the rest of us . . . Well, I'm glad you like it. Mrs Cam. was tickled to death when it was done, though it took a whole lot of argy-bargy before she'd say go. She's a mule, if ever there was one. . . . You'd better buzz off and change.'

Kif's bedroom was a replica of the sitting-room. Gone was the crazy basket-chair thinly smeared with hard turkey-red cushion and bristling like a porcupine with broken cane, gone the defaced linoleum, gone the drawers reluctant to open and impossible to shut. Kif rummaged happily among the clothes which had been laid in the new chest-of-drawers, finding, as is the way with everyone after a long absence, garments he had forgotten he possessed. It was Angel calling to know if he were still alive that recalled him to passing time, and the impatient one came upstairs and sat on the edge of the bed while he completed his toilet.

141

In that hour Kif felt that the barriers to his knowledge of Angel had been broken down. He knew, too, that they had reached their last reserve—Baba. And that that reserve would for some reason remain.

After the midday dinner it was Mr Carroll who took a holiday while Angel went to business, and Mr Carroll suggested that he and Kif should go up West together. It was almost as if he had guessed Kif's ache to see the town again. As they walked up Piccadilly from Hyde Park Corner Carroll asked him if he had any plans. Kif, who was sniffing the atmosphere delightedly, would have preferred to leave ways and means to a future occasion, but he said:

'I want a job.'

'It would be better,' said Carroll, 'but it won't be easy.'

Kif fumbled in his breast pocket. 'They gave me this,' he said, handing over the address with which the governor had provided him.

Carroll examined it. 'Ah, yes,' he said kindly. It was the tone one uses on being asked to admire a kindergarten drawing. 'Well, there's no harm in trying them.'

'What's wrong with them?' demanded Kif.

'Oh, nothing, nothing,' said Carroll. 'A most excellent institution. Of course,' he added, 'there is no immediate need to find work. There is your share of the last eighteen months still untouched.' He paused pleasantly before delivering his bomb, and then lobbed it gently into the warm afternoon. 'Your share of the Cannon Street business and of the two affairs which, contrary to my custom, I put through alone, amounts to——' and he mentioned the sum.

Kif's eyes opened wide, and the world swung suddenly into a new perspective. A lump sum like that—why, it altered things completely. With that sum he could begin bookmaking again; and presently, if things went well, own horses of his own, make a steady income, have a house on the river—long ago he had decided that when he had a home of his own it should be by the river—and perhaps Baba for his own.

But the delicious mirage faded in the desert of second thought. There would be too many questions to answer if he reappeared on the Turf just now. Everyone in the bookmaking crowd had known that he was a partner in Hough & Collins. He had no evidence to show that he had been a sufferer in the absconding of his two partners. And any inquiry would unearth the fact that he had just served a sentence of hard labour. He could not risk yet that warning-off which would definitely put an end to the hope which he secretly still hugged. But—supposing he got a job and hung on to it?

They were crossing the circus when he came to himself. 'All the same,' he said, as they pushed open a bar door, 'I think I'll look for a job. The busies are too inquisitive.'

Carroll assented with his tolerant air of letting everyone decide their own course. As a Bass and a stone-ginger were set before them—Mr Carroll drank only soft drinks—Kif heard him say: 'Hullo, Sammy!' and swung round with an eagerness he had not meant to betray. Here was the man who had caused him so many tortured moments.

Carroll turned from shaking hands to introduce Kif. Sammy looked at him curiously for a moment and then nodded, but as he and Carroll talked his eyes came back always, curiously, to Kif. Sammy was long and lean, and pale, and loosely put together, with shoulders too square and too flat. He had a thin twisted cynical mouth, rather kindly grey eyes, and a perpetual air of having slept badly. They discussed the failure of the Derby favourite, the possibility of Donoghue's doing the hat-trick next year, the thinness of beer and its iniquitous price—all the subjects, in fact, that are common to bars and clubs.

'I see Murray Heaton was married yesterday,' Sammy said. 'No end of a splash. Duchesses and what not.'

'Oh? Didn't pay much attention to the papers this morning. Who's he married to?'

'Don't know. No one I'd heard of. The chorus as like as not. The duchesses would be all on Murray's side. He was a dam' fine jock.'

'He was. A great jockey. It's a pity he isn't riding now. Were you at Liverpool when he won with Purple Pest on three legs and his hand half chewed off at the wrist?'

They exchanged reminiscences until Kif was moved to give them later news.

'He was a jolly good soldier, too. He was my captain in France.'

At that they turned eagerly to him, and Kif told them stories of Heaton, authorised and apocryphal, until their second glasses were drained. But going home to six o'clock tea at Northey Terrace his mind was occupied more with speculation about Sammy and thoughts of the evening he was going to spend with Baba than with memories of Heaton, though he cast him a friendly thought. (Old Heaton married! Good luck to him! One of the best, Heaton.) Why was there this queer gap of silence in the apparent frankness about Sammy? They all liked him, apparently, and they all talked freely about him, and yet Kif was conscious of an uneasiness in the atmosphere when his name was mentioned.

Danny came in at tea-time, a little more round-shouldered than when Kif had seen him last, but with black eyes alive and friendly, and Kif tried to thank him for what he had done in his rooms.

'Oh, that's Baba's work, not mine,' he said; and as Baba had said, 'Oh, Dago did that,' Kif was left with his thanks undelivered. Kif noticed that his eyes followed Baba as intently as they had on that night more than two years ago, when he had met Danny for the first time. He had it rather badly, poor little devil, Kif thought with a spasm of pity; and he hadn't a chance—not an earthly. And yet what had Baba said about his not being jealous? But he was jealous once. He had been jealous—furiously jealous—that first night, when Kif, the new-comer, had helped Baba in the kitchen. Strange!

Kif helped Baba again to-night, partly to be alone with her, partly because she had to dress afterwards. But the clearing process had so many interludes that the first reason proved to be the only valid one.

'For goodness' sake get a move on,' she said at last, 'or we'll be coming home before we're there.'

She spread a newspaper on the sink and scraped the refuse from the plates into it before consigning them to the water in the basin, and Kif stood by her side drying expertly, his absent eyes on the newspaper.

'It is rumoured that very shortly a new arterial road will be commenced from . . .'

'The state of Mysore has been famous for a generation or more for the statesmanlike character . . .'

'Yesterday at the junction of Bedford Street and the Strand a collision occurred . . .'

'At St. Margaret's, Westminster, yesterday there was solemnised the marriage of Murray Heaton, the famous jockey, horse breeder and trainer, to Miss Ann Barclay, only daughter of Mr and Mrs T. R. Barclay of Golder's Green and granddaughter of . . . large assembly . . . the bride who looked charming wore . . . retinue . . .'

The cup he had been drying crashed on the tiled floor.

'Butter-fingers!'

'I'm sorry. I'm—I—I'm sorry,' he stammered stupidly. Murray Heaton and Ann!

She looked at him surprisedly and said: 'Well, you are a ninny, getting white in the face over a broken cup. You don't suppose it matters really, do you? Even if it did, it's done now.'

'Yes, that's true,' Kif laughed. 'Spilt milk, 'm?' He was still looking at the pieces.

'Well, at least you can pick up the bits!'

'Can I?' He squatted on his heels and began to collect the fragments, laying them in his palm as carefully as though they were fragile and valuable.

'And don't be all night about it. It's nearly eight o'clock. Chuck them in the ash-bin. It's outside the door.'

Kif carried the remains outside and trickled them slowly into the ashes.

As they danced—languidly, for the evening was warm—Baba glanced curiously at him once or twice, and then she said: 'You're tired, aren't you?'

'Well, it's long past my usual bed-time,' he said, but his smile was unconvincing.

'We shouldn't have danced to-night. Let's beat it. I'll come to Eighteen with you.'

She went to collect her wrap and they walked across the park. The cool damp air rose round them from the dim grass, and the lights—the lights of London at the climax of the season—came and went behind the purple brown of the trees. Outside, taxis hooted, the horns of cars called long and low, klaxons choked; but here it was very quiet. Their footsteps sounded in faint thud and swish over the grass.

'Funny to think it was only this morning you came out,' she said.

'Yes.'

144

They took a taxi at the other side of the park and sat in their respective corners without a word, the man abstracted, the girl puzzled.

As they came into his sitting-room she said: 'You do like it, don't you?' and looked at him again with that doubtful glance.

'Oh, rather,' he said. 'Rather!'

As the door closed behind them he sank on to a chair, drawing her down to the arm of it, and buried his face against her shoulder, clinging to her despairingly.

'Baba!' he said 'Oh, Baba!'

Her face cleared. She laughed, and rumpled his dark straight hair.

24

It was a dull hot morning, heavy-aired and full of thunder. Kif, having dutifully reported himself, determined to do the politic thing without delay and provide himself with work of some sort. With considerable curiosity and not much faith he betook himself to the address furnished by the governor. There he was interviewed by a small rotund gentleman who looked like Mr Pickwick—though Kif, who did not read Dickens, was unaware of the fact—and whose benign expression seemed to have something to do with his glasses, for when he removed these appendages for a moment his eyes revealed themselves as hard and shrewd as any lawyer's.

'What have you done in the way of work? Have you a regular profession?'

Kif explained what he had done since the war.

'And before?'

Kif was just about to suppress the farm experience when he recollected that now that the police had his dossier nothing could be hidden any more.

'Ah, farm work!' said the little man, seizing eagerly on the information. 'Now the best thing you can do is to go abroad. I think I can arrange about the fare if you engage yourself for three years. An entirely new start for you and a splendid opening.'

Kif, breaking in, said that he had no intention of going abroad.

'Dear me! and what are your intentions?'

'I want a job in London.'

'And do you know that about ten thousand men are wanting the same thing at this moment?'

'I shouldn't be surprised.'

'And what chance do you think you have of being successful?'

'One in ten thousand.'

'Oh, much less. You forget your disabilities.'

'You mean that I've done time?'

'Exactly.'

'That doesn't prevent me being good at a job.'

'Perhaps not, but it makes you undesirable from an employer's point of view.'

'Oh yes. I forgot. A bad lot, in fact.'

'You must see that in your position it is not possible to pick and choose the kind of work that appeals to you. We take the risk of recommending you, and if you desire to go straight, the work is there for you and the opportunity. We can find you work that you can do, but it is not possible for us to supply the ideal occupation.'

'Oh, I'll do any kind of work provided it's in London,' said Kif cheerfully.

'Why London?' asked his interviewer suspiciously.

'Why not?' said Kif.

'Because,' said the little man, slightly non-plussed by this March Hare attitude, 'it seems to me that it is the worst place for you.'

'It's the only place,' Kif said.

The little man subjected him to a mild stare through his glasses and a keen examination without them, and said at last: 'Come back to-morrow afternoon.'

On the morrow Kif was provided with an introduction to the manager of a garage off the Edgware Road, and for the next six months he earned forty honest shillings a week as washer there from nine to six daily.

The manager had received him without comment beyond explaining the conditions and the work, and had dismissed him to his labours with a casual: 'I expect you'll do all right.' The foreman had not been so reticent. When he had finished a harangue on what was and what was not to be done he added: 'And no tricks. You see, I know all about you.'

'Well, you have the advantage of me,' said Kif, 'but I expect I'll learn all about you in time.' And after that the foreman, except for some nagging, let him alone.

The work was monotonous but cheerful. New faces came and went continually, and Kif found it bearable. He planned to stay there at least a year, by which time he would have earned a recommendation which had no taint of prison about it, and then to make an attempt to get back to the Turf. Without doubt the happiest months of all his life were those he had spent as clerk to Hough & Collins, and he wanted to get back to the life—with a stake in the game. He felt vaguely that the concentrated excitement of one night's 'job' did not compensate for the monotony, however comfortable, in between adventures, and the risk of several years super-boredom thrown in. Life was so short—so short—that he must pack it with the maximum of living. So he was willing to trade twelve months' monotony with Fate for the chance of living the kind of life he wanted afterwards. It was a gamble. And it did not come off.

He was hosing a car after coming back from his mid-day meal one muddy December day when Rice, the foreman, appeared and said: 'Hand it over before there's trouble. We don't want the place to get a bad name just through you.'

'What are you talking about?'

'I'm telling you to hand over that fur. The lady who left the Daimler this morning left it in the dickey and it's gone.'

'Well, she should have locked the thing.'

'You have a nerve. Have you pawned it already? If not, hand it over.'

Kif was stammering with rage. 'Do you actually think I'd touch a mangy bit of ratskin——'

'It's sable,' said the literally minded Rice.

'What do you think I am? A shop-lifter?'

'I don't know what your department in thieving is, but I do know you're a dam' jailbird, and we've no use for you here.'

'Nor I for you,' said Kif, and hit him. 'Take that.'

He picked up the hose he had dropped, turned off the water and, having removed the hose to its appointed place, rolled down his sleeves.

'I'll have you up for assault,' said Rice, hugging his jaw.

'Do,' said Kif, 'and I'll sue you for libel. You can tell the boss I've quit.'

But he met the manager at the office door on the way out.

'I'm going, sir,' he said. 'Every time someone's mislaid a spanner since I came here they looked sideways at me, and now someone's lost a fur, and I'm supposed to be able to produce it. They didn't teach conjuring in quod.' He turned up his coat collar preparatory to braving the winter atmosphere.

'That's a pity, Vicar,' said the manager. 'Don't you think you have been too thin-skinned, perhaps? There's bound to be a lot to put up with for a little. You'd find things easier after a bit, I'm sure. Think it over!'

'Well, I've just landed the foreman one,' said Kif.

'Oh?' the manager's eyes were almost amused. 'Hit Rice, have you? In that case I think perhaps it would be better for you to go. Your resignation is accepted with regret. Come into the office, and I'll give you what is owing to you.'

'There's nothing owing to me,' said Kif. 'Thanks all the same.' And he moved away.

'All right, Vicar. If you ever want a job in the future, come and see me.'

Kif was halfway down the street before it occurred to him that the manager had accepted without question his implied statement that he knew nothing of the theft.

Kif made three more attempts to earn the recommendation he hankered after. One was in a garage, and one was as packer in a West End store, but in both places his history leaked out, and things were made very much more unbearable than they had been under Rice. Indeed his fellow packers—youths of nineteen and twenty who had been just too young to see active service—struck work when they found that the management, who knew Kif's record, expected them to work with a 'convict'. They weren't over particular, they said, but they had their pride. So Kif went.

A week later by a piece of sheer luck he obtained work as traveller to a firm of crimped-case makers. This he secured through his own efforts, and, afraid that if he enlisted the aid of the only people who would vouch for him the truth might cause a rebuff, he resorted mistakenly to covering his tracks by inventing a past for himself. He had been in Ireland for the last two years, he said, and though he had done travelling work, he had lost his job when the firm went phut. But before that he had been with Vidor & Pratt, the soap people.

He risked that scrap of truth, hoping that the London address would be sufficient to reassure them without further investigation. Once more it was a gamble, and this time it came off. An agent had died suddenly and they were in a hole. Kif was given his credentials, his samples, and was sent out. He spent a busy and profitable five days among the bakers and confectioners of the suburbs, and though he disliked the work he was elated as he turned in to the office to report on Saturday morning at the prospect of keeping it. The distributing manager was complimentary and pleased, and Kif received his paltry pay with more satisfaction than he had ever had on taking the contents from a safe. He had one ambition, and one only: a clean sheet for a year, and then the Turf. And he had what looked like a chance.

He went out of the office with his head in the air, brushed past another of the salesmen coming in to report, and went downstairs three at a time.

The new-comer stood looking after him and then came slowly in to the desk.

'Who was that?' he asked.

'Our new man on Denny's round.'

'Was he ever with Vidor & Pratt, the soap people, do you know?'

'Yes, why?'

'Because I was with them too. Is his name still Vicar?'

On Monday morning by the first post Kif received a note saying that Messrs Blewbury would require his services no longer, and enclosing a cheque in lieu of notice; and when Kif went to the office to attempt an explanation and understanding the office boy assured him that the manager was out.

'What kind of out?' Kif asked.

'You know,' said the boy. '*Wash*out.'

Meeting Kif's eyes he instinctively lifted his elbow in a protective gesture, but Kif turned on his heel and walked away. Down on the pavement again he stood looking through a mist of anger at the world. He felt physically sick with rage and disappointment. He grabbed the rail of the bus he boarded as if he would wrench it from its socket. From its top he viewed Holborn, shining after a spring shower, in unseeing bitterness. He was finished. Never again would he subject himself to that, even to get the thing he wanted most. There were other things in life besides the best. He had had high-falutin notions, that was what was wrong. And life was too short for high-falutin. He would take the best of what came his way from now on, but he wasn't going to sweat blood for anything. Nothing was worth that.

As they came into Oxford Street his eyes lighted on a familiar doorway and woke to intelligent vision. That was where he had run into Angel that morning two—three years ago now. He remembered his cracked boots, his soaking clothes, his semi-starvation and weariness. Well, thank God he didn't have to go back to that. He had learned a thing or two since then.

Over a very good lunch in Regent Street he continued to review the situation. He had been a fool, anyhow, to save the money Carroll had banked for him. Look what had happened last time he put all his eggs in one basket. As for his dreams of making Baba his wife, that too was a wash-out. If anything she cared less for him now than when she first refused to consider marriage with him. He would hold her better by a present prodigality than by any glory to come. He realised that now. And as for racing, there were other ways of enjoying the Turf besides bookmaking. There was nothing to hinder his going racing any day as a private individual.

But he knew suddenly and quite certainly that he would never do that. The second-best theory did not apply to this. A sick stab shot through him. He got up hastily, paid his bill, and went out.

At Northey Terrace he found Baba poised in front of the living-room mirror engaged in deciding the most suitable situation for the *boutonnière* which was to be the finish of her toilet. At sight of Kif she arrested the dabbing movements with which she was pursuing her experiments and said in surprise:

'Hullo! I thought you were selling paper frills.' In her voice was the faint scorn—a scorn so faint as to make even its existence doubtful—with which she invariably referred to his attempts at work. Her attitude had annoyed Kif without dismaying him—he still took his own line in most things; now he was almost unaware of it. For once it coincided with his own view of the matter; he had been a fool.

'Wash-out,' he said. 'But I've got a week's pay for nothing. They gave me that rather than see my face again. Were you going out with anyone?'

'No, I was just going shopping.'

'Well, it's too late for a matinée. Let's go and have tea somewhere.'

He pinned the *boutonnière* on the under side of the lapel for her and they sallied forth together. It dawned gradually on Baba that the Kif by her side was not the Kif she had known yesterday. He no longer hankered after straight jobs for no earthly reason. (Kif had never told Baba of his great ambition; that, quite typically, he would have kept to himself until it was on the point of realisation.) And there was in the recklessness of his expenditure a suggestion of celebration which she did not understand.

'Are we celebrating something?' she asked at last, having revolved the matter and arrived at no conclusion.

'We're blowing my last pay,' said Kif succinctly.

'Oh? Have the employment agencies turned you down for good?'

'No, the other way about.'

'Oh!' She thought for a little, and then smiled at him dazzlingly. 'I think Father's been missing you. He says he's getting old, and that's something new for the old boy.'

Mr Carroll had refrained from the day on which Kif obtained his first work from suggesting his participation in any 'job'. Kif was, in fact, ignorant as to whether in the nine months that had passed since then, Carroll had worked at all. (It may be said here that he had not.) Baba's remark was meant as encouragement to a prodigal, but Kif changed the subject abruptly. His only interest at the moment, it seemed, was to spend what he had received that morning; to buy things for her. And in that Baba came happily to his assistance.

A week later Kif and Mr Carroll did a job in Grafton Street, the staff-work of which had been simmering pleasantly in Carroll's brain for six months or so. The job, which occupied them from Saturday night until early on Monday morning, involved a dizzy climb to the roof of a five-storey building, a promenade over two neighbouring roofs, the breaking of a skylight, the lowering of themselves into a questionable dark, the forcing of two doors, the boring of a hole in the floor of an office, through which they dropped to their goal below. In this last drop Carroll slipped and broke two fingers of his right hand. He splinted them with Kif's help, handed over his tools, and with Kif's coat and his own settled himself comfortably in a near-by corner. 'This is your affair, my boy,' he said. And after that he said nothing; he watched in silence. And Kif faced the safe in that mixture of pride and trepidation of a small boy who has been asked for the first time to come out to the floor and do the sum on the board for all to see; the board looks queerly perpendicular and the floor as big as a desert, but he knows how to do the sum! Kif went to work unhurriedly, his hands choosing and rejecting with their habitual neat deliberation, his reckless eyes absent, absorbed. When the door of the 'fire and burglar proof' swung on its hinges, he turned suddenly to the silent Carroll and smiled a whimsical smile that was very good to see.

'After you, sir,' he said, with a little gesture of his hand to the yawning door.

Carroll's mild blue gaze caught and reflected his pupil's laughter.

'I congratulate you,' he said. 'That was as pretty work as I ever did myself.' And he came over to inspect the contents with the gratified air of one accepting an invitation.

The safe contained two ledgers, share certificates, a letter written by a famous society hostess to an actor, and ten pounds.

Carroll, who had made no secret of his hope of from two to three thousand pounds as the result of the week-end's work, said: 'Dear, dear! Who would have thought it!' And at the inadequacy of the remark Kif, whose mind was already thronging with curses, sat back on his heels and laughed helplessly.

Carroll pocketed the bank-notes, examined the ledgers to see that there was nothing of value between their pages, and came back to the letter. They both knew by reputation the woman who had written it, a diplomat's wife, liked and respected both by her own crowd and by her more casual acquaintances. Since the owner of the safe was not a friend of the lady and since the letter was exceedingly compromising, its preservation could only be for blackmail. Carroll, having read it a second time, lit a match and applied it to a corner of the sheet.

'I didn't know he was as black as that,' he observed mildly, as he powdered the last ash to dust with a plump forefinger. 'Let us have some sandwiches.'

'Yes, but—' Kif paused, weighing one of Baba's neat little packets in a contemplative hand.

'But what?'

'She won't know that it doesn't exist any longer. He'll just go on as if it were there.'

'Yes. Quite true. I hadn't thought of that.'

'Let's write and tell her it's gone up in smoke.'

'And present the police—— Oh, but of course—I see. Yes, we could do that. Yes, certainly we could do that.'

It was Sunday afternoon, and broad daylight, and there was no hope of making their escape for nine or ten hours yet, and they settled happily to the composition of a letter which would inform their host's victim that she need be a victim no longer. By the time they had finished the production—execrably typed by Kif on their host's paper—they both felt friendly and warm toward the woman they had never seen, as one does to a life one has saved.

'MADAM' (they wrote):

'This is to inform you that we have to-day, Sunday, March 4th, at the above address destroyed a letter written by you which we found in the course of our business. We feel sure that you will be glad to know what has become of it, and since we do not believe that the late owner would be anxious to inform you we have taken it upon ourselves to do it. We also undertake never to mention the existence of the said document, though for obvious reasons we refrain from signing our names.'

The style was Carroll's, but the moving spirit was Kif's, and I have reproduced the letter so that the woman, if ever her eyes light on this page, may know the story of the boy whose idle thought brought her out of hell.

They amused themselves with the ledgers until the early quiet of a Sunday night had settled on the streets and they deemed it safe to make their get-away. To retrace their steps with their impedimenta and the handicap of Carroll's maimed hand was an uneasy business, and Kif breathed a sigh of relief as they dropped safely to the deserted pavement of a yard and walked out unchallenged into the street. As he let himself into 18 Dormer Street in the chill dark of the early morning he was sleepy and tired, but satisfied for the moment. There had been no tangible reward for all their effort, but that did not matter much; he had had twenty-four hours of very good entertainment.

So Kif drowned in the excitement of adventure the forlorn ache that ate sometimes like a toothache into his indifference, and between times did his best to ignore it. He took to spending his mornings in and out of the West End bars with one or another of 'the crowd', spotting winners, discussing the day's news, and exchanging mild drinks, exactly as his more fortunate fellows were doing all along Piccadilly, St. James' Street and Pall Mall. Baba, who had disapproved strenuously but ineffectually of the washing and packing jobs—she had found the pliant Kif as malleable as stone when he so pleased—was delighted at the change. This was Kif as she would have him; well dressed—her interest in the dongareed Kif had waned perceptibly—and possessed of leisure and money. And presently Kif, almost unconsciously, resigned himself to his milieu. The Carrolls and their friends were the only constant quantity in a life that lacked foundation; and his natural egotism was satisfied by being accepted as one of themselves and a personality. He accompanied Baba here and there when she expressed a wish to be squired—to the Old Bailey or to one of the sale-rooms which she haunted—but usually he was to be found in one or another of the rendezvous of his acquaintances.

To provide the necessary spice in such a life he betted cheerfully and recklessly on anything that provided an adequate gamble, and when he was unlucky went short until the tide turned. In the following November—almost a year after Kif's final attempt to tread the path of his ambition—Carroll and he had planned a raid on the house of a Levantine diamond merchant who lived with a plump, famous, and notoriously unfaithful wife at Kew. It was the first 'villa' affair that Kif had taken part in since Carroll had screwed up the scullery window on that wet night more than three years ago; most of Carroll's business was concerned with office safes and jeweller's premises. The layout had been studied with the care that Carroll habitually gave to preparing the plan of attack—he did few jobs, but those he did were perfect. Mrs Lisman was in Biarritz at the moment, and her maid was on holiday. Mr Lisman dined at home every night except on Thursdays, when he attended some weekly festivity and returned home between two and three o'clock just sufficiently sensible to be able to put himself to bed. There were three maids and a butler, all of whom retired at eleven, when the butler went round switching off lights and locking up. One of the maids had insomnia, but she was also dull of hearing. There was a burglar alarm of a well-known and almost infantine design, and a safe on which Mr Carroll was itching to try his quality. It had been agreed that on a certain Thursday Carroll and the safe would try conclusions, but on the previous Tuesday Carroll developed influenza. Since postponement would mean that the attempt would be hampered by the returned Mrs Lisman—who had no habits—only impulses, and whose comings and goings were incalculable, Carroll after some persuasion agreed to let Kif, who was broke and correspondingly eager, attempt the work himself. Angel was hot and shivering and obviously sickening for the same malady as his father, and was therefore no help. So Kif was given one or two of Carroll's most precious possessions to supplement his own equipment, and departed from Northey Terrace in the early afternoon with these and Carroll's blessing. He spent the evening at Danny's rooms, but Danny, who seemed restless and depressed, did not share his jubilation over the night's work.

Kif wondered if he were annoyed that he had not been asked to take Carroll's place, and then dismissed the thought as being not in accordance with the evidence where Danny was concerned. Jealous of his own he might be, but envy did not exist in him.

'Are you sickening for 'flu too?' he asked as he was departing with two books.

'Don't think so,' said Danny. 'Got the hump just.'

'None of the various theories any good to-night?' Kif grinned.

'Not a bit. Everyone comes up against the fact of luck in the end. They've all tried to explain it away, and no one's ever succeeded. It's just there and you can't dodge it. A monstrous iniquity. And no theories are any use.'

'Have ten grains of aspirin,' said Kif, but his hand on Danny's shoulder had an affectionate touch.

'I wish you'd call it off to-night,' Danny said for the third time.

'You are an old grouch,' Kif said. 'And that reminds me—lend me your automatic. I almost forgot to ask you. My old gat weighs half a ton, and I can't afford to give away weight to-night—even if I did beat Angel on points the other night. Did you hear that? We sparred six rounds . . . What?'

'I say don't carry a gun at all to-night. It's much safer not.'

'Safer for who?' Kif grinned again. 'Don't be afraid. I'm not going to use it. But if presenting it is going to make a good get-away out of a tight place for me I'd be a fool not to take it. You don't imagine I'm going back there' he jerked his head vaguely to indicate prison, 'if I can help it?'

So Kif left Danny's rooms with the automatic in one pocket and two books under his arm.

At Number Eighteen he collected a muffler, an attaché case and an umbrella—the twin of Delilah—and laid the two books on the table by his bed, where Danny found them long afterwards.

25

It was nearly one when he found himself in the garden of the house at Kew. It was a dark night, with a light frost and no wind. The house was in complete darkness—a mere thickening in the blackness in front of him—but in his head was a clear and accurate map of his surroundings. He moved over the grass, avoiding the beds as though he could see them, until he came to the edge of the carriage-sweep. He followed that on the grass until he reckoned that he had left the carriageway behind and had only a path between himself and the house. He crossed that slowly. The paths, he knew, were made of exceedingly fine bright

153

red sand. As he took each step he obliterated the mark of the last by a scuffling movement of his toe. His gloved hand touched the wall, and he felt along it for the beginning of the study window. It was longer in coming than he had anticipated, and for a moment he was afraid that he had lost his bearings after all. And then his hand slid into nothingness where a moment before there had been brick; he was all right. Six or seven minutes' work at the window, six seconds with the burglar alarm, and he lifted a cautious leg over the sill, laid his case on the floor, and stepped into the centrally heated warmth of the house.

He stood there listening. The door of the room must be open because he could hear the pompous thud-thud of the hall clock. Another ticked fussily near at hand, on the mantelpiece, presumably. Still he waited. There was another ticking, sharp and irregular, that puzzled him, until a sharper report than usual enlightened him; it was the cooling cinders of a dead fire. Still he waited, standing by the tall curtain, a cold light air at the back of his neck, the warm cigar-scented atmosphere of the house in his nostrils. Nothing stirred. In all the night nothing stirred but the two clocks, one agitated and one aloof. Gently he pulled the heavy silk curtains across the window and took out his torch. It lighted a small table set with a siphon and sandwiches. So this was where old Lisman ate on his return if he were sober enough. Well, that was not often, and in any case he would be away by then.

He moved carefully to the open door and stood there looking into the dark hall, listening. Not a movement. He closed the door soundlessly, switched on the light, and returned to his case. He knew where the safe was, perfunctorily hidden by a marqueterie bureau; Mr Lisman relied more on the workmanship of the safe than on any subtlety in concealment. If he cracked this it would be a feather in his cap, and Carroll would have to admit that the pupil was nearly as good as the master. He looked at the drinks wistfully for a moment but decided against them. Apart from the necessity of keeping a clear head, he wanted, if he did the job neatly, to leave the fact of the robbery unsuspected as long as possible.

He had been working for perhaps ten minutes when a dull thud sounded somewhere. He stopped instantly, his ears strained, his eyes on the door. Would he have time to get to the switch before the door opened? '*Now* you're going to be caught! Now you're going to be caught!' chattered the clock exultantly. But nothing happened. The silence hung thick and still as ever.

And yet that thud had sounded in the house somewhere. He drew Danny's automatic from his pocket and laying it within easy reach resumed his work. For two minutes he worked; and then everything happened at once.

He heard the breeze of the door opening, and turned to see Lisman, apparently perfectly sober, his hands in his coat pockets, surveying him and saying: 'Oh, you vould, vould you!' He saw Lisman see the automatic, reached out his hand for it, saw the army revolver appear as if by magic in Lisman's hand, heard the report of it, and heard something sing beyond the open window in the night. And even as the report came he had fired instinctively—as instinctively as he would have fired on the enemy confronted suddenly in patrol—and he saw Lisman sag at the knees and drop.

His first feeling, staring at the obscene bundle of flesh, was anger at the wrecking of his night's work, his second was realisation of the need to get away. In ten seconds the household would be awake. He crammed the precious tools into the case, risked the loss of several seconds to put out the light, and was through the window and running across the lawn before the first light appeared in an upstairs window.

God! he had put his foot into it this time.

There were footsteps coming from the gate to meet him. Someone from the lodge. He had forgotten the lodge. He pulled himself up. The steps had started to run. He was being hemmed in between the house and the gate. He wheeled sideways and made across the garden to the far side-boundary. There were pear-trees against the wall, he remembered. Hampered by the dark and the case to which he still clung, he climbed the wall, his sensitive hands feeling ahead of him, and dropped down the other side into soft mould. He bent and felt. A flower-border. He took two steps straight ahead of him on to grass, obliterating his footsteps as he went. Where now? The front way would be too unhealthy. But he had to put as big a space between himself and Lisman's as soon as possible. The telephone would be busy. He would have to risk it. He could not remember where the gate lay, but he knew where the road was, and made for that, stumbling over shrubs and afraid to show a light. There seemed to be no gate. To and fro he went in the blackness, desperate and trapped. But there *was* a gate; it had been part of the knowledge he and Carroll had gathered in their preparation, that gate. He would have to use his presser. Not using it was just a fad of Carroll's. There was no time. . . .

And then he came on the gate. It was unlocked. He was through, walking down the open naked road at a pace as leisured as he could make it. It took the whole force of his will to keep his rising heels in subjection. The effort exhausted him as a physical strain would have done. At each step he felt that another at the same rate was more than he could achieve. And yet they went on, those difficult even paces.

Someone was coming in front. A man. They had passed. He had done it. This hell of a street ended in another hundred yards. At the end of this wall. No, that man was coming back. Looking round he saw the flicker of a half-touched torch in the man's hand. His heart leaped sickeningly. There was no time to think. Without stopping he heaved the case over the high wall at his side and heard the 'hush' as it dropped into some shrubbery. In a moment the man behind overtook him and the torch-light ran over him.

'Late to be out, isn't it?'

Kif stopped. 'What d'you say? Do you mind taking that beastly thing off my face?' He felt surreptitiously in his pocket for the automatic—the mere feel of it would give him courage. It was no longer there. God! he had dropped it somewhere. Where had he dropped it?

'Sorry, sir,' said the constable, pacified by his inspection of Kif's clothes, his lack of impedimenta and his Barclay manner. 'We've got to be careful in this district. Too many good hauls lying about for us to take any chances.'

Kif made his stiff lips smile. 'That's all right, constable. Cold work on a night like this.'

'You may say that, sir! And beginning to snow, too.'

It was, but Kif was aware of a much more portentous phenomenon; the hum of a motor filled the night in a rapid crescendo. He must get away.

'Well——' he said, beginning to move on.

'Have you got the right time about you, sir? The cold's made mine crazy, I think.'

As they compared watches a car whizzed round the corner and came to a sudden halt with a squeal of brakes a yard or two past them.

'What's this? What's this?' said an irritated voice, and a man came to them from the car. The constable, seeing the shape of a police-helmet in the rear of the car, said:

'I was just making sure of the time from this gentleman, sir.'

'You on the beat?'

'Yes, sir.'

'There's been trouble at sixty-four. Who's this?'

'I was making my way home when the officer thought he had better make sure of my respectability,' said Kif. With the only part of him that was still capable of emotion, he prayed that the new-comer would be content with the dim backwash of light from the head-lights.

But the new-comer took the torch from the constable and turned it on Kif's face with a quick flash up and down his person. 'What are you doing here, and where have you——' he stopped. Then with a change of tone he said:

'Do you mind taking off your hat for a moment?'

There was nowhere to run to. The constable was on his left, and the new-comer on his right. At his back was the wall. Kif removed his hat.

'Well, well, Vicar! This is a pleasure. It's a long time since we met, but I remember it very well. *Very* well. You've become quite well-known since then.'

'I don't know what you're talking about,' said Kif, utterly without hope.

'No? Well, you'd better come along with us, and we can have further explanations in a warm station. It's a cold night.'

'Are you arresting me?'

'That's what I'm doing.'

'But you have nothing against me. You can't arrest me just on spec.'

'Nothing against you!—*Hayward!*—That's good, from an old lag like you! What about acting suspiciously, just for a go-off? Are you strolling round Kew at two in the morning for your health? You and your respectability! That's a good one. Put your hands up. Run him over, Hayward.'

'Nothing,' reported Hayward, having examined Kif.

156

'Well, we're not taking any chances. Put these on him. He ruined one of my best collars once.'

'Get in!' he added, and Kif got silently and despairingly into the car between the two men, and while the man on the beat stood on the foot-board, they were borne back to the Lisman gate.

'You take him to the station,' said Wilkins, 'and come back for me.' He disappeared into the lodge gate with the constable, and Hayward escorted Kif to the police-station in the car.

26

Baba was cutting up steak for beef-tea and listening to an account of scandal in high life as recounted by Pinkie's successor, whose brother was a footman in the best circles, when Mrs Campany arrived, her thin face flushed and her expression a mixture of dismay and importance. Mr Vicar had not been in all night, and this morning two plain-clothes men had come and searched his rooms.

Baba gaped at her, obviously trying to drag her mind from the delightful inconsequence of Lady Blank's indiscretions to the contemplation of immediate trouble. When Mrs Campany had told all she knew—which was very little, since the officers had been uncommunicative—and had some of the importance wiped from her face by Baba's unrestrained scorn of the meagreness of her information, Baba stood looking long at the chopped and oozing fragments under her knife, and then said:

'All right. Have some tea. Gladys'll give you some. I'll see what can be done.'

She poured some soup into a bowl, and leaving Mrs Campany to be fortified by Gladys went upstairs to her brother's room on the second floor. There was no help in her father—he was really ill this morning, and she was waiting for the doctor—but perhaps Angel would have some ideas, even if he had a temperature.

Angel turned his flushed face on the pillow, and seeing the steaming bowl said: 'Oh, give me something cold, there's a good kid,' and then immediately: What's the matter?'

She set down the bowl beside him. 'They've got Kif.'

Angel started upright, gazed incredulously at her, and sank back with a groan of dismay.

'Oh, hell! . . . How d'you know?'

Baba explained.

157

'Nothing in the papers?'

'No.'

'Perhaps they haven't got him. Perhaps he's just lying low. What did they search his rooms for? He's probably got away. You'd better go round and warn Dago though. Oh, Lord! what a mess! And everyone tied by the leg!'

When Baba asked Barney, the half-Irish half-Italian owner of the hair-dressing establishment where Danny worked, if she could see Danny he was delighted to oblige Miss Carroll, and Dago would be sent for immediately. He ushered her into a small room and left her.

One glance at Danny's dark face when he appeared was all that Baba needed.

'How do you know?' she asked. 'Has he been to you?'

'No, I'm afraid they've got him.'

'Then how did you know?'

'It's in the paper.' He pulled forward a chair and pushed her gently into it.

'What did it say? Did they get him with the stuff on him?'

'Haven't you seen a paper?' he asked.

'No, Mrs Cam. came round to say he hadn't been home, and that they'd searched his rooms this morning. So we hoped he'd got away. How do you know he didn't? What does it say?'

Danny went out and came back with the latest edition of the morning paper.

'You'd better read it,' he said.

GREEK MERCHANT MURDERED AT KEW
Mr Lisman shot

'Oh, Danny, he *hasn't*!'

'You'd better read it,' he said again gently.

At an early hour this morning, Mr Lisman, the well-known diamond merchant of —— Street, was shot dead by burglars whom he had interrupted in the course of their operations. According to his butler, Mr Lisman had returned from an evening engagement rather earlier than usual. That he was aware of the presence of the intruders is indicated by the fact that he was grasping in his hand a heavy service revolver, which was contrary to his habit, and which he must have fetched from his bedroom. One shot had been fired from this weapon, but had apparently missed Mr Lisman's assailants. The thief or thieves made their escape from the garden by a side wall, and in their haste dropped an automatic revolver which is regarded as a valuable clue. Nothing was missing from the safe, which had not been opened, though the attempt showed the work of an expert.

Mrs Lisman, who is at present in the south of France, is a well-known beauty. It is understood that an arrest has been made.

Baba's eyes, stony as green agate, were once more on Danny. He moved uneasily.

'Don't mind so much, Baba,' he said. 'They may not have him.'

She was still speechless.

158

'They always say that about an arrest being made.'

'No, they don't,' she said, 'and you know it. When they have nothing they say a clue. They've got him. And there's nothing we can do. There's Tommy and Father in bed with flu' and no one to do anything!'

'There's me,' said Danny.

'Yes, there's you, but what can you do?'

'I'll do whatever I can. You believe that, don't you?'

'Of course I do,' she said impatiently. 'We all will. I'll have to go back to Father and Tommy. Oh, Kif! Why did he!'

She left Danny, a mournful little figure, without a backward glance, bought the later morning papers, and took the truth home to Angel.

Angel's aghast blue eyes lifted from the welter of shrieking headlines to his sister, rocking herself in pent emotion on the edge of his bed.

'Old Kif!' he said. 'What a damned mess!'

'The fool! Oh, the fool!' she said between her teeth.

Angel was cogitating.

'Look here,' he said at last, 'if they haven't got him, by any chance, let's say he was here all last night. You can say he stayed to help look after Dad.'

'Not I!' she said. 'Do you take me for a fool?'

Angel looked genuinely astonished. 'Why?' he asked. 'What are you afraid of?' And as she did not answer immediately he added with a twist of his mouth: 'Your reputation?'

'Now *you're* being a fool. No one can prosecute me for my reputation. But I'm not going to find myself in the dock for perjury.'

'You wouldn't risk that even for Kif?'

'I wouldn't risk it for *anyone*. Why should I? I didn't ask him to do that job at Kew and make a fool of himself by killing someone, did I?'

'No, but you'd go dancing on the proceeds,' said her brother brutally. 'He's taken all the risks so far, and you've had the good times. It's surely up to you to take a risk to help him out of as tight a place as this?'

'Not that risk,' she said. 'Think again!'

Angel lay and looked at her in a half-curious disgust. 'Well, I always thought even the rottenest women did decent things when they were stuck on a man.'

'Oh, shut up,' she said, 'you make me tired. Put your great brain to some use instead of playing parson.'

She picked up the untouched bowl of cold soup and went out.

Angel lay looking at the closed door for a moment or two, clutching his head with feverish hands in an attempt to think clearly, and then he got slowly but determinedly out and began to dress. Baba found him there, half-dressed and only half conscious, an hour later, and her rage knew no bounds.

That afternoon Danny, very well brushed and neat, walked into what he always referred to as his favourite police-station. It was not clear whether his liking for it was due to its familiarity, its locality, or the shade of the paint on the walls. He found Wilkins there in earnest talk with the sergeant.

159

'Hullo, Dago!' said Wilkins, friendly but surprised. 'I've just sent for you. You haven't had my message already?'

'No, I've come to save you trouble by giving myself up.'

'Oh? What for? Have you killed someone at last? I always said you'd do it some day.'

'Yes. I killed Lisman. And you know it.'

'I know nothing of the sort. When did this happen? Lisman seems to have been a popular sort of target.'

'I don't know what you're trying to pull. You've found my gun, haven't you! And it's just my luck that you happen to know it's mine.'

'Oh yes, I know the gun's yours. It's the one I took from you that night at d'Agostino's. But you didn't kill Lisman, all the same.'

'Why? Isn't he dead?'

'Because at a quarter to one your long-suffering landlady went up to ask you to stop playing your fiddle, and Lisman was killed about one-fifteen.' Wilkins smiled triumphantly.

Danny's eyes, which had been unfathomable black pools, became suddenly hunted things.

'You don't know my landlady,' he said in a moment. 'She'd perjure her immortal soul if she thought it would keep her house respectable. I think you'd better arrest Mrs Frazer too. Or will you let her off now that you have me?'

Wilkins ignored him. 'When did you give your gun to Vicar?'

'Never,' said Danny. 'He has one of his own,' and bit his too-ready tongue.

'Quite so,' said the inspector. 'It was reposing all last night in his collar drawer.'

'He doesn't carry one,' Danny said, trying to retrieve his error.

'No, just keeps it to look at,' agreed Wilkins facetiously.

'Look here,' said Danny, beginning to draw one hand through the other, 'you've got a perfectly good confession with perfectly good evidence. I was there—with another chap—and I shot the fat rotter. Isn't that enough for you?'

"Fraid not, Dago. There was only one in the business last night, and your feet are three sizes too small. Besides, we've got all we want. Vicar was charged this morning. Do you mind identifying this as your property?' He produced the automatic.

'Of course it's my property! I've said so.'

'Well, when did you give it to Kif Vicar?'

'I didn't.'

'Was Vicar with you last night?'

'Yes'

'Till when?'

'About eleven.'

'What did he come for?'

'He often comes.'

'And he took nothing away with him?'

'Yes, he had two books.'

160

'Oh?' The inspector grinned. '*Three Weeks*, and *How To Open a Safe*.'

'No,' said Danny indifferently, 'a *Heraclitus* and a *Sophocles*.'

The inspector's grin vanished. 'Well, you'll hear further from me, I expect. It has still to be discovered how Vicar had that gun.'

'I've been offering you the explanation, but you don't want it.' Danny buttoned his coat, and the inspector watched him curiously.

'What makes you so keen to go through the drop?' he asked as Danny turned to go.

'I thought I might as well have the honour and glory of croaking that fat swine. But you're so —— particular.'

And Danny went out into the grey afternoon.

27

The shooting of Philip Lisman created a sensation without any adventitious aids; for once the press came panting in the rear of public interest. Lisman was well known—and universally disliked—in London, and Mrs Lisman was famous throughout Britain and a large section of Western Europe. The trial for murder of the man who was said to have shot him became a *cause célèbre*. In those days Angel lost for ever the bloom which had made his beauty the singular thing it was. He became merely a good-looking youth who dressed well; his clothes no longer looked mundane and incongruous. Mr Carroll too had lost something which could not be accounted to the after-effects of influenza; and Danny looked like one crucified. Only Baba flourished among the horror and the strain and the fight against despair which occupied the men around her. Instead of being involved in the squalor of an obscure murder trial, as she had feared, she found herself a central figure in a case of intense public interest. She therefore forgave Kif his criminal folly and spoke kindly and affectingly of him. When an admiring reporter said: 'It's on the stage you should be!'—he referred to her looks, not to her histrionic ability—she played with the thought and turned over the possibilities in secret delight. She would become famous one day, see if she didn't.

The combined resources of the two Carrolls and Danny proved insufficient to brief the greatest criminal lawyer of his time, Stanley Arden-Davis, in whom lay what seemed their only hope. Mr Carroll, making an attempt to see the great man and perhaps get him to accept what was the most they could offer, was met by the bland refusal of his secretary, and the assurance that the case did not present sufficiently interesting features to make defence worth while. At least, that is how it sounded in Carroll's ears. It was Murray Heaton who proved the god from the machine and gave Kif all the chance that remained to him. He came, grave, self-possessed, solicitous, into their hot distress and helplessness and 'got things done' as of old. He interviewed Arden-Davis, pointed out the popularity of the case, guaranteed his fee, and left that famous man cancelling an engagement.

When he was ushered into the visitors' room he occasioned the first spark of real interest that Kif's face had shown since the hand-cuff closed round his wrist in the light of Wilkins' torch. He shook hands warmly, as one war veteran with another.

'I came along,' he said, 'to see if I could do anything. I didn't know until last night that you were a friend of Ann's. I had forgotten that you and Tim used to be chummy. I've just been to see Arden-Davis and he'll undertake the wangling business for you. You seem to be always butting into trouble. Last time it was that little —— of a corporal—forget his name—who had to be saved from your clutches.'

'Blyth,' said Kif. 'Well, that wasn't exactly the last time.'

'Oh? What have you been doing since then?' Heaton sat down as one would sit down to chat with a club acquaintance, and when the warder indicated that time was up they were discussing the best method of making a sprinter into a stayer, and Heaton had learned the salient points of Kif's history since his discharge from the army, and had guessed the rest with his uncanny accuracy.

He shook hands again and said that he would come as often as he could wangle it. 'Tim's in Canada, but we expect him back in about a fortnight. Ann said to give you her good wishes and to say to keep your pecker up.'

The door clanged, and Kif came back from the atmosphere of cheerful good-fellowship and legitimate adventure to the realisation of his loneliness. Ann had sent him that message, but it was a small weak echo in the cold vastness that his life had become. It was meaningless, irrelevant, in this numb immensity of horror. He tried to picture her saying it. 'Tell Kif to keep his pecker up.' He pictured her in the drawing-room at Golder's Green, and then remembered that she did not live there any longer. She had married Heaton, and he had had Baba, and it was very long ago that they had taught each other dance-steps, and been curious about each other's ideas, and made toffee with Alison in the kitchen at Golder's Green. 'Tell Kif to keep his pecker up.' The words sang in his head, but it was like listening to unrelated voices on the telephone—thin, far-away voices that had nothing to do with him. What had Ann to do with the thing that had happened to him? What had anyone to do with it? They were all outside—spectators. He was alone with the thing.

Arden-Davis found him an uninspiring client when he came to interview him.

'You confessed to the police. What made you do that?'

'They had a gun that I borrowed from a friend. So I just told them the truth.'

'What was the truth?'

'That he fired first. I never meant to kill him.'

162

'Did you say that of your own accord?'

'Yes.'

'They didn't suggest things to you?'

'No.'

'Well, tell me exactly what happened that night.'

Kif told him wearily, Arden-Davis watching him the while. Good living had thickened the lawyer's jowl, but the eye in the fat face was keen and clear as a bird's. When Kif finished, and had answered his questions, he said:

'You needn't be so despondent, Vicar. You have a good fighting chance.'

'Of what? *Of what?*' said Kif, with a passion so sudden that the lawyer was staggered.

'Of getting off, surely,' he said.

'Getting off! There's no getting off. Do you call fifteen years getting off? *Fifteen years!*' Kif's hands came together white-knuckled and beat a despairing tattoo on his knees. His eyes, staring at the opposite wall, reminded Arden-Davis of the eyes of a horse he had seen whose back had been broken at a point-to-point. He could find no words.

'Perhaps we may get it to less than that,' he said mendaciously, and got himself away to where he could forget unpleasantness in Italian cooking and French wine.

But that was the only occasion on which the drowning, helpless Kif became articulate. He came into the packed court to stand his trial pale and quiet, his heavy dark eyes seeking round for familiar faces. When he found them a smile that was more a ray of light than a movement of feature went over his face, and after that he did not glance their way again. The small wizened piece of concentrated acuteness that was his judge examined him minutely from his hooded eyes, and the jury glanced furtively or stared curiously as their several natures were. But Kif did not appear to care, or even to be aware of the battery. He and the custodian on either side of him were mere onlookers—the only onlookers in the arena. They would argue and fight, all those others; strain their wit and understanding, whip their straying minds back to the narrow path of attention, take oaths and declare and deny, weigh the worth of phrases, snatch a doubtful word before it fell, and juggle with it till the nut became a tree sprouting new meanings; they would steep themselves in a hot mesmerising bath of words and struggle to keep their brains cool, the jury because it was their duty, the judge because it was his habit, the prosecution because the Crown counsel had a new appointment in his eye, the defence for the greater glory of Arden-Davis and the ultimate advancement of his two juniors. But Kif and his stiff large guardians could only watch. Nothing he could say or do would arrest the spate of words, put an end to the heavy mockery of the play. He, Kif, was the subject of it all, but no one in the arena remembered it now. He was translated for them into an abstraction, a cause. He was a real person only to the pleased mob that breathed and coughed subdued coughs and exchanged surreptitious whispers beyond the pale, and to them he was something between a monster and a hero. His very presence filled them with a delightful entrail-gripping mixture of horror and pity; his smallest movement, for which they watched with greedy eyes, thrilled them as would a sign from Heaven. When he blew his nose they remarked it with éclat and felt themselves privileged among mortals that they had witnessed it. They had scamped their too-early breakfasts in order to procure a good place at this free show, they had planned and manoeuvred to be here, and the value of the show was enhanced accordingly. Now they sat breathing comfortable breaths of achievement and content, the sandwiches they had prepared the night before resting reassuringly in pocket or bag, or lying careless and casual in newspaper on complacent laps.

Through the preliminaries—that careful setting out of facts with all the jealous relevance of the law—the court stirred gently and continuously with the slight indeterminate sound of wind over grass. They had heard all this before, this why and when. All this minute explanation of the game, this dreary prologue demanded by and beloved of the law, was but tedious recapitulation of an old tale. Had there not been an inquest to enlighten them? To say nothing of a police-court and the press of a whole nation. The law was a self-conscious bore. And so, with the eye that was not occupied with Kif, they searched the court for amusement, criticised the jury, compared the fleshy power of Arden-Davis with the lean acuteness of Kinsley, the Crown counsel, decided that in a tight place they would like to have Arden-Davis on their side, speculated as to who was paying his fee in the present instance.

And then the first witness was called; there was a quick concerted movement as the whole crowd leaned forward, and complete silence fell.

The first witness was Lisman's butler, Allen, who described the habits of the household, his being roused from sleep by revolver shots, and his discovery of his master's body. He was unable to say how many shots there were. He had not actually heard any shot. It was merely the noise that had awakened him. His master did not habitually carry firearms, though he was apprehensive of burglars.

Arden-Davis: Was Mr Lisman a quick-tempered man?

Allen thought not.

Arden-Davis: Was he habitually clear-headed?

Allen thought he could say he was.

Arden-Davis: At one-thirty in the morning?

No, Allen must say that by evening Mr Lisman was not often clear-headed.

The butler was succeeded by Wilkins, who gave his testimony in the usual model police fashion. He described his finding the body—he had been at the police station on other business when the call from the Lisman house had come in—and his search for clues. There were no finger-prints, but outside the window of the room were two perfect footprints, one of a whole foot and one of a toe. He took a cast of them, which, as could be seen, fitted in every detail the boots which the accused was wearing at the time. On the far side of the wall separating the Lisman house from that on the east side of it he found the revolver from which the bullet that killed Mr Lisman had presumably been fired. The bullet from Mr Lisman's own revolver had been found in the soil of the garden. Behind the street wall of a garden further along the road was found a case of burglars' tools. The tools had been thrown into the case carelessly and evidently in great haste. On his way to the Lisman house he had met the accused and caused him to be detained, since he could give no proper account of himself. The spot where he had stopped and interviewed the accused was less than twenty yards from the place where the case of tools had been found. The accused was charged on the following morning.

Arden-Davis did not cross-examine, and Wilkins was succeeded in turn by the constable who had talked with Kif before the arrival of Wilkins, and by the officer who had charged him.

Next came Danny, who was shown a revolver and identified it as his. His appearance was hailed by the mob with a sigh of ecstasy. A real crook—and a thoroughly bad lot, no doubt! Anyhow, he certainly looked it. They prepared themselves for drama. The hostility on Danny's face as he turned to Kinsley was unmistakable, and his slight round-shouldered figure in the tight-fitting navy blue coat had the quality of a bent spring. But they were disappointed. Having claimed the revolver as his, Danny was dismissed. He hesitated a moment as if surprised, and then went. Neither when he came in nor as he went out did he cast a glance at Kif. A faint unexpected colour had mounted in Kif's weary face at sight of him, but no one noticed it except the little blinking brown image in the red robes, who noticed everything.

As the day wore on the weariness that marked Kif's face deepened, until one of the jurymen, catching sight of it at a moment when his thoughts were elsewhere, was jerked suddenly into realisation and humanity. For two painful minutes he contemplated things as they were, and then pulling himself sharply together became once more an unthinking plumber and a juryman. It didn't pay to see things like that.

When the case for the defence opened Kif was preceded into the witness-box by the Lisman housemaid. She said that on the night of the tragedy she was not asleep. She suffered from insomnia. She had heard the shots quite distinctly. Two of them. They differed in sound, the first being louder than the second and not so sharp. She was quite sure about the order of the sounds. She was slightly deaf, but not deaf enough to be unable to hear sounds like that. On the contrary her very deafness made her more aware of the character of sounds as detached from their meaning than she would otherwise be.

And then Kif came, quiet and very white. He told his story in answer to Arden-Davis very much as he had told it to the lawyer in the first instance; bald bare phrases without explanation or excuse. When the lawyer wanted a qualification he had to ask for it. Kif made no attempt to justify himself. What did it matter? What did anything matter?

Arden-Davis brought out all the defence there was: that Lisman had fired first and left Kif no choice, that Kif had had no intention of using his weapon. And the great man sighed with pleasure as he sat down. What a model witness! Would all witnesses were so amenable. There was a lot to be said for indifference in an accused person. The over-anxious always spoiled the game.

'You say Mr Lisman shot first?' Kinsley asked Kif.

'Yes.'

'Then how is it that he did not kill you? He did not even wound you. How was that?'

'Because he was a bad shot, I suppose.'

'He would have to be a particularly bad shot to miss you by a yard, wouldn't he?'

'Yes.'

'Was your gun in your hand when Lisman came into the room?'

'No.'

'Where was it?'

'It was lying on a chair by my side.'

'Not in your pocket?'

'No.'

'Then you were prepared to use it at a moment's notice?'

'I was prepared to present it. Not to use it.'

'When did you first pick it up from the chair?'

'When I saw Lisman.'

'But if he had you covered how could you pick it up?'

'Lisman hadn't a revolver when he came in.'

'Then you were the first to present a weapon?'

'No. I reached for my gun, and when I looked up he was covering me.'

'Then if he had you covered why did he shoot?'

'I don't know.'

'I suggest that you shot Lisman before he had time to take aim at you.'

'No. What I told you is the truth. I shot because he meant to kill me. I never meant to shoot.'

'But *you* killed him, and *his* shot went a yard wide of the mark?'

Kif did not answer, and Kinsley abruptly sat down. Arden-Davis glanced at the jury and wondered how far sob-stuff would go and how far the straight-from-the-shoulder touch. He got to his feet still debating.

In convicting a man of murder, he said, they had to prove the will to kill. The accused had said that he had no intention of killing anyone, and since in law a man was presumed innocent until he was proved guilty they might accept the accused's word for it, as hypothesis if not as fact. Let them, in the absence of evidence, consider the probabilities. Here was a man who had joined the British army in 1914. He was then fifteen. They taught him how to kill, and for the next four years—that was, for the whole period of what would normally have been his boyhood—he killed and risked being killed daily at the bidding of his country. At the end of the war he was discharged, and invested his gratuity in a perfectly honourable business. His partner swindled him and he was left

166

penniless. His grateful country showed no anxiety to help him to the work he sought for. On the other hand, an old army acquaintance, met by chance, proved a good Samaritan if incidentally a bad friend. The friend and *his* friends were what is popularly known as crooks, and the accused assimilated their point of view. When on business he carried a revolver as naturally as another man carried a heavy-headed stick on a lonely tramp; not because he anticipated having to use it, but because he felt happier with it. For a man who had spent his 'teens as a fighting soldier on the western front to go into any adventure without a potential weapon would be as unthinkable as that a soldier would be willing to go into no-man's-land without a rifle. The accused had not the faintest intention of killing anyone when he put his friend's gun into his pocket that night. Even at the moment when he was confronted with Lisman, gun in hand and intention in eye, he had no will to kill. He answered Lisman's attack as mechanically as his training had taught him to do. That he*killed* Lisman was also due to the mechanical reaction to his training. If he had been deliberate he could have disabled Lisman without doing him serious injury. He had no reason to kill him. It was enormously to his advantage that he should not. That Lisman was killed and the accused unscathed was due to the fact that Lisman was a bad shot and had had too many drinks, and to the fact that the accused was taken unawares, and without time to think, shot by instinct, as he would at an enemy, to kill. If his country had never taught the accused the trade of killing Philip Lisman would be alive to-day. His country had taught him that and nothing but that, and as long as he killed in their service they approved of him. But now that in a mad unthinking moment he instinctively fell back on what they had taught him they called him a murderer and wanted to hang him. They called that justice. 'But justice is for you to dispense, you twelve persons of the jury, and for no one else. It is for you to say how blameworthy this boy is. There is nothing in his favour but the probabilities and the sworn evidence that of the two shots the first was the heavier report. Beyond that you have only his word. Do you think it is so difficult to accept?'

Arden-Davis waited a long silent moment, and then sat down slowly.

It was late afternoon when Kinsley rose to address the jury.

There was no need, he said, in this instance to decide whether or not the accused had fired the fatal shot. Even if the evidence for the Crown had not been sufficiently conclusive on that score they had the accused's own word for it that he had shot Lisman. Since his word was backed by incontrovertible evidence they were ready to believe his statement. But they were then asked to believe, with no more corroboration than that of a half-deaf woman who had been half asleep at the other end of the house at the time, that the shot had been fired in self-defence. That was to say, they were asked to take the uncorroborated word of a man who was confessedly on the premises with criminal intent. The net of the law had closed so quickly and so securely round him that he had no chance to deny, with any hope of belief, the fact of his presence there on the night in question. Now he said that he would never have fired at all if his victim had not used his weapon. If that were true it was strange that it was the man who had fired first who had missed his target, and that the man who had fired in flurried self-defence was the one to kill. It might, of course, be a mere matter of marksmanship, as counsel for the defence had suggested. But if probabilities, in the absence of evidence, were to be taken into consideration, it was much more probable that the very erratic course of Mr Lisman's bullet was due to the fact that he had already been shot.

Again, whether or not he had fired in self-defence, the accused was responsible for the killing of a human being, and that killing had become necessary, as the accused would term it, only through the accused's own criminal practices. Was that to be termed manslaughter? Was a burglar who shot one when one showed signs of defending one's possessions to be described merely as criminally negligent, or something equally absurd and inapplicable. It was for the jury, under the judge's direction, to decide, of course. He held that the shooting of Philip Lisman was murder, and should be punished as such.

Kinsley's gown made a soft s-s-sh in the silence as he turned to his seat. The court stirred, and breathed, and fell to silence again. In the quiet the small, awful, red and brown god above it turned over the pages of his notes with the stealthy rustle of dried leaves. Below him in the hot stillness they waited for the oracle. The blood thudded thickly in their ears. But in Kif's ears was a sound that was more the beating of his heart than any artery's spasm—the sound of London's traffic. Sudden and distinct it sounded, and a wave of agony rose in him.

Out there. Just out there. Just that little distance away. People would be going home now; it was raining probably; it had been raining when they brought him in the morning; the pavements would be wet and the buses full. He could see the yellow *Star* placards wrinkly and damp. People buying evening papers and going home and to theatres and things, just as usual. All over the world people doing things just as usual. But he——! What was it Danny had said? 'Luck always gets you in the end'—something like that. Luck—that's all it was. And he'd drawn a loser. Or perhaps he'd played badly. Who dealt anyhow? Oh, well, what did it matter? It was done now. This was the card he was left with.

Mr Justice Faver began to address the jury. His slow precise words fell into the silence as if they were distilled from some precious retort. The jury were there, he said, to weigh the worth of facts, not to decide upon matters of sentiment. As the prosecution had pointed out, the accused had gone to a certain house on the night in question to commit a burglary. When confronted with the owner of the property he shot him and killed him. The accused said that the owner was the aggressor, and that he, the accused, shot in self-defence. That was to say, he asked them to believe that a householder, well armed, well aware that there were trespassers on his property, and having the intruders at a distinct disadvantage in that he could take them by surprise, was yet so devoid of all reason as to shoot without provocation. Well, there were distinct limits to human credulity, and quite frankly he did not find that story credible. Provocation there must have been, and provocation could have been provided only by the accused, either overtly with his weapon or covertly in a gesture. It was, he thought, too unlikely for credence that Lisman, having all the advantages of the situation on his side—having, quite literally, the accused at his pistol's point—should go to the extreme course of firing. There was evidence that Mr Lisman was of a placid temperament. The defence, it was true, had in the course of evidence suggested that Mr Lisman was not habitually responsible for his actions at that hour of the morning. But subsequent and incontrovertible evidence had been led to show that he left his friends about half-past twelve in a perfectly sober condition. It was not, then, any inflamed condition of Mr Lisman's own mind which induced him to use violence. The defence had brought forward a witness who swore that of the two shots the first had been the report of Mr Lisman's revolver. The witness was very positive on the question, and there was no reason to suppose that the facts were other than she had stated. There was nothing in her statement incompatible with the case for the prosecution. It was quite possible that Lisman had fired first. It was even probable. He was the more prepared of the two. But it was something which the accused did which caused him to fire. Did they think that if the accused had meekly held up his hands on the appearance of Lisman that there would have been any further trouble?

The defence had sought to enlist their sympathy by pointing out at what school the accused had been taught the use of firearms. His readiness to shoot, they had said, was a weakness for which the nation and not the accused was responsible. But half a million men—many of them as young as the accused—has also been taught to use firearms with speed and accuracy, and had evidently found no difficulty in resisting any inclination to use the talent for their private ends. It was not unwisdom on the part of the nation, but idiosyncrasy on the part of the accused which had brought about the tragedy. It was that very idiosyncrasy—that predisposition to recklessness—which led to the accused's being on the premises. Illegally armed, illegally on the premises with criminal intent, the use of his revolver came, it had been admitted, fatally natural to him. But one could not provoke a man to a trial of arms and then attribute his death to self-defence on one's own part. One could not threaten a man to the point where he defended himself with violence, and kill him, and call it manslaughter. Let the jury go and consider it, without bias and without sentiment. Let them not say: 'The accused is young and badly brought-up.' Nor, on the other hand, must they say: 'There is too much of this type of lawlessness. One must be ruthless.' Let them consider this one case and this alone, on the facts as they were before them.

As the court rose respectfully at the talking god's slow departure a man whispered to his neighbour: '—— little devil! How he loves himself! And *how* he hates Arden-Davis!'

'Hasn't much of a chance, has he?' said his neighbour, indicating Kif, who was being led below.

'Not an earthly. Shall we wait? I do want my tea.'

But they waited.

In seventeen minutes the jury came back. They would have been back in five if it had not been for one juryman—a plumber—who was filled, it appeared, with queer theories. Some heated minutes passed before the other eleven could convince him that they were not concerned with ideas, but with Facts and Justice.

They found the prisoner guilty of murder, but recommended him to mercy on account of his youth. (That was the plumber's salve.)

The bright hooded eyes turned to the boy in the dock, the sunken mouth opened for speech. But the expected speech did not come. The god paused. For the first time in history Mr Justice Faver quite obviously changed his mind. What was it? Had he suddenly recollected the lateness of the hour? Had he caught himself on the point of being inartistic? Or did he find in the indifferent dark eyes that met his a wholly new estimate of himself, an estimate that made him, shockingly, of less account than the hum of the traffic outside? Mr Justice Faver paused and became mechanical.

The recommendation to mercy would be passed on to the proper quarter. Had Kif anything to say before sentence of death was passed on him?

Kif shook his head.

The judge picked up the small black square.

28

Baba was not going to see Kif. She could not bear it, she said. Besides, she could be better employed otherwise. Every minute of every day must be used in adding signatures to the petition for his reprieve. The signatures of influential people. Anyone could get the man in the street to sign his name, but that didn't get reprieves. It was the influential people who counted, who must be persuaded, and it was she who would see to the persuading.

Angel, coming in one afternoon, found her entertaining a delighted cub-reporter in the living-room. He surveyed the situation for a moment with bitter eyes. Then he said to the newspaper man, who had risen at his entrance, and was waiting an introduction, 'Git!' and jerked his head at the door. And the reporter, surprised but politic, went without ado.

Angel went out of the room behind him—hastily, as if he did not trust himself—leaving an indignant Baba with nothing on which to vent her rage. But later he said: 'If you ever have one of that crowd here again I'll beat you till you're half dead.' And Baba, appealing to her father for sympathy and protection—'It's to Kif's advantage to be as nice to the press as we can'—was disagreeably surprised to have Angel's prohibition confirmed.

Kif, when Angel, nervous and explanatory, broke the news of Baba's defection, seemed to his friend unexpectedly acquiescent.

'Oh, I understand,' he said. 'Tim's the same.' And he handed over the letter he had been fingering for Angel to read.

'My DEAR OLD KIF,

I meant to see you as soon as I could after the trial, but I have been thinking it over, and have come to the conclusion that a letter will perhaps be less painful for you as well as for me, and will say better what I want to say.

I have a horribly guilty feeling that I left you in the lurch, somehow, sometime, and that all this mess is somehow due to me. I can't put it clearly even to myself, but I have the feeling all the same, and I want to say that I'm as sorry as a man can be about everything. If it would do any good to see you I would come, but I can't see that it would. I would rather wait and meet under happier circumstances. I have a real belief in the prospect of a reprieve, a belief so strong that it amounts to a hunch.

If there is anything in this world that I can do for you, I'll do it.

Yours,
TIMBARCLAY.

Angel's features were carefully expressionless as he handed back the letter.

'He's quite right, you know,' Kif said with a hint of defence in his tone.

'About what? Leaving you in the lurch?'

'No, no. About it being best not to come.'

'Oh, yes. . . . Do you not want him to come?'

'Not if he feels like that about it. Things always worried him when they didn't go right.'

And Angel went out into the road thinking what a rotten world it was.

But there were others. Ann was in her sunny Surrey nursery playing with her son when Tim came in. The baby was lying on the hearth-rug kicking its seven-month-old legs in an ecstasy of enjoyment, but its mother's eyes were absent as she raised them to meet her brother's. It was the morning after the trial, and though Ann had not been there at all—'There'll be enough to stare at him,' she had said—Tim had attended from beginning to end. It was he who had telephoned the news of the verdict to the waiting Ann and Heaton.

'Well?' she said.

'I know now what the people who came back from Calvary felt.'

'Yes,' she said. 'Yes, it's like that. Have you seen him?'

'No, I couldn't.'

'What do you mean? Wouldn't they let you in?'

'Yes, but—— I just couldn't, Ann. I just couldn't!'

'Tim! You don't mean that you're not going to go at all? You're just waiting to get your courage up, is that it?'

'I haven't any. I'm a moral bankrupt. I just can't go. It's beyond me.'

'But he'll be expecting you. Murray told him you were coming home, and he probably saw you at the trial. And anyhow——You can't possibly *not* go, Tim!'

'I've written to him. He'll understand.'

'You've——!' Ann sat a long time silent and looked at her brother. 'I sometimes think we're a rotten family,' she said. She picked up the crowing infant, and deposited him in his cot.

'Murray will be in the stables. I heard the second lot come back. I want to see him,' she said, and went out.

And that was how Kif was told by a warder that Mrs Heaton would like to see him, and Ann came in smelling of frost and furs and violets, ignoring the warder as if he had been a shadow.

It was some time before Kif found his tongue, but Ann talked easily and happily until he recovered himself. Kif could not see the shaking hands that were hidden in her pockets. He saw only her bright small eyes with their good-fellowship, and the kindness of her mouth and chin, and he was conscious of a wave of strength and wholesomeness that flowed from her to him. So miraculous was it to have Ann—*Ann*—sitting there that he forgot for a little what lay in front of him, and talked and smiled and exchanged ideas and experiences as if he were once more sixteen and sitting on the beach at Birling Gap. She talked of Heaton and her baby and of horses, much of horses—'You see, I'm a much more interesting person from your point of view nowadays!'—and when she rose to go at a slight movement from the warder, Kif lifted his hand in a wholly unconscious gesture as if to deter her.

'I hope I haven't taken time that your fiancée might have had,' she said. Heaton had told her that there was a girl.

She was not coming, Kif said. It was better that way.

'Perhaps you would rather that I didn't come again?'

'No, I'd like you to come, only it's pretty rotten for you.'

172

'No, it isn't. It's very nice to get to know you all over again. I'd forgotten there was so much to know. And you see, I'm going to know you for many years yet.'

She left him her violets and a vague new sense of self-respect. 'Keeping his pecker up' didn't apply merely to trust in a hope, but in being able to take the obliteration of hope like a man. Ann had not used the phrase to him, but something in her personality had given a new meaning to it.

She came twice more in the time that lay between the sentence and the day fixed for Kif's death, and each time put, for a little, some meaning into existence for him. Two days after her third visit the Home Secretary saw (officially) no reason to interfere with the course of justice; and it was Danny who said in a blaze of anger to Kif's friends, hanging back, 'Are you going to leave Kif to a — — parson when he hears that?' And it was Danny who went to him first.

'It's better that way,' was all Kif said. 'I know what you tried to do, Dago. Bluffing Wilkins. It was dam' good of you. . . . You'll look after Baba, won't you?'

'I will,' said Danny.

'I haven't been any little plaster saint, but there's a whole heap worse about. You'll look after her, won't you?'

'Do you want to see her?'

'No.'

'Anyone you'd like to see?'

'Yes, Angel. . . . And Mrs Heaton, if she comes of her own accord. Not unless. Don't ask her. Promise!'

'I promise,' said Danny, giving him his hand in farewell. 'I wish to God it could have been me, Kif!'

On the last evening Ann came.

'Isn't that girl going to see him *now*?' she had asked her husband, and he had said no, that she was a rotter and a funk, and there wasn't enough publicity in it for her.

'And she can leave him alone like that! *Alone!* Good God!' she had cried.

'So it's a washout, Kif,' she said, her lips trembling.

'Yes, don't mind, Ann. It was that from the beginning. The other way would have been worse. It's only the waiting that's bad now.'

Her heart was crying: 'But this is the end of everything for him! Going out, like a flame.' To-morrow there would be no Kif, nor ever any more. Finished. This boy, alive and lovable. The end of him. Nothing any more. God, how awful!

And his was saying: 'I've got to do it decently. It's the only thing that's left. I've got to do it decently.'

'I want to thank you for being so good. I wish I could have seen your kiddy. Is he like you?'

'Well, Murray says he is, but I think he's like Murray. Very natural. Parents are like that.' She kept it at that level for a few minutes. Then she said:

'I'm going, Kif,' and took both his hands.

173

'Ann,' he said, gently, contemplating her. 'Do you remember that first night I came to see you, and you came down in the black-and-gold thing?'

'Rather!'

'I was awfully scared to come. Scared stiff. Did you know?'

'No, I didn't guess.'

'It was you who cured me of being scared.'

'Bend down,' she said.

He bent his tall body. She put her ungloved hand on his hair and kissed his cheek.

'You've been a brick, Kif,' she said.

29

The woman unbolted her cottage door and set it wide to the clear morning. Pearly and high-heavened it stretched to the far round-backed hills, daffodil gold in the first sunlight. The dew lay grey on a shadowless world, and no bird sang. The sound of the drawn bars dropped into the stillness and was lost in the wide waiting loveliness.

The woman's eyes were wet as she turned from the door. Her man came down the wooden stair, stocking-soled because of the sleeping children. He sat by the hearth to put his boots on, and she bent to the kindling fire.

'I used to save him candle-ends,' she said. 'He was always great for the reading. And give him tea sometimes in the mornings. Poor Kif! Poor boy!'

Her tears hissed in the crackling wood.

Made in the
USA
Middletown, DE